BLUE
SUICIDE

BLUE SUICIDE

Jennifer Venner

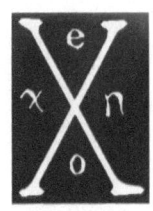

Copyright © 2015, 2018 Jennifer Venner
Published by Xenoproductions
1272 Danforth Avenue
Toronto, Ontario, Canada
M4J 1M6

Front cover design: Ellen Yu

Library and Archives Canada Cataloguing in Publication

Venner, Jennifer, 1971-, author
          Blue suicide / Jennifer Venner.

Issued in print and electronic formats.
ISBN 978-1-988393-00-1 (paperback)

          I. Title.

PS8643.E565B58 2015   C813'.6   C2015-906177-6
                                                                    C2015-906178-4

Blue Suicide. First Xeno Edition. January 2018

Thank you to my family for their patience,
and to GJ for the inspiration

"Haro, Haro, Haro! À mon aide mon Prince, on me fait tort!"
("Haro, Haro, Haro! To my aid, my Prince! One does me wrong!")

Ancient Norman legal injunction (10th century)

Prologue

Scarborough, Suburb of Toronto

June 28, 2000

Wyn Rhys was an investigator for the Special Police Oversight Agency, and as such he worked the night shift, the time in which it was most likely that a crime would be committed, and if police discharged a weapon and a perpetrator was injured or killed, SPOA would be called immediately to attend the scene. Though he shared this shift with other investigators in the Greater Toronto Area, the person closest to the location of the crime was the one dispatched, and because he worked Metro, he was called often. Much of the shift was spent in SPOA's headquarters on Bay Street, analyzing evidence from other investigations or report writing, but he was always highly alert, waiting for the call. After 4am it could be expected that whatever chaos had been perpetrated would have come to its irreversible conclusion. By that time, anyone with a grudge or a plot to unleash fresh hell was safely tucked in bed, dreaming dreams of revenge, windfall, or victory. They might rise a few hours later and tumble down the rabbit hole, but then they became the next shift's problem, not Wyn's.

Sometimes, instead of simply waiting for the call at his desk, Wyn would sign out one of the fleet vehicles and take long, leisurely drives around the city. As he slowly drove the residential streets, straight and unwavering as lines on a circuit board, he would smoke and think about whatever case he was working on, about other cases he'd completed, sometimes about more mundane things, like conversations with his wife. Occasionally he turned on the radio and listened to broadcasts from other, day-lit countries, but even as he half-listened, he was closely observing his surroundings, on the lookout for suspicious behaviour. Sometimes he went to high-crime neighbourhoods and surveyed the young hoods on street corners, slowing down and making his presence felt when he could sense trouble brewing. But once in a while he patrolled serene Canadian suburbia, if only to enjoy the unexpected curves and cul-de-sacs. The streetlights were far apart, casting some homes in an almost impenetrable darkness, giving the illusion of peace, of privacy. But darkness was hardly the friend of a potential victim of violent crime. And there were far fewer police officers out patrolling in suburban neighbourhoods than in urban ones, allowing for even more opportunities for the enterprising burglar or rapist.

Wyn had once been a police officer, but only as part of his training to become a criminal investigator for the London Metropolitan Police in Britain, which, in turn, had provided him the skills he needed as a police investigator in Canada. As a law enforcer, he'd been involved in one or two dodgy situations with suspects and, during the Brixton riots in 1985 had worn riot gear and pressed marauders into compact clusters for arresting. Though he never carried a deadly weapon in the UK, he had been involved in a takedown where a suspect had run out into traffic and got himself killed. The straight-backed authority of the police officer still clung to him even now as he sat in the SUV, his seat pushed as far back as possible to accommodate his above-average height, window open to the intimate warmth of a late June night into which he exhaled Rothman's smoke, one hand leisurely draped in the crook of the steering wheel, the other, his cigarette hand, on his knee. Mostly, nothing happened on these patrols. But on this night, something did.

It started as a keening sound in the distance and seemed to come from more than one direction, then, into the thicket of houses, blue and red and white beams glanced and ricocheted. Rounding a corner, police cruisers suddenly swung into view and streaked past. Wyn stuck his cigarette in his mouth to free up both hands and made a tight, screeching three-point turn in the middle of the broad street and followed them. From other streets other emergency vehicles came into view: fire trucks, paramedics, all converging on an urgently blinking point on a map. Technically, he was supposed to wait for a dispatch from SPOA before attending a crime scene, and he was certainly not to be present when a scene was unfolding and put himself in danger, but the police officer in him wanted a taste of the action if there was any to be had. He had no weapon, though that strangely made showing up all the more compelling.

The emergency crews had all congregated near a modest bungalow set back on a large expanse of green lawn that was fenced on all four sides. Two empty police cruisers were parked out front; likely officers had been first on the scene and had called for back-up. Wyn knew not to park onsite; he drove by at normal speed and parked around the corner, grabbed his notebook and cigarettes and checked his jacket pocket for his identification, then made his way to the residence on foot. By the activity at the scene, he knew that something very serious had transpired but the time of danger had definitely passed. He approached a police officer holding a roll of caution tape and displayed his ID. "What's going on?" he asked.

"Jesus Murphy, you guys are quick," said the constable. But knowing that Wyn was from SPOA, he was taciturn. The cops didn't like SPOA investigators and had several colourful nicknames for them. Wyn had heard them all. The officer pointed to the house. "Civilian, a guy, in the basement. Shot by two officers from 42 Division."

"Dead?"

The officer nodded curtly and began unrolling the tape.

"Was he the resident, or an intruder?"

"Resident. Made the 911 call. Got a casualty in the garage."

"Any officers injured?"

The cop shook his head and focused on creating a perimeter. Wyn saw activity in the backyard near the garage and went to take a closer look. The lights from the ambulance rotated red and blue and white, ranging in long beams over the interior of the building, illuminating its dark corners in which ordinary garden implements – rakes, spades and the like – cast long, malevolent shadows. There was some shouting of "step back, step back" and hasty instructions among a huddle in the centre. Wyn was stopped by a paramedic, who tried to block his view. "No one past this point," he ordered.

"I'm with SPOA," said Wyn, reaching for his ID, but the paramedic shook his head.

"No way. Got a victim back here. Medical personnel only."

Wyn, who was six and a half feet tall, craned his neck a little to see beyond the paramedic, over the bristling activity of the ER crew. A woman hung from a rope tied to a rafter, her face somewhat obscured by long, blood-draggled hair. She wore a pink pyjama top but nothing from the waist down. There were stab wounds to her abdomen and lacerations on her bare legs, likely sustained before she was asphyxiated. Three large men carefully prepared to let her down, one cutting the rope with a box cutter, the other two alongside her, bracing themselves for her descent. "Easy does it," someone said. By her head's mournful droop and the supplicatory way her hands rested against her thighs, she looked like a funerary monument. The police must have found vital signs, otherwise they would not have called in the paramedics, but whether or not she was alive still he couldn't ascertain. In the strange, circuslike glow of the flashing lights, she crumpled, limp as laundry taken from the line, into the basket of hands below.

Wyn looked away and retreated back to the driveway, trembling a little, and lit a cigarette. Despair tried to scale the walls of his dispassion, but he held firm against it by remaining focused on facts, or possible facts. The man had been shot dead by the officers who'd responded to the call, so he must have been armed and dangerous. If he was the killer, he had called the police in a panic, or out of remorse. In cases like this, the police had to be cautious that the suspect wasn't luring them into a trap, or, on the flip side, into killing him. Officer-assisted suicide had been on the rise in the last few years.

Death was part of the job and most of the time it bothered Wyn little. On average, he had to look at a dead body every four weeks or so. He'd started out as a police officer at age twenty-one and was now thirty-sex, so he'd seen approximately one hundred and seventy corpses in his career. Far less than a paramedic, but far more than a parking-meter attendant, a lawyer, a retail salesperson or the Prime Minister. He'd been present at horrific car accidents, seen bodies bifected, decapitated, bearing the brands of flame or swollen after drowning. Once confirmed dead, the victims were left in the places fate had abandoned them to be photographed, examined, discussed. They were just part of the scene and, in the case of high-impact deaths, such as car accidents, sometimes ineradicable from it. Tissue could be embedded with glass and glass with tissue, blood could sneak under carpets and floorboards and drip through ceilings onto the heads of people residing below. In one of his examinations of a car wreck, Wyn had once discovered a finger under the back seat. The bodies he'd stepped around weren't fathers or someone's children, just evidence that had to be examined as one would bullet trajectories. At post-mortems he'd stood by as forensic pathologists disassembled bodies with the efficiency reserved for unpacking a suitcase and with the same intimate knowledge of what was contained therein. Organs removed and cradled carefully, almost lovingly, before being immersed in formaldehyde solutions that turned them into murky jewels. Saws from Home Depot were deployed to the skull to remove a brain in which all recollections of childhood wonder, first love, the sensory memories of petting a cat or being kissed, were secreted and forever locked in its coils and volutes.

Finishing his cigarette and tossing it into the street, away from the scene itself, Wyn started for the house but was summoned by a youngish woman at the taped-off perimeter. She looked very anxious, almost tearful. "Are they okay?" she called to him.

Wyn came closer. "Did you call 911?" he asked, taking out his notebook.

"No. We heard an argument but then nothing – oh my god," the woman interrupted herself, placing her hands on her temples. "They have kids. I know their kids. Oh my god. Are they okay?" She put her hands over her mouth, staring at the garage.

Wyn said, "Could you please give me their names and ages? Ma'am?" She was looking over his shoulder at the garage, but he sidestepped to block her view. "Names, please?"

"Oh my god … I don't know. Um … Adele is the mother. Her husband is Kevin. Liam. Sean. Little boys, twins. They're just babies. Oh my god." This last refrain, or punctuation, was involuntary, like a hiccup. A man approached her and put his arm around her shoulders. "Are you a cop?" he asked.

Wyn showed him his ID. "Do you know the family?"

The man nodded gravely. He gave Wyn the names of the dead man and his wife. "They have three kids. We heard some arguing about an hour ago, but they argued a lot, so…" he seemed uncomfortable with his decision to not call the police himself, sooner, and jerked his chin at the building. "Are they okay?" he asked.

Wyn ignored the question. "Did you say three children?" he asked.

The woman opened her mouth and coughed, like she was about to be sick. "Three," she said. "There's a girl. Jennifer? Julia? I can't remember." She shook her head and turned to her husband, who drew her away from the scene.

Heart thrumming, Wyn returned to the site of the hanging, touched the shoulder of one of the medical personnel. "How many victims have you found?" The woman held up three fingers. "This woman, and two toddlers, drowned in the bathtub," she said.

Somewhere on the premises was a third child.

***

He didn't question emergency personnel on the main floor of the bungalow to confirm that it had been searched and that no other family member had been discovered; this was his own small quest. The kitchen and bathroom had been the sites of the murders, so he was careful to not intrude. At the other end of the house there was little activity. Wyn quietly checked the bedrooms. The room where the little boys had slept still smelled of talcum powder, milk, and faintly of urine, and retained some of the ambiance of their slumbering bodies. Kevin and Adele's room was no more haphazard than any bedroom shared by a couple. The room of the third child, a daughter, was the smallest and the most tidy, straddling the boundary between childhood and young womanhood: stuffed toys on a miniature wing-backed chair, posters of pop bands on the mauve walls. The bed was unmade, though in the least disruptive way possible, the corner of the coverlet turned down to form a tidy triangle, the rest undisturbed. Wyn noticed the pillow was missing. It lay on the floor near the open closet door. He peered into the closet, holding his breath, but it was empty.

That left the basement and the room in which the father had been killed. As everyone had been occupied by the scene in the garage and only Wyn knew of the possibility of another victim, and because he and his team were the ones in charge of the scene where the officers had deployed their weapons, no one had yet infiltrated it. Like a man under hypnosis, he moved automatically to the door to the basement and opened it. The air changed about halfway down the stairs, from warm humid to cool humid, from embrace to release. The people upstairs became just foot thump and murmur, with the occasional clatter and shout.

At the bottom of the stairs was a corridor with doors, all closed, along one side. Wyn turned on the light and the white walls glowed. There was nothing to denote violence, but he knew from experience that violence jumped out at you from clouded corners, waited, breath held, around the edges of doors. The only open door was at the end, and the darkness that seemed to encroach on the light pulsed with iniquity. The hall was carpeted, and Wyn noted how his tread was completely absorbed. The dead man may not have heard the police closing in.

As he walked he knocked at, and then opened doors into small rooms: a laundry room, an office with file boxes stacked to the ceiling, a toilet with a tiny vanity. None of the rooms had closets or beds, nowhere to hide for even the smallest child. Like the rooms upstairs, they were reassuring for their unremarkableness. As he came closer to the shadowy entrance to the last room, Wyn thought he could taste blood on the edges of his tongue, shiny metallic red. That was where the man had been killed. Perhaps it was also the locale of his last murder. There may be two bodies waiting for him. Wyn sucked the inside of his cheeks into the space between his teeth and bit down hard, hard enough to taste his own blood.

At the entrance lay a toy, a small stuffed animal. He crouched and picked it up, not certain why. It was soiled, but only by love. He put it under his nose and sniffed. Child smells of milk spit and snot rubbed deep into the nap. He put it in his pocket, then felt along the inside of the door frame for a light switch. He found it and turned it on.

The first thing he noticed was the bottoms of two pairs of feet on the floor, side by each, both barefoot. One pallid pair belonged to a man and was lax, only the heels touching. The other pair was a child's and was pinkly upright, alert. In three short steps he was in the room proper. It was also unremarkable: TV, sofa, toys strewn about. There was a spray of blood on the wall above the sofa and some gore. Below him he could see that the man appeared young and healthy, by his body alone, as his head had been almost completely blown off. The place where his face should have been was only a bubble of black-red, featureless, indecipherable, and because Wyn had never seen him before, he could not imagine him ever having one. His hands had been placed on his chest, one over the other. A girl between the age of eight and ten lay alongside him and mimicked the pose, her own arms folded over her breast and her eyes closed, but Wyn could hear her breathing, quick in and quick out, like any child. She wore only scant shorts and a tank top in silky fabric – pyjamas. Their heart pattern was obscured by dark splotches of blood, but Wyn was certain it wasn't her own.

He knew he'd made virtually no sound, and perhaps should have spoken to alert the child to his presence, but he must have touched her foot with one of his, because her eyes suddenly flew open and she stared up at him in the disconcerting way sleepwalkers look at things, like she was looking through him, or over him, at something quite frightening beyond. They were black, the iris and pupil indistinguishable.

Before she could move, he quickly crouched again and touched her ankle. "You're safe," he said. "My name is Wyn. What's your name?" The girl didn't move, her black eyes didn't blink. She opened her mouth, but no sound came out. "That's okay," said Wyn. "You don't have to tell me yet. Are you hurt?" The girl slowly shook her head. "I'm going to pick you up, all right? Just nod to show me you understand." She remained motionless, so Wyn, remembering the stuffed toy, now took it out of his pocket and placed it on her chest. Instinctively, she clutched it. She was part of the crime scene, but he couldn't leave her in it. He should have called someone down, but he didn't want to scare her by shouting. In this hushed room, with a dead man, it would be unseemly to move too abruptly or speak too loudly. He had to extract her from the horror as gently and carefully as he could.

Slipping one hand into the warm hollows behind her knees, he placed the other under her neck. She had long black hair, quite curly, and as Wyn lifted her head, some of it stuck to the carpet where her father's blood had soaked through. Though lanky, she was narrow-limbed and rather light, but Wyn, cautious as he was to leave as little evidence of his own presence in the room, stumbled a little because he didn't want to step too far back. She put her arms around his neck, one hand still clasping the toy, and he felt her breathing, soft and normal, against his collarbone. Shock, he knew, expressed itself in remarkable ways; this child was so serene, so trusting.

He looked at the scene. The lights had been off. The door had no damage, so the officers likely did not have to force their way in. The intensity of the impact of the bullet suggested the man had to have been shot at very close range. There was no weapon nearby, so he'd been unarmed. What had the girl seen? Had she been in the room when the shooting took place? Had she seen the officers open fire, heard her own father plead with them? Had she been visible to the officers, they would have removed her immediately, so all Wyn could think was that she'd been concealed somewhere (behind the sofa, maybe) and only emerged when the room became silent again.

He could tell by holding the child that she had no broken bones; indeed, she seemed completely unharmed, and had not cried out or stiffened when he lifted her. The ocean of death all around had not so much as dampened the tips of her feet. After what he had seen in the garage, he felt a surge of gratitude and relief so intense that it actually brought tears to his eyes. Alive, he thought, over and over. He held the child tight against him and put his chin against the top of her head, on her luxurious hair, inhaling her young, biscuity scent. He was not a religious man, but this moment had a holiness to it. The girl's heart, beating against his own, had a million more beats to mark the rest of her long, complicated life.

***

By exceptional chance, Wyn managed to talk to the involved officers before the Police Association could get a lawyer to the scene to remove them. They were both on the sofa in the living room. Their eyes had the faraway, thoughtful look Wyn recognized among people involved in a traumatic event. They were watching it unfold in front of them, over and over.

Wyn segregated them and spoke to the younger one first. Constable Jameson told him that the 911 call had come from Kevin Wolfe himself. "He was really panicked," he said. "We thought that someone had broken into the house and attacked his family. He didn't tell us nothing. Just to come quick." Jameson sniffed, but it sounded more habitual, a tic in times of stress, not emotion. "We got there and the house seemed quiet, but we noticed a light on in the garage and went there first. We found the mother and called for medics right away. Called for back-up. We didn't know what we were up against. Didn't know about the little boys until after we took down the father. Found them in the bathtub." He sniffed again, ran one hand under his nose. Wyn noticed a tattoo on his wrist, of a black heart. "Got him in the basement. Rec room. You know when I was a kid I used to think it was 'wreck' room. Like a car wreck. Sure is now." He fumbled in his pockets and took out some cigarettes. They weren't supposed to smoke in residents' homes, but Wyn didn't stop him from lighting up. "We thought it must have been a domestic when we couldn't see evidence of a break-in. Or maybe it was the fact that when he saw us coming to the house, he took off for the basement. I mean, we announced ourselves and everything, but he fled."

"Did you see him before you shot him? Did you see the child?"

"Lights were off in the room. No, we didn't see the girl. Didn't know about her until they brought her upstairs."

Wyn thought of the commotion among the paramedics, who'd only just emerged from the calamity of the garage and the bathroom, when they'd come upon him with the girl in the basement. He had handed her over to another large man, feeling a strange sadness, letting her go. She had stared at him, clutching the small toy. When he came upstairs, he saw the two gurneys with small bodies strapped into them in the hallway near the bathroom. White bundles. He shuddered and held his pen tighter. "You know you endangered her life, firing a gun into that room," he said, feeling his face grow hot. "You're lucky it hadn't been her who opened the door. Very lucky."

"This is bullshit. I want my lawyer," said Jameson, moving to stand.

Wyn used the officious tack. "You have to comply with an SPOA investigation," he warned, though, technically, involved officers could plead trauma and remove themselves from a scene, or be removed.

"Fuckin' right I do." Jameson lumbered away with his coffee and cigarette, the blanket that a medical officer had draped around his shoulders slipping to the floor.

***

The other officer, Constable Woloshyn, was much older and more prepared for Wyn's questions about motive. "We didn't know for certain that he was the suspect," he said calmly. "We were responding to threats. He said he had a gun."

Wyn didn't need to check his notes, but pretended to anyway. "Your partner didn't mention a gun. There's no weapon at the scene."

"Yeah, well, he did. In the heat of the moment we're not gonna remember the same shit, right? It was a tense situation. We just saw his wife hanging from a rafter in the garage. Found the two kids–" he broke off, his voice like a saw caught in the cut. "It gets you in a state of – you know, like, shock. We were shocked. But it didn't mean we couldn't carry out our duty. We wanted to take him away in cuffs – you bet we did. See him brought to justice. But it didn't work out that way." Woloshyn didn't make eye contact with Wyn as he spoke, choosing to look down at his hands, which were methodically reducing a Styrofoam cup to tiny specks that fell to the floor like snow.

"How many shots were fired? And by whom?" asked Wyn.

Woloshyn sighed. "I shot him. Don't hang this on the kid. He's just outta college."

Wyn wrote this down. "We can tell if he discharged his weapon," he said.

The constable finally looked at Wyn, a look that was at once pleading and disdainful. "Geez, you guys are somethin' else. Y'know, you're lucky we're even talking to you. You should be talking to our lawyers," he said, then sighed. "I'll take the heat for it, okay? Don't fuck him over."

"The evidence speaks for itself," said Wyn. "You are the more experienced officer. You should have been the one to confront the suspect. Shooting in the dark is extremely dangerous."

Woloshyn suddenly touched the back of the sofa, behind Wyn. His fingers came away red. Wyn turned to look. They were sitting on evidence. He quickly rose. Woloshyn said, "All's I know is, if I saw what I saw in that garage when I was in my first year of duty, I would've shat myself. In my opinion, that officer's a hero." He curled his upper lip at Wyn. "But I guess that's not how you guys would see it."

***

By the time Wyn had finished talking to the involved officers, an early summer dawn was breaking. Sylvia Hughes, a recently hired Police Association lawyer, appeared at around 5am to take charge of them. Her small black eyes had launched grenades at Wyn when she learned that he'd spoken to them, which, while not expressly prohibited in the Police Services Act, was considered to be poor etiquette, given that the men were shaken up by events. Wyn would later testify that he had asked for and received permission from the involved officers to submit to questioning, thereby making their statements admissible in court. This would be the beginning of a long history of mutual mistrust between him and Sylvia. He then remained on the scene, interviewing neighbours, talking to the forensics team as they collected data from the room in the basement where Wolfe had been shot. Smoking and smoking and smoking. Drinking coffee that just kept appearing in his hand. Sometimes images of the bodies on the gurneys or the drooping head of Adele Wolfe leapt from his peripheral vision to taunt him, but he subdued them with his black pen and notebook, with facts. He filled page after page of his small notebook with his cramped, incomprehensible script. He was the only person who required the notes, so it didn't matter that only he could read them later.

The neighbours said that Kevin Wolfe had been a young lawyer with a large firm downtown. It was a stressful job and he had a busy family life, but not extraordinary. There had been some late night arguments and tires squealing out of the driveway in the wee hours, but nothing to lead anyone to believe that Kevin had homicidal leanings or was losing his grip. He sometimes drank too much at parties and had once accused Adele of cheating on him in front of a group at a barbeque. Otherwise the family seemed all right, if a bit private. The neighbourhood was friendly; someone would have alerted the police if they had suspected that Kevin Wolfe was dangerous. About the wife and children little was learned. Adele was friendly, if a bit remote. She had her hands full with the twin boys and looked tired, much of the time. The daughter was seen on her bike frequently, riding in circles in front of her house, supervised, usually, by her mother from the front porch, but sometimes alone.

Allan Guthrie from the city's homicide department had arrived only twenty minutes after the bodies had been taken to the hospital, where, he reported, they'd been pronounced DOA. The boys were most definitely dead before they'd been drawn from the bathtub, where they should have remained for investigative purposes, but no one could bear the sight of them. Adele had been faintly alive when she'd been cut down, since the chair beneath her feet had not been kicked away, but she succumbed to her injuries in the ambulance. The murder of the family was Guthrie's investigation, but he congratulated Wyn on dealing with the third child and thanked him for his help. The girl had been taken in by a neighbour pending pick up by one of her mother's siblings.

Guthrie stood for some time smoking a cigarillo near the garage as the forensics team worked, watching them but not interfering, as the scene was delicate and any intrusion, even by a seasoned expert, could contaminate it. When the team finished, he joined Wyn as he stood in the backyard, himself smoking and ruminating in the rose-peach glow of dawn. There was no rule prohibiting Wyn from sharing his notes on the officers' testimonies, so he briefed Guthrie on what he'd been told, particularly the words of Woloshyn about young Jameson being a hero. Guthrie listened with the same stillness evident in the way he surveyed crime scenes, taking in each detail and mentally turning it over in his hands, like a fascinating artifact. Finally he shook his head as he looked around the meticulous garden. "Y'know I'm retiring in a coupla months?" he said. "Been dreading it for years. Retirement just gives you more time to remember shit. At least at work I always have new shit to look at. This is some swan song, if this case is gonna be my last. Ever worked in homicide, investigator?"

Wyn pulled out his own cigarettes, Rothman Kings, had one in his mouth and lit before he even realized he'd decided to smoke another. Habit. He really should quit. He was up to three packs a day. "For about ten years. But then I married and my wife didn't fancy me working in that field. Too many unquiet dead."

"The dead are quiet enough, which is just fine with me, even if it would make my job easier if they could talk," said Guthrie. "But I don't want to know what they were saying, thinking, feeling in those last hours. You guys at SPOA, at least you always know who pulled the trigger."

"We may know, but we're powerless to charge when we think there's been misconduct or negligence. We can only make recommendations." Recommendations that resulted in less than a one-percent rate of charges. To date, not one of those few charges had made it to trial, let alone a conviction.

"Yeah, and I know Henry. He doesn't like to rile up the Police Association." Henry Schell was the Director of SPOA, the fourth person to hold the post in less than seven years. The directorship was among the least sought-after portfolios in the provincial government for two reasons: SPOA's mandate was difficult to reinforce – Police Chiefs routinely ignored the stipulation that they contact SPOA in the event of a death or serious injury precipitated by one of their officers. And secondly, the police union was powerful and vocal; it deemed SPOA an interference in an officer's duty to serve and protect. Oversight was a new concept; heretofore, the police had investigated themselves.

"I'm not sure how you plan to handle this particular case," Guthrie went on, looking at some point in the distance. "But if you recommend a charge of manslaughter, I wouldn't stand in your way."

This was a rather shocking admission, but Wyn wasn't taking it at face value. Guthrie, though usually incorruptible enough, could be fishing for information from Wyn that he would share with the Chief of 42 Division later. "It would never stick," he said only.

Guthrie kept staring into the distance, his eyes squinting against the advancing sun. "As I told ya, I'm retiring; I don't really give a shit anymore, so I'll say this: if that cop was off-duty, say, or was just a civilian neighbour who cornered the man in his basement, as these officers did, and killed him with a weapon, legal or not, I'd recommend a manslaughter charge. Add to that the fact that there was a kid in there with him who could have been caught in the crossfire, and you have a charge of negligence endangering life. Imagine if the guy took his kid and made off in his car and they pursued him and caused an accident. This is no different. And after seeing what Kevin Wolfe did to his family, you can bet emotions were running high when they chased him to the basement. I was down there. The man had no weapon, 'less you count Tickle Me Elmo."

"I was told he made threats," said Wyn.

"No judge would rule this as a case of self-defense on the part of the officers. I think you can make a case for intent to harm the suspect, due to a heightened emotional state after seeing the casualties."

"Intent is almost impossible to prove, Al. They'll just say they were doing their job. That's what they always say."

"Not to put too fine a point on it, but this is a death of an unarmed, middle-class white man, not a drug-crazed thug packing heat in a back alley of Regent." Regent Park was a notorious part of East Toronto that had a high Jamaican immigrant population and trouble with gangs. There had been a few police incidents there that had resulted in the deaths of young black men, which had aroused public condemnation.

"Ah, but what about blue suicide?" Though better known as "suicide by cop," Wyn preferred the more poetic term.

Guthrie shrugged. "The guy may have lured the officers downstairs with the idea of provoking them to kill him. But he had to have put himself in the kind of danger – like running into traffic or jumping in front of a train – that forces a cop to disable him to save him. There was no imminent danger in that rec room. Threats from behind a closed door to kill himself or someone else don't cut it."

"I know all that, Al. But we'd have to have a watertight case before recommending a manslaughter charge. The third child is key, but she may not talk, or we may not be able to access her testimony because of her age."

"If the Crown wants to prosecute, and the charge is manslaughter, she will be assessed to determine if she's a competent witness. She was in the room, she is a key witness," said Guthrie.

Wyn's eyes burned from the powerful light of the summer sun, which was drying the dew off the grass now, making it steam. The new heat intensified the smell of death in the garage. "I'm not sure I'd be comfortable putting a child on the stand, especially after all she's been through. Don't you think we'd have enough evidence without her testimony?"

Guthrie shook his head. "Not for a serious charge. Against a cop to boot. I've had to bring child witnesses into investigations plenty of times. You'd be surprised how well they remember shit. They're also pretty fucking resilient. Kids have ways of coping, with the proper therapy and whatnot." His voice was calm, cool. Years of this kind of work made a person this way. Indeed, it was the sort of profession that attracted people like him in the first place.

"Any idea why he didn't kill the third child?" Wyn asked. "Why he called the police?"

"You worked in criminal investigations. We don't care that much about motive when we've got a mountain of physical evidence to support a conviction. Why does anyone kill the innocent? And what mechanism makes them stop killing? If we knew the whys, Rhys, we could maybe prevent the hows and whens, and who. Frankly, I don't want to know. I don't want to spend any more time than I have to in the mind of a killer. In a way I'm relieved that the cops did take him down, saves the long process of convicting the bastard. I bet he's glad to be dead too. Won't be haunted by the images of those poor kids and that lovely woman hanging in his garage. Wish we could say the same."

Wyn moved to pull out his cigarettes again, then stopped himself. "You say you're retiring, but perhaps you might consider a post-homicide career as an investigator at SPOA?" he suggested. SPOA was thought to be less stressful, and for fifty-year-old retirees who didn't like golf, a decent-paying diversion. He could use someone like Guthrie on his side. Wyn was not exactly popular among his investigator brethren.

"Tell me something, you got any kids?"

"A daughter. She's two."

Guthrie squinted at the sun. "Well, if you stay in this profession, might as well say goodbye to her now, 'cause you're not gonna speak to her again 'til you retire. I've got a second chance with my grandkids, who seem to like old Grampa Al. I wanna travel, see some of the achievements of the human race, not the crazy stupid shit people do to each other. That family." Guthrie shook his head, sad, but not disbelieving. "I'm done with it. You're young," he said, taking in Wyn's unstreaked black hair, his still-youthful features. "But I reckon by around fifty you'll be ready to pack it in too."

Wyn pondered this. The image of the dead woman, the bundles on the gurneys, grotesque as they were, did not infringe on his love of this kind of work. If anything, they intensified it. He could have been like Guthrie and been a homicide detective, but he preferred dealing with the police. And finding that girl in all the chaos, lifting her out of it, holding her and feeling her breath on his neck, smelling of innocence … there was nothing in the world like it. She was a miracle. Not many professions proffered miracles.

Part I

Chapter One

December 18, 2014

It was only when Wyn was putting on his coat in the dim foyer of his house did he notice the framed photograph propped on the staircase, about halfway between the main and second floors. It was a new photograph of Rebecca, in graduation finery. Her usually black hair had been recently dyed blonde with disappointing results, and she had the expression of someone who was resigned to similar ungratifying experiences. Beneath her face, on the part of the gown that covered her heart, was a note written in his wife Anna's hand: *This is your daughter. She lives with us. She will be accompanying us on vacation.*

This was very much in keeping with Anna's sense of humour. When Wyn had met her he had considered it playful. Now he thought it was aggrandizing.

He put on his galoshes, then gently released the bolt from the lock of the front door and turned the handle, its click a toy pistol shot in his brain. Outside lay a mute and ambivalent winter dawn, the lazy northern sun slowly unpurpling the darkness. It had snowed the night before but not very much. He surveyed the generous sweep of the wide street and the large houses, built, like his own, in the 1920s, his vision obscured by his own exhaled breath, and quickly buttoned his coat. He then raised his chin to the morning, resolute. Lifting his briefcase, he made his way down the steps. Anna didn't know where he took himself on Saturday mornings, but she knew it wasn't to work, because she'd called the supervisor inquiring after him once or twice. Where Wyn was headed was his secret.

Several months ago his wife had decided that the family needed to take one last vacation together before Rebecca finished high school and embarked, hopefully, on a university career. "One last" reverberated hollowly with Wyn; he couldn't remember their first vacation, and he had not taken holidays with his family in over a decade, and only to Britain, to which Wyn would have gone anyway, to see his parents. Mother and daughter frequently vacationed together and Anna long ago had given up inviting her husband. But she asked this time and he'd acquiesced – had no choice but to acquiesce. His wife had demanded so little and put up with so much in the twenty-one years they'd been married that the very fact that she made the request had a momentousness about it, almost a finality, like a dying wish. But, unfortunately, he was only blurrily aware of what he'd agreed to. All he could cobble together in his mind were bird's-eye-view mirages of sun, sand, margaritas, people walking on a beach. They were the backdrops in screensavers, they weren't *lived*, as far as he could comprehend.

As he came to the end of the block, the wind picked up a little and chilled his ears. He wore no hat. Winter always came as a surprise to Wyn; he could never prepare himself for it, even after he'd spent twenty winters in Canada. He was still more accustomed to the temperate, if monochromatic, weather of his native Britain, and found Canadian extremes of heat and cold burdensome. Usually he avoided confrontations with weather whenever he could, but today he couldn't take his car anywhere because Anna had promised Rebecca she could use it. The girl had only just gotten her G2 licence and now routinely harassed her parents into letting her drive everywhere, even though the subway was only five blocks away. Anna had asked Wyn, several times, to take his daughter out driving, but after several evasive manoeuvres he finally declined, citing work and a wish to see his fiftieth birthday. She hadn't asked him since, but had once or twice confiscated his keys, and he did not berate her for it. He just took the subway.

He stopped at the top of the main road and put his hand to his holster for his phone. It wasn't there. Heart fluttering, he felt around his coat pockets. He couldn't go back to the house and risk waking up Anna or Rebecca, but he couldn't imagine getting through the day without it, either.

Wyn had a long and intimate relationship with communication devices. It had started with pagers, which were commonplace when he'd begun his job as an investigator years before, and which were invented for people in professions where response times were crucial. Back then, when his pager had beeped, his response was reflexive and instantaneous; he reached for the nearest phone, gathered up his keys and found his shoes. He could be on the road to a scene in less than a minute. His wife had wryly joked that the only thing he did quicker was achieve orgasm. He came to see other activities as intrusions in the continuum of waiting for a beep and responding. As a result he drove too fast, ate too fast, fucked too fast. If he lingered over some mundane endeavour too long he was reneging in his main duty: responding to a call for help.

But now that he was Director he found that he mostly resented his phone. He was not in the front line any longer, so most of the beeps and chirps were to alert him to messages with updates on cases, reports, excuses from his team for delays in completing tasks. Or they were emails from the man who was technically his boss, the Attorney General, about policy developments or the mandate, which Wyn had been toiling to change since he took the leadership. Or it was invitations to conferences. Or it was Barb, his secretary, reminding him about his dentist appointments. A few hours without it might actually be a good thing. After all, he didn't want to be contacted. But he checked one more time anyway, and he discovered there was a device in the inner breast pocket of his winter coat, slender and smooth, too small to be a phone, with a cord attached. Mystified, he pulled it out. It was a pink iPod and headphones.

It was obviously not Anna's, who only listened to music on the radio. That meant it was Rebecca's, but how did it end up in his winter coat? His investigator mind pondered; Rebecca must have worn his coat to take out the garbage or something. She was always hooked up to some device, so it was not that peculiar that she would have put it in a pocket, but an inner one? He shrugged. Who knew what went through teenagers' minds.

The day was unusually silent. It was December, and therefore not quite light, even at almost 7am, and the world was how Wyn liked it best – uninhabited. During his years working the night shift, dawn had come to have a special significance for him. At dawn he could breathe in the purity of a day in which no one had yet been shot, stabbed, beaten, robbed or run over. After his shift, he should have gone to bed but he never did, the time was too precious to be slept through. So what he'd usually done upon returning to his silent house was pad around with his coffee and the paper, even go for a walk, if it was a nice day in May. When he was made Director five years ago and locked into a roughly nine-to-five schedule, he lost dawn's asylum. He went into the office very early, but it was a twenty-four-hour outfit and there were always people around. At home were the insistent demands of his family, and if he wasn't running errands for his wife and child or fixing something (or hiring someone else to fix things; he wasn't handy) he suffered under the persistent conviction that he was neglecting them, even when he was present, and this drove him to sequester himself in his basement office for hours at a time. Indeed, in his office – a converted laundry room that still smelled of fabric softener – the pounding footsteps on the floor above him had one, oppressive note: disappointment. He needed time to himself.

Did Anna know where he went? Did she care? He usually came home from his Saturday excursions around 2pm, leaving enough time to undertake any chores assigned to him, and he always had dinner with his wife and daughter, if they weren't out doing things. But whether Anna wondered if he was merely out for extraordinarily long walks or having an affair with his secretary Barb (though had she ever met her, she would be reassured this was not the case) he never determined. If challenged he would tell the truth; he always told the truth, and Anna knew this, which may be why she didn't ask. She didn't want to know.

As he stood on the underground platform he took the iPod out to examine it. He reckoned that when he returned home Rebecca would be churlish, thinking he'd filched it from her. She and her many devices were virtually inseparable; at least, that was how it seemed to Wyn, though, to be fair, he didn't see her very often. Their communication was limited to his flaccid greetings and her shrugs on good days, but when he was in bad humour and called her "The Heiress" and "The Girl Who Will Marry Into Wealth" because she refused to get a part-time job to help pay for her schooling, she retorted with snorts, huffs and "Oh my *god*'s" as she marched away from him.

He turned the device over in his hands, a bit embarrassed by the colour; the pink screamed girlhood. But there was no one else in the station, so he decided to turn it on, see what dreck kids her age were listening to these days. Some auto-tuned poptress wearing a sno-cone bra? Or a boy band comprised exclusively of hair gel, leather pants and glitter? Or maybe she fancied herself a "classic rock" kind of girl and bobbed her head to Led Zeppelin, Pink Floyd and the Beatles, all bands that Wyn had never liked. He let his thumb drift over the screen and watched album covers carousel and present themselves to him like contestants in a beauty pageant. Some of them looked familiar. He held it at a distance (he hadn't conceded to bifocals yet) to bring them into focus. The Police, Elvis Costello, Talking Heads, Pater Gabriel, David Bowie (*Low*? Rebecca liked *Low*?) and more of what he'd been lugging in milk cartons from flat to flat, across the ocean, from basement to attic – all of it nestled in his palm. Wyn was shocked to see so many songs of his evaporated youth (which had left a sticky residue on his middle age, like gum on a shoe) and that somehow, somewhere along her meandering stroll to adulthood, Rebecca had appropriated them for her own personal soundtrack. Did he dare to talk to her about it? After she freaked out at him for "stealing" her iPod, would she like to hear how when he heard the first Sex Pistols album in 1977, when he was only thirteen, he declared them the worst band of all time, destined to go nowhere? Or the time he met Joe Strummer in a pub and played darts with him, and won? How he listened to "So Lonely" over and over when he got dumped by the first girl he ever loved until the record practically bled, then never listened to it again? Could he talk about these things with her without inviting her derision or, worse, her contempt?

The train entered the station, pushing burned-smelling air in front of it, the brakes a supercharged metal squawk. The car he entered was completely devoid of people. Who else would be going somewhere at 7am on a Saturday? Shift workers might be going home, or revellers who'd outstayed their welcome at a party, but there generally weren't enough of them to populate a train. Still, Wyn sat in the most private seat (at the back, where the cars connected) with his large square briefcase, but instead of using this blank time to read a report on a car chase, he fiddled some more with the iPod, intrigued by the possibilities. He didn't know what he wanted to listen to. He couldn't remember what he liked from his collection; it had been created almost thirty years ago and the last time he'd put a record on the stereo must have been sometime in the mid-nineties, after a few drinks maybe.

Joy Division. When the *Peel Sessions* album cover appeared he instantly recalled a song that in 1979 had sent reverberations cascading through him on the first listen: "Love Will Tear Us Apart." Feeling himself trembling a little in anticipation, he selected the album and the song, then put the earbuds in, leaned back in the hard seat and pressed PLAY.

The song commenced its flourishing crescendo of electric guitar riffs. Then the haunting, heartbroken synthesizer and the simple melody in D. And finally Ian Curtis's voice, that baritone that sounded like a man who'd despaired of ever being rescued from the bottom of a well.

Wyn's faulty memory convinced him that this song was about lust turned toxic. But the real metaphor resembled a curtain. Two lives woven together that had been cleaved and pulled asunder, slowly and agonizingly. He could actually hear the fabric ripping in the monotone of Ian Curtis's voice. And what had done the tearing? Ennui. He had a vision of himself in bed with Anna, she on one side of the desert of their Sahara-sized bed, he on the other, dunes of sheets between them. They'd forgotten what the other's mouth tasted like.

Wyn tried to remember something from the past eighteen years that wasn't work-related. There was no cicatrix in his brain that reflexively twinged when he smelled certain foods or perfumes, or touched an old piece of clothing, that might take him back to the days when he'd been dating Anna, or the first years of his daughter's life. Back in his glass office were stacks of reports, binders full of memos from the Ministry, on his computer were hundreds, thousands of emails. Every minute of his professional life had been tediously documented. He could choose any random day from the last decade and find a corresponding agenda. His personal history had no index or table of contents.

Now, when he actually wanted to read some of it, all the pages from that manuscript had gone skittering across an empty parking lot in his mind, and even when he caught a few he'd found them blank. This thought elicited a bit of a panic, so he forced himself to take a deep breath and gave himself milestones: the first time he'd had sex with Anna, his wedding day, Rebecca's birth. From a couple of the pages, watermarks glowed when held up to the light of his yearning: what Anna had worn the night he made love to her (a black velvet dress), the slick of their kiss at the altar (well, at the registry office, they'd only had a perfunctory service with a few friends), how his thumb had had an infected hangnail but he let Anna hold it throughout the birth of Rebecca anyway, unable to complain about his agony while witnessing hers. Wyn squeezed his eyes tight – Rebecca as a little girl. A school concert? Christmas day? Something, anything. Out of the vagueness an image surfaced – the white part dividing her dark hair, seen from his parental eyrie. Sitting at his feet, chirping in child-lisp to a Barbie doll.

These frugal images, accompanied by the song, brought on an unexpected attack of melancholy, an ache that probed deep into his gut and made his eyes sting. Opening them he found that everything in front of him was blurry and wet, like he was underwater. Why couldn't he see properly? A drop fell on his coat and he realized, confusedly, that it was a tear. A tear. Jesus. He hastily touched his eyes with his sleeve before anything else fell out.

At the hotel, Wyn went through the motions of producing his credit card (he applied for it at another bank, and had the bills sent to his office), ordered a pot of coffee and picking up the key, wandered to the elevator and rode up to the sixth floor in its padded silence. He set his briefcase on the bed and pulled out his laptop and printouts of the reports he needed to review. He had his red pen.

This was his secret. He came to hotel rooms on Saturdays to work. Rather a dull secret, but a fiercely guarded one nonetheless. And such an important part of his routine that even the dully pleading gaze of his photographed daughter and Anna's stinging note did not chastise him enough to change his plans. Wyn took out his pen and settled into a chair by the window with a report on a police car chase where a civilian had been killed. Another police chase.

He set down his pen. How many reports had he written as an investigator? At least five hundred. Given that they took him usually twenty to thirty hours to write, that meant that the accumulated time spent just report writing was somewhere in the vicinity of twelve thousand hours. How many had he read since becoming Director? Another two hundred, at least. Another thousand hours or thereabouts spent reviewing and correcting. That did not even take into account the number of hours he'd spent collecting data, interviewing people, discussing cases with colleagues. A frugal estimate of how many hours he'd worked at SPOA was an astonishing seventy-five thousand. Add to that the twenty-five thousand or so hours he'd put in as an investigator for the Met and he had dedicated approximately one hundred thousand hours of his life to his career.

So was he tired of it all, finally? More pressingly, why hadn't he gotten tired of it sooner? It was as though the time he had on this earth was stored in a bank account, and he'd been carefully drawing on it, making sure that each hour was spent in a useful and important way. No fucking around, no dithering with TV or pubs or sex or daydreaming. No mountain climbing or beach lounging or going to the cinema. But on the subway with the iPod, he hadn't thought about where he had to be (well, not much) or what he needed to be doing. He'd simply existed. The hotel sojourns had been merely a cautious, incomplete move in that direction, because he would still take calls, answer email. But now he was in the hotel room without his phone and didn't have to work *if he didn't want to.*

With the realization that he was free, for a few hours at least, Wyn tossed the report on the floor. Just threw it on the floor. It was not even 8am but he opened the mini-bar, thrilling to the wickedness of tearing the seal, incurring a ridiculously high charge on his bill. But after one hundred thousand hours, fuck it. He poured some Jack Daniel's in a glass, took the iPod out of his coat pocket, turned the chair to the window, opened the curtains and sat down. Put the headphones on and pressed PLAY.

He listened to songs he hadn't heard in thirty years for about an hour, his eyes closed, sipping the whiskey. For much of that time he thought about nothing, but then slowly, memories emerged. His father had had bad psoriasis, so he washed his hands with tar soap that would form black bubbles when lathered. He remembered sitting on the stiles between country fields of sheep in Yorkshire in summer and passing a can of ale back and forth with Amy (who was a mate, not a girlfriend, though he had longed for her). Then stepping off the train in Waterloo station and seeing London for the first time as a teenager and falling in love with it instantly. He thought about policing in that city with the Met, about his crazy partner who loved to drive fast, almost got them killed a few times. Then Canada, SPOA, his early career as an investigator. Then he thought about the case that changed his career. The Wolfe murders.

He rose from the chair now and went to fetch his laptop, making a detour at the fridge to retrieve another small bottle – vodka – from the mini-bar. He poured it into the glass that still had a few drops of whiskey in it. He wasn't going to do work. He was going to do something he had wanted to do for years but never permitted himself to do: look up the third child on the internet. She was twenty-five now. Was she as beautiful as she was that day? Was she happy? Wyn knew some things about her: where she'd gone to university, what she'd studied, where she'd travelled when she received a settlement of five million dollars in a civil suit against the Police Association. He knew that she had changed her name. All of this he had found out from staying in contact with her lawyer. But he had never gone online to find her, because he knew once he started searching, he would want to find out more and more. He might not know where to stop. And because he was an investigator, he could find almost everything there was to know about her: her lovers and friends, her interests. Too much information was dangerous, but he suddenly had an appetite for a bit of danger.

After a few bracing gulps of vodka, which made him grimace (he was not a spirit drinker), Wyn trembled only a little when he typed "Justine Lyons" into the search engine.

***

When he came home later that afternoon, the photo on the stairs had been removed and no one was home. Out driving, he reckoned. He put the pink iPod in the keys basket where his daughter would see it. More than slightly intoxicated, he instinctively went to his basement office, where he found his phone, lying on his desk, innocent of any misdemeanour but looking apologetic nonetheless. He turned it on, feeling guilty himself now for not having missed it more, and waded, somewhat distractedly, into its shallows. Usual dross in his email: updates on cases, excuses for why certain reports hadn't been submitted yet, complaints about uncooperative officers, witnesses. If he went back to the same day a year ago, the litany would look the same. He thought he'd never tire of SPOA, of his power. Maybe it was Joy Division's fault, or maybe it was the Jack, or his two hours online finding out everything he could about the third child (not everything, but almost, almost), but the narrow cot looked inviting for once. The weight of the entire house pressed into his shoulders and spine. Sleep might be the only refuge from this disquiet.

Above him noise of thumping boots and the whoosh of a slammed front door – Rebecca's hand, no doubt. Anna never closed doors that way. The buzz of their female voices intermingling – one pitched in querulousness, the other subdued. Wyn could only hope that his cherished vehicle had not suffered the vicissitudes of their quarrelling. He should go upstairs and be pleasant, jovial, rumple his daughter's hair (he couldn't remember the last time he'd touched Rebecca), offer to order pizza or something. Be the man of the house.

Instead Wyn lay down on the hard cot and closed his eyes.

Chapter Two

December 26, 2014

Boxing Day dawned inauspiciously, its too bright snow glow an affront to Wyn's hangover from Christmas dinner, when he had consumed a quantity of red wine unusual for him. Some of Anna's relatives had been visiting (she was part of a very large family, something that had always intimidated Wyn. His parents had been only children and he had just the one brother) and Wyn, obligated to sit through a multi-course meal and not look at his phone, had to content himself with imbibing to dull the chinking sounds of cutlery and chatter, contributing little to the conversation. But he wasn't expected to. Anna's family could talk about practically anything, as long as it wasn't politics, religion or culture, because those topics were not conducive to mirth or, more importantly, did not pertain in any way to their personal enjoyment of a solid, middle-class existence. To them, the world beyond their material needs was a vast blank landscape of death, so against it they erected terrific barriers of noise, listing towers comprised of tinkling observations on food (turkey cooked to perfection, not too dry at all), the weather (cold, but last Christmas had been colder), Rebecca's hair (blonde made her look more like her mother, which was presumably a good thing), and Anna's taste in cutlery, linen, glassware and butchers (consensus: excellent). In the swagged and mahoganied splendour of the Rhys dining room, they rebuffed death with their easy laughter, fork tines punctuating their jokes, and discussed plans for the near future: ski trips, holidays south, engagements, weddings, secure in the knowledge that they would live to see them all. Wyn admired their resoluteness; not to them would sudden tragedy strike with its poleaxe, first bludgeoning them senseless, then slitting their throats with its keen blade.

Rebecca had been just as taciturn, but not quite as pleasant about it, sighing and flopping in her seat adjacent to his place at the foot of the table, missing, he was sure, her own gadgetry. He had wanted to ask her about the iPod and about the small galaxy of music from his own spent youth stored there, but couldn't find a way to introduce the conversation, having had very few father-daughter discussions over the course of her adolescence. Even generous alcohol consumption had failed to give him the courage. He'd had to deal with hardened criminals and murderers over the course of his career; why couldn't he talk to his own child? The origins of the playlist, and how the device came to be in his coat, remained a mystery.

He had gone to bed with his wife last night, but they hadn't cuddled or made love. Like two effigies of their former selves, they had lain side by side, indifferent to everything but slumber. Now when he woke he observed Anna deep in sleep in her silk nightgown, one bare arm draped over the edge of the coverlet, the fingers of her left hand adorned in the hard-earned diamonds and gold Wyn had bestowed at their engagement to prove his undying love and devotion. To see them together one would think he was older than his wife by at least ten years. She looked even younger while sleeping, her soft blonde hair a small storm on her pillow. Under her closed lids were the bluest eyes Wyn had ever seen and even though she was of Norwegian extraction, she had the features of a classic Englishwoman: sharp-nosed and thin-lipped but with ample cheeks that prevented her from looking weathered. Her body was slim and gently angled in all the right places: she really was a beautiful woman. In the early years of their marriage he would notice other men's gazes on her, slyly raking the outline of her breasts and hips, coveting her, and had felt the smugness of proprietorship, was charmed at her lack of self-consciousness. She had a job that was not too stressful, working as an underwriter for an insurance company. She had a Master's degree in Art History but never really bothered to pursue a career in that field; it would have required more education. Her nine-to-five job gave her abundant free time for other interests: yoga, gardening, decorating their home, reading magazines, watching reno and cooking shows. Wyn recalled her taking classes associated with those pursuits. She was keenly interested in Rebecca's education and extracurricular activities. She had never smoked and kept to a strict healthy diet. For years she had given Wyn grief about how much he smoked (he'd quit twelve years ago) and tried to get him to eat regularly, but she lost interest after a while. He could probably smoke a coal fire plant's worth of carcinogens now and she wouldn't notice, as long as he did it outside and not around his daughter.

Wyn had bought her many expensive presents in recent years, especially since he'd commenced travelling more to conferences. Most of the gifts were purchased in airport duty-free shops that took advantage of busy men like him who only had time to shop while waiting for connecting flights. As a result, Anna had an impressive collection of designer perfumes, a couple of Louis Vuitton bags, Hermes scarves, diamonds set in earrings and pendants. Glamour, but anonymous glamour – thousands of other women all over the world had these items. Anna had always been appreciative, but likely she would have preferred gifts that demonstrated a deep love for her, carefully chosen in boutiques in the Distillery or in Yorkville, things engraved, or something she had always wanted, a painting maybe. He didn't know what she wanted, though he had his suspicions, when he permitted himself to contemplate them. It was unspoken but mutually acknowledged that Wyn spent so much money on his wife out of guilt. And not just for not being home very often, or, when he was home, for not paying much attention to his family. The real unspoken truth about their relationship was the most awkward one: they didn't have sex anymore.

Back in the UK, when Wyn had a stressful job as a criminal investigator, he always had the energy for and interest in making love to her. But after they moved to Canada, he had gotten his job at SPOA and Rebecca was born, their sexual encounters lost their frequency. Wyn would come home from an all-night shift and find mother and daughter had usurped his place in the marital bed; he would end up on the sofa in the rec room, watching old American sitcoms until he fell asleep. Then, when Rebecca could finally be persuaded to sleep on her own, Anna had complained of Wyn waking her with his nocturnal schedule and, after he put his back out sleeping on the rec room sofa, finally set up for him another bedroom/office in the old laundry room in the basement. For years his wife had had their large beautiful bedroom almost exclusively to herself.

He left his wife to her slumber, when he could have woken her by tracing the constellation of moles on her back, between her shoulder blades, like he had done in earlier times, fashioning pictures: a bird, a teapot, a closed fist. She may have turned towards him and smiled the way she used to smile when she was in love with him; one side hitched higher than the other, eyes half-closed, and perhaps slid her hand down his torso, clasped his penis, drawn him to her. Now he couldn't hazard making any overture for fear of being politely rebuffed. He would merely do what he did every day: take a shower, shave, put on clothes.

He stayed in the shower for a long time, having the luxury to indulge in its cascading warmth, which loosed the tendrils of his slight hangover, sent them swirling down the drain. For the first time in years he had no plans for the day save packing and driving to the airport. What would he wear in Mexico? All he really owned were pyjamas and suits. And what would they do once they got there? He suddenly felt anxious. The idea of a week in a hot place with an endless horizon, staring at nothing, talking about nothing, was deeply unsettling. Relaxing? Reading a book? Anna told him he couldn't bring his laptop, had only very grumpily conceded that he needed his phone. What had she said to him? "You are convinced that the entire universe will collapse if you're not available twenty-four hours a day. No one is that important, and nothing is that urgent, that you can't take a week off." But she was wrong.

He could hear Anna moving around their bedroom as he dried himself and set about shaving. His hand trembled – how much had he had to drink? – and he nicked his chin. Swearing and bleeding, he opened a vanity drawer and moved things about, looking for antiseptic. At the very back of the drawer he felt a packet with a familiar ring in it. He drew it out. It was a condom.

He didn't look at the package, but at himself in the glass, at the blood that was now making its way down his neck, thinning as it stretched from the source.

A condom. Wyn had had a vasectomy back in – when? 2000? – because Anna didn't want any more children and thought the pill would give her breast cancer. Or something. He couldn't remember the rationale, but Wyn had complied because, naturally, he wanted to continue having sex with his spouse, though it was, ironically, the beginning of the decline in their marital relations.

He had never worn condoms with her in all the years they'd been together. He turned over the packet now and looked for evidence that it predated his operation, not knowing precisely what the shelf life of a condom was, but reckoning that they weren't much use after ten years. The expiry date was later this year.

So, the vacation was meant as a farewell, something he'd suspected when Anna had made the request. Would they fight to stay together, or would they let their sagging marriage, sodden and stained like a tent left out in the rain, finally collapse upon itself? What kind of woman was she now? In their daily interactions her identity had devolved in his mind and was replaced by roles: Mother, Homemaker, Professional, Wife. Perhaps, to her, Wyn was also just a type now: the workaholic type. The ambitious type. The English type, with all the attendant qualities of stiff upper-lippedness, repression, cynicism. Their relationship no longer possessed the alchemy that at one time made them indissoluble as partners, lovers, friends. He recalled that day on the subway, when he'd struggled to remember moments that should have been easily retrieved. He sensed now that such forgetfulness was the symptom of a much larger problem, he'd lost the plot of their story a long time ago, and Anna had forged, was forging, a new narrative in which Wyn was not cast among the main characters. There was a man out there somewhere for whom this condom was intended, like the glass slipper on the foot of Cinderella.

When he exited the bathroom in just a towel, he found Anna awake, dressed in jeans and a turtleneck, bustling about and packing, looking for all the world like an ordinary middle-aged woman preparing for a family vacation, not the lover he had momentarily craved when he woke, not the adulteress he now suspected her to be. She had laid out some things on the bed that were intended for their holiday. "I shopped at that place on Avenue Road you like. You had nothing suitable for the climate. This must be your first time south, except for work," she said, not looking at him.

Why wasn't he furious with her? Why was he standing in the bedroom in a towel, watching helplessly as his wife pretended that she didn't have condoms stashed in the bathroom? Wyn was not the kind of man to suppress his anger. But perhaps he knew that he had no right to call her out and accuse her, because he'd given her far too much ammunition for a counterattack: he'd had a lover of his own for two decades, his job.

Anna said, "Hard to believe we haven't been away together on holiday since we were married."

"We've been to England."

"Seeing your parents is not a vacation."

She was right. Wyn's parents were not pleasant people and Leeds not a very pretty place to spend two weeks, at any time of the year. He picked up a shirt. "Er, thanks," he said dubiously. Khaki pants and golf shirts in colours he never wore: red, turquoise, yellow and a kind of seafoam green. They looked like they were meant for someone far more interesting and fun-loving than him, for a man who relished walks on a beach or exploring tropical undergrowth. Perhaps she'd been dreaming of her lover while perusing the racks, choosing what he might like, rather than what her husband would prefer? But what did her husband prefer? Staying home.

He put on a pair of khakis, the red shirt and observed himself in the full-length mirror. Casual Wyn. Vacationing Wyn. Wyn the golfer, sailor, tinker, tailor. Middle-aged, successful, confident. He attempted to ascertain his worth not by Anna's standards, but those of another woman. He stood up straighter and lifted his chin. He wasn't a bad-looking man. He'd never carried excess weight because, as Anna once observed, he had the metabolism of a hamster. He had all of his hair, which was satisfyingly thick and wavy with enough grey in the black to make him look distinguished, and his face, while a bit forbidding, had firmness, had character. His eye colour was the first thing Anna had fallen in love with – not quite green, not quite hazel, but a peculiar shade that she said was like a cat's, gold green, sometimes amber.

Perhaps his wife didn't want him anymore, but another woman might. After all, another man seemed to want Anna, maybe several men. Maybe she'd had many lovers over the dry course of their years as a couple. He tried to picture it: Anna naked in front of another man, flicking the condom on his bare chest. What did the man look like? Would he be younger than Anna, or was he some phlegmatic gent from her office, soft-bellied, outwardly trepidatious but inwardly thrilled to have scored with such a vibrant woman? Wyn could only think from the point of view of the lover, not from that of Anna herself. Perhaps he didn't know her well enough anymore to guess what kind of man she wanted now, or to what purpose, except that she was lonely and neglected by a husband who felt almost as lonely, but not lonely enough to traverse the desert of their alienation.

As he stood before the mirror he saw his phone blink from his bedside table. It was probably someone from work. It was always someone from work.

The call display showed that it was Stuart McIntosh, the day supervisor at SPOA. Wyn hesitated, perhaps he should ignore it. But he was the Director, he had to take it. Still, he deliberated as the device rang and rang.

"Are you going to pick that up?" It was Anna's voice, behind him. Wyn didn't turn around. "They know you're on vacation, right?" she added.

Wyn slid the lock on the phone's screen. "Wyn Rhys," he said wearily.

"We got an altercation at Gerrard Square Mall," said Stuart, forgoing all niceties such as greetings. "DOA white male, late forties. Causing a disturbance. Security called in 55 Division at 9:15am."

Wyn looked quickly at his watch. It was almost 11am, later than he thought, but he had slept in and had contemplated the condom for a while.

"Cause of death?" he asked as he unbuttoned the khakis and slid them awkwardly over his legs, then walked to his closet and the rows of dark trousers and white shirts hanging there. They didn't mind that Wyn would never birdwatch while wearing them.

"Tasers were used to subdue him. Maybe a heart attack. Behaviour was erratic; could be drugs or alcohol involved. About thirty witnesses."

"Frank's on call today. Did you speak to him?"

"'Course, but he's in fucking Niagara Falls, with his daughter. Weather's acting up. So I called in Nick; he's the closest in Metro."

Frank O'Shaunessy was his most senior investigator and Nick Chirila was the new guy. This would be his first death in custody case. Today would be a veritable test of his capabilities, as there would be a post-mortem to attend. Hopefully the post-mortem would take place too late in the day for Wyn to accompany him. Worse than blood in his clothes was the stench of formaldehyde, which he had learned through experience was almost impossible to eradicate.

"Nick's never been to a scene."

"Yeah, well, we gotta work with what we got."

Wyn thought about his impending vacation, an abstract image of two hopeful-looking margaritas on a table with a sunset in the distance, then mentally swept them aside and replaced them with one stark priority. "I'm going," he told Stuart.

Directors did not go to scenes of incidents, ever. Stuart asked him to repeat himself, then said, "I don't think that's a good idea. Lucci would have a fucking bird."

Since Tony Lucci had become Toronto's Chief of Police, he had been vocal and belligerent about the powers of SPOA, especially about a new change to the regulations that obligated subject officers – ones who were directly responsible for a serious injury or death of a civilian – to remain on the scene to be interviewed in the immediate aftermath of an incident. It had been one of Wyn's hard-won achievements as Director and very controversial. "I don't give a rat's arse about Lucci. We need a lead on this. Get Frank in there as fast as you can. We can't leave Nick on his own. Sylvia will show up and try to snatch away the subject officers." After a number of run-ins, he knew what Sylvia Hughes was like.

After he rang off it took only a minute and a half to remove the red shirt and don the official uniform of Director Rhys: dark trousers, white oxford shirt with French cuffs and the two top buttons undone, no tie. He was adjusting his cuffs and putting links in them when he heard Anna's voice behind him again. "You're not going to the office." In his peripheral vision Wyn saw she held in her hands some silky things, lingerie or dresses, he couldn't tell. "You're on vacation," she said.

Finishing with his cuffs and sitting on the bed to put on his socks, Wyn said, "Yes, I'm on vacation, but I'm also in charge." And I'm not carrying any condoms in the event that I meet a lusty tart at a crime scene, he thought. He stood and moved past his wife like she was a piece of furniture placed inconveniently in the room. He couldn't look at her without seeing in her eyes disappointment, or worse, disinterest.

Downstairs, Wyn put on his overcoat and checked his briefcase. Dictaphone, notebook, battery charger. The pink iPod was still in the keys basket, where he'd left it over a week ago. He wondered, for only a moment, if Rebecca had left it there for him before taking it and shoving it in his pocket. He didn't know why.

Anna had remained at the top of the stairs and was observing as Wyn prepared to leave. "It'll be only a couple of hours," he said, though it was likely to be at least five. The flight was at 7pm. "I can meet you at the airport. You can have my car."

"Wyn," she said. He turned, looked at her finally. From her position at the top of the stairs his wife resembled an angel of judgment. "If you're not at the airport by 6pm, don't bother coming at all." He thought he heard something break in her voice. She turned, entered the bedroom and shut the door.

Chapter Three

The mall was awash with people, kids mostly, flush with gift card booty. Gerrard Square Mall was not a glitzy establishment, merely a neighbourhood plaza serving the slowly gentrifying East Chinatown and Riverdale community. Most of the shops were discount stores selling clothes and shoes that may as well have been made of paper and plastic bags, they were so cheap and shoddy. At one end was a greenly lit grocery store with a large bulk food section. The clientele was almost exclusively South Asian or Asian, with a smattering of low-income white people from the high-rises near the train tracks. The few tinselly Christmas decorations looked tired and uninspired, nothing like the crystal and flourish in the Eaton Centre downtown.

Many of the curious were milling around the part of the mall where the confrontation had occurred, and all seemed to know that Wyn was an official person by his stride and his briefcase. People stepped out of his way. Already, police tape had been stretched across the entrance to the large Staples outlet and officers were posted along its boundary. The media had arrived, too, with cameras, and Wyn, reading texts from

Stuart on his phone as he walked, could see them in his peripheral vision. They may have been a little surprised, seeing the Director of SPOA in attendance and on a holiday no less. No doubt most of them had already received the standard response from the office that all was going according to procedure and that an official statement would be forthcoming, but they moved, herd-like, towards him nonetheless. Blinking a little under the glare of the lights being held above his head, he said only that there had been an incident in the Staples store. "The scene has been secured and our forensics team is on its way," he said. Asked if he could confirm that someone had died, he said only, "A person has been injured. We'll let you know more when we know more." He then flashed his ID card to the officers guarding the entrance to the store. Bending under the police tape, Wyn's back spasmed sharply. He feared for a moment that he wouldn't be able to straighten up again, but he managed, wincingly. It was once something he could do with little effort, even though he was so tall. Getting old, he thought.

The scene had been taped off by police, and Wyn knew to not cross the inner periphery where the altercation took place, but he could get a glimpse of the outline of where the man had lain when he fell. He also noted the unusual-looking structure that had been fabricated from the shop's supplies. It resembled a barricade, but an artful one: boxes of paper were arranged in a symmetrical way, with gaps in between, forming shelves, on which other items were arrayed: boxes of pens, DVDs, iPods and the like. It was about ten feet long and seven feet high. What was it supposed to resemble, a castle? A fortress? How long had it taken to build, and why hadn't someone stopped the man? Somewhat bizarre, but Wyn had seen some strange things. Along a couple of the other aisles some inventory had been scattered and a DVD display capsized. Otherwise, there was no evidence of violence, even though a man had died. After a rash of gun-related deaths in recent years, Tasers had been introduced and frequently deployed in situations where a civilian may not be a direct threat, but required stringent subduing. However, for all the manufacturer's promises about their efficacy and safety, Tasers still carried risks, after all, they carried fifty thousand volts of electricity, and a civilian had died in Vancouver a few years earlier after having been tased. They may be mess-free, more precise and less traumatic to witness than a person being shot with a gun, but they made it far more difficult to determine a cause of death.

For all that it was unfortunate for the family of the victim that this man had died so ignominiously in a public place, Wyn was secretly grateful that he had not been grievously injured instead. With the severely wounded it was imperative to get as much information out of them as possible before they lapsed into a coma or succumbed to their injuries. Highly disagreeable as it was, it was often necessary for investigators to chase ambulances to hospitals and run alongside gurneys with tape recorders, trying, usually unsuccessfully, to get a half-dead victim to talk. Some investigators refused to do it on principle. Wyn had done it, many times. Anna had called him a "justice vulture." There were many things about his profession that she found annoying, but chasing ambulances was, to her mind, deplorable.

A couple of officers stood alongside Sylvia Hughes, the Police Association counsel. Wyn noticed her first because of the orange parka she habitually wore, favouring it probably because it distinguished her from all the black uniforms, but Wyn thought it made her look like a crossing guard. He wondered how long she had been at the scene. Typically, SPOA was called in first.

Nick Chirila, SPOA's newest investigator, stood near Sylvia, looking aggrieved and somewhat confused. He was young and quite handsome and would probably never defloresce into stoutness and jowliness, the way most cops-turned-investigators did. Wyn recalled his own early days as an investigator. He, too, had been the youngest on the team and for the first year chided about his accent, his height, his private school vocabulary, which, among men with scarcely high school educations, distinguished him even more than his European background. But he had already been an investigator in a world capital before coming to SPOA and that earned him some respect. Nick was smart and ambitious but a bit soft. After years of negotiating with his team, Wyn had finally gotten the green light to hire a civilian investigator instead of an ex-cop to join the staff. Nick may not have known it, but he was an experiment, a hypothesis – that civilian investigators were as competent, and less biased, than ex-police officers – the veracity of which had not yet been revealed. Frank, the most senior investigator after Wyn, had grudgingly agreed to a six-month probation period for the man, during which time the ex-police officers would endeavour to train him.

At SPOA's inception, acting police officers were seconded to the agency, most of them from Homicide. The idea had been that these men (they were all men) would train civilian investigators, to avoid criticism that it was a conflict of interest for police officers to investigate their fellow officers in what was supposed to be an arm's-length agency. However, the seconded officers soon became permanent staff, and the new recruits came mainly from the retired police force. They didn't want to get out of the game quite yet and perceived SPOA as safer and less stressful. Unfortunately, no training program for civilians ever made it past the theoretical stage, the Attorney General citing lack of resources and bowing to the insistence by the investigators that they had hardly enough time to do their job proficiently, let alone show someone else how to do it. Like the union from which they had lately departed, these ex-cops knew how to present a stubbornly united front against the policy-makers and politicians and blue-sky thinking. They felt threatened, and put the fear of God into the AG with assertions that civilian investigators would be the ruin of the agency. You had to walk a mile in a cop's shoes before you could be tasked with investigating them, they claimed.

Sylvia seemed to have taken advantage of Nick's lack of experience; everything appeared in disarray. The witnesses had not been segregated. The forensics team had not yet arrived. Even though the body had been taken away from the scene, the vast white fluorescent space still looked like the locale of a hastily organized funeral awaiting a priest, with lots of pale faces, whispering, and apprehension. But with Wyn's arrival a new expectancy arose, his presence lent the atmosphere logic and meaning. He recalled the years he was an investigator and felt a familiar whoosh in his bloodstream, a feeling that had never been replicated in his large glass office, as Director. He never thought he would miss it, but even on the drive over he had felt his pulse quicken. Now he could almost feel the atoms in the air aligning themselves to his authority.

Even before he was close enough to make eye contact with her he noticed that Sylvia was alarmed to see the Director at a scene. She was a long-time employee of the Police Association, and she and Wyn were well-acquainted. She had participated in the Wolfe case twelve years before, when they were both relative newcomers to the world of police oversight. Sylvia had been part of the team of lawyers who defended Constable Jameson, and lost. The conviction of Jameson had changed Wyn's career, eventually leading to his promotion to Director, the first investigator ever to assume that role. Since then, his interactions with Sylvia, while sporadic, had been scarcely cordial.

"Mr Rhys, we have to insist–" she began, but Wyn put up a hand and addressed Nick. "I've received notification from Stuart that we've got about six guys coming to help out, and Frank will take over for me as the lead." He glanced around at the witnesses and mentally calculated their number and how much time would be needed to interview each of them. They were going to be on these premises for at least three hours, by his estimation. After that, there was the next of kin to notify, always the most difficult part of the process. Maybe he could just send Frank, or if time was really tight, a police officer could do it.

Sylvia was hovering, buzzing really, with the urge to attract his attention, but Wyn ignored her and turned to the young men in uniform. "You are the involved officers, I presume?" he asked.

Looking at Sylvia, the two men slowly shook their heads no. Wyn's mouth involuntarily twitched. "Where are they, Ms. Hughes?"

Trembling slightly, which made her voluminous coppery curls shake, Sylvia said, "Mr Rhys – Wyn – it's a *holiday* for god's sake."

Wyn took her puffy elbow and drew her aside, out of everyone's hearing. "You are aware of the recent change to SPOA's regulations?" he said, bending his much larger body to keep his voice low near her ear. "Surely I don't have to remind you? There was a great deal of press around the decision, and many memos from the Chief."

"I know about the change," said Sylvia, wresting her elbow free of Wyn's grip. "But those men were traumatized, and I made the decision, with Chief Lucci's permission, to let them go home."

Wyn looked at his phone. 12pm. He really didn't have time to argue. "I don't care if he sanctioned them to marry each other; this is my bailiwick, not his. Were you called in before the report was made to my office?" Sylvia looked about to retort but Wyn waved it away. "I know you were. Not your problem. I'll take it up with the Attorney General. In the meantime, I will ask you very politely to step aside and let us do our jobs. Get a coffee. Relax." He was about to move along but Sylvia intercepted him, the soft, entreating expression gone and her real character in evidence, calculating and fierce. "Do you think that because you decided to show up at a scene as

Director that you can throw your weight around?" she said, crossing her arms with difficulty because of the bulk of her jacket. "I've always wondered: why'd you give up policing? Was it too stressful for you?"

"If the Police Association was honouring the change to SPOA's regulations, I wouldn't have to come down here and 'throw my weight around.' They were changed for a reason, Ms. Hughes: to ensure that the involved officers are held accountable to the same rules as civilians and witness officers. You should be glad. Means less work for you. No more need to vet officer's notes, or prepare their 'official' statements. In fact, you really should be at home yourself, putting your feet up, not concerning yourself with SPOA matters."

Sylvia, whose finger had been raised scoldingly the entire time Wyn was speaking, said, "My job is to protect our boys in blue from being intimidated and bullied by your agency."

"'Our boys in blue'? You've been spending too much time in the company of the Chief, Sylvia. A bit outdated, that expression. There are at least three or four women in active duty now, I think? Maybe even more. I expect you to arrange for the involved officers in this incident to report to SPOA by 2pm. Consider that as me doing you a favour."

Undeterred, Sylvia said, "And if I don't?"

Furious now, Wyn lowered his voice again. "If you don't, I will write a complaint to the Police Board. I don't care how long you've been around, if you pull another stunt like this one I will get you fired." Before she could detain him any longer, Wyn walked away, back to the befuddled new investigator. "If you haven't yet canvassed the witnesses, do it now. Make sure to get everyone's contact information in case we need to follow up. They can't share anything with the media or go about chatting with friends and family. Strict confidence. Barry's bringing the laptop to collect phone data." Nowadays, people used their phones to record practically every moment of their waking life, so in recent years SPOA and the police had taken to carrying computers onto which they could upload videos shot on cellphone cameras, as they were not permitted to confiscate devices and civilians were generally reluctant to turn them in.

Wyn opened his briefcase and took out his digital recorder and notebook. As he shepherded the witness officers out of the store, he noticed the forensics team had arrived with their equipment. They would mark out a grid in the store, each square diagrammed and each piece of evidence photographed in situ before being placed in plastic bags and labelled. The victim had been transported to hospital, meaning that paramedics had found vital signs when they'd examined him. The Tasers used would be taken to the officers' police station and their cartridges examined to determine when and how they were deployed. Time, with its insistence on moving in only one direction, meant that while the team couldn't precisely relive the moment Tragedy swooped through the shopping centre, it could harness and analyze its traces.

Wyn had conducted enough interviews with suspects, victims and witnesses to deal with them expediently. His time as Director had in no way threatened his capacity to do that part of the job, and he felt a comfortable warmth, settling into the standard questions to the witness officers about where they'd been, what they'd seen, how they carried out their own duties. They both claimed to have seen little of what had happened; most of the action had taken place out of their visual range, again, because of the obstruction of the wall, which had been erected by the victim and which had precipitated the call to the police. Officers Sadiq and Maguire had been in place mostly to protect the crowd of curious onlookers in the event that the suspect knocked down the wall, or to jump him if he made a dash for the door. About their impressions of the suspect (on drugs? making threats? suicidal?) Wyn learned almost nothing. Neither of them saw him alive for more than a few seconds, and nothing he may have said had been audible. They reiterated that they were only present as back-up. Whether or not they had been advised by Sylvia to keep their testimony vague or had really witnessed so little Wyn would not be able to determine until after he spoke to the subject officers, when they decided they were fit to be interviewed, after Sylvia had coached them to say nothing to incriminate themselves.

In other parts of the store other versions of the story were being recited to Nick and the other investigators, including Frank, who had arrived to assist him. For some people, drama unfolded unnaturally slowly and each second had a hard-edged brilliance that endured. For others everything was a Gaussian blur, wet and floppy and useless. The investigators would be able to distinguish between the two, and were aware that tantamount to accuracy was timeliness: memories deteriorated quickly. Even with video data there would be gaps, or a poor vantage point, or ambient noise.

Frank, as lead, observed the forensics team work on the scene itself, as he would be the one to put together a picture of what happened when assembling the investigative plan. Once the forensics team had finished and all the witnesses were released to carry on shopping, or to recover from the shock of witnessing a man die, Wyn texted Sylvia to inform her that she could come collect her charges. The investigators, five in all, then congregated around Wyn and he divided the next tasks between them: calls to the cops' division, informing the Chief that forensics would be over to search all the vehicles that had attended the scene. All recordings of communications among the officers and emergency personnel would be seized. Forensics had to gather clothing from the involved officers and eventually, at the post-mortem, from the victim. The office would have to be updated on how things were progressing and the communications assistant, Chantal LaPierre, would write the press release appealing for any other witnesses who may have been passing by at the time of the incident.

Out of a peculiar habit, or perhaps it was a superstition, Wyn always waited, if possible, until after the mess had been disposed of to get information on the person who'd been killed. When it was just "a body" or "the decedent," the person who'd suffered, be it a cop or a suspect, could be anyone and no one. As soon as they were tagged with an identity, it was tempting to speculate about their ethnic or economic background or some other detail that could skew his objectivity. Of course, there was an element of respect that came into the equation as well. No amount of procedure or protocol could detract from the fact that these incidents ripped holes in the lives of the affected and that a death, in particular, scattered suffering in all directions, to places even Wyn's relentless muzzle couldn't sniff out and define.

Before removing the man from the scene, the paramedics had removed his personal effects and submitted them to the investigative team. Nick had given them to the most senior investigator, Frank. Frank had left the building with them so he could smoke in the parking lot, and it was there that he and Wyn convened once the rest of the team had dispersed.

Frank was the last of the original investigators who had been hired upon the inception of SPOA almost twenty-five years before. Hailing from Newfoundland, where he'd served as a homicide cop in St. John's, he had suffered a back injury and was forced to retire early, but couldn't sit around doing nothing for the rest of his life, so he moved to Ontario and joined SPOA. Wyn guessed he was around sixty years old now, but appeared much older because of his bent back and the way his jaw never seemed to close completely, giving him a hangdog, desperate look. His hands were museum specimens of gnarled bone, and his completely bald skull was a newel post of scratches, dents and, if possible, worn paint. His enormous nose and ears had long ago won the battle for supremacy over his eyes, which were small and rheumy and always bloodshot. Wyn had wondered if he had a drinking problem, but he was never late and never missed a day of work.

The overcast sky had the opalescence of the inside of an oyster shell, and it was getting colder and more windy, but Frank would smoke in a tornado, he was that dedicated. When Wyn used to smoke they had spent many a break smoking in other parking lots, in driveways, on street corners, in vehicles. Frank enjoyed the fieldwork as much as Wyn had, and right up until the latter's promotion, they'd worked closely together on cases, sometimes bickering, sometimes dismissive of the other's theories, but always companionable. When Wyn was made Director, Frank never quite got around to being deferential to him. Wyn wasn't sure if he was resented for getting the post, as Frank had seniority, but Frank was edgy with everyone and it was almost impossible to get him to bow to anyone's authority, not the Chief, not the Ministry, not the Premier. There had been some tense moments in the past few months between them, and Wyn had more than once had to be stern with Frank, especially in front of the other investigators, but while he didn't seem to hold grudges, he wouldn't change, either.

Frank had an Old Port cigarillo clenched between his teeth and was struggling to type a message on his phone. If Wyn's phone was his best friend, Frank's was his mother-in-law.

"Fockin' shite piece of fockin' crap," he muttered as he put it in his pocket. "Saw you talking to Sylvia."

Wyn sometimes swore, but he chose the time and manner carefully. Frank had no such restraint. "Fuck" was concurrently a verb, adjective, expletive and noun, occasionally even an adverb. No amount of remonstrating eased it, though, and with his accent, "fuck" came out as "fock" and was therefore moderately less abrasive. However, a few of the younger investigators had, out of some kind of allegiance, emulated him and, as a result, their professional interactions were veritable orgies of fucks. Wyn found it very tiresome.

"Well, she'd sent the bloody involved officers home to have their naps, hadn't she?"

Frank dragged hard on his cigar as though it contained oxygen in an oxygen-deprived environment. "Told you the change to the mandate wouldn't make no difference, didn't I?" he said.

"Yes, yes you did. If I have to show up at every scene in person to ensure that this doesn't keep happening, the Attorney General will hear about it. Then the Chief and the Police Association will think twice about obstructing us."

"Don't hold yer breath," said Frank, exhaling some smoke. The subject of bureaucratic and procedural issues bored him. He took out a ziplock bag and handed it to Wyn. "Travelled light, this focker," he said.

The bag contained only a single key and a bank card. "Did the paramedics take his health card?"

"Nope. Weren't on him. This is it."

Wyn examined the bank card. It had "David Drobac" impressed on it. "Well, at least we have a name," he said.

Frank held up his phone, displaying a close-up of the dead man's face: heavily lined, drawn, dead blue eyes vacant. Masses of curly hair. "And a photo. Sent it to the Ministry. Confirmed it's him." The Ministry of Health issued photo ID cards to everyone in Ontario.

Wyn handed the bag back to Frank. "We will need to find his next of kin and get proper identification, if it exists. How old is he?"

"Forty-seven, though he looked older, sad bastard. Some hard living, I reckon. But he's got a home and Abby got the name of the NoK." NoK was an acronym for "next of kin." "Lives on Grant Street. I mapped it and it's about fourteen blocks away. But get this. Abby tells me that the NoK is only sixteen fockin' years old. It's his daughter, for fock's sake. Abby don't know how come no one noticed it sooner."

Wyn closed his eyes momentarily and another girl's face appeared before his mind's eye. Justine Wolfe. He opened his eyes and the image dissipated. "Did Abby give you the name of any other relatives?"

"No other Drobacs in the directory. No mention of extended family on record, but we can go to the residence and ask around. Neighbours, if need be. Or we find the kid and talk to her."

Today. It had to be today that he'd be faced with a complex and potentially volatile situation. Wyn looked at his watch. "I'll come with you. Let's hope there are other adults living there we can talk to. He could have a wife or a girlfriend."

Frank said, "When I said 'we' I didn't mean that I'm doin' it. Makes no sense, if I'm the lead, I gotta put together a plan back at the office. You do it. You're better'n me anyways. Take wee Nick. Be good for him, don'tcha think?"

Circumspect rather than confrontational, because they'd argued so much about hiring civilian investigators in the past, Wyn said only, "Certainly. Good idea."

As they walked back to the mall under the pearl and pewter sky, Wyn thought about calling Anna but didn't really know what to say. That he was going to make his best effort to be at the airport on time? He wasn't quite sure he could keep that promise. Besides, if she was cheating on him, what right did she have to judge? And to tell him not to bother coming to Mexico if he didn't make the flight, what did that mean?

Chapter Four

Nick drove. Wyn could tell he was nervous. Nick's background had been in law and he had considered working for the Police Association at one point, but his ethics didn't fit with that organization, the police having such a poor reputation for accountability and transparency. Wyn had heard about his interest in the police and approached him with an offer to join his outfit. There was no official college or university training available anywhere in Ontario, so Nick was learning on the ground, and what better person today than Wyn to observe doing one of the most difficult aspects of the job – breaking news of the death of a loved one to a next of kin? Wyn gave Nick no pointers as they made their way to the dead man's address, except to observe and be respectful of the family of the deceased, no matter what they encountered when they got there.

Wyn speculated on what they'd find at the address Frank had dug up. A crack house? A meth lab or grow-op? Or perhaps the family hadn't lived there in ages and he and Nick would have the laborious task of deciding where next to turn. Without any identification they couldn't run the post-mortem and would have to preserve the body until all the protocols were followed. But there must be someone, somewhere, besides his daughter, who cared about David Drobac and would have more information about him.

As per procedure, Wyn called the central police data control office to run a check on David Drobac. It would be several hours before they'd get back to him with the results. Social services, however, were closed for the holiday, so it wasn't possible to get them to run a check on the family to find out if Children's Aid had ever been involved or if there was a mother in the picture. So Wyn called the head of Victim's Services, Maria Rosetti, directly on her cellphone and left her a message, just in case help was urgently required.

Grant Street was just off Broadview Avenue in a part of downtown east below Little Chinatown, an area that only very lately had begun to enjoy the first tentative stages of gentrification. There was a street mission a block away but also new condos behind what had once been a strip club, now under renovation on Queen. Many of the old grand houses had been turned into boarding houses, but some had been rehabilitated. Further along the thoroughfare the laundromats and pawnshops had been slowly replaced by gourmet organic food purveyors and lushly lit nightspots. Dangerous Dan's burger joint still had old car seats for booths, but the vibe was definitely shifting towards the young and affluent.

The Drobac abode was the last of a row of spinsterly Victorian townhouses, prim and straight with delicately pointed gables, but shabby and neglected looking. The door was painted a last breath shade of lilac. SPOA investigators were accustomed to far less salubrious abodes in neighbourhoods like Regent Park or Jane and Finch, which, for all their geographical disparity (Regent Park was in the core of the city, Jane and Finch on the northern edge of Metro), possessed the universal hallmarks of poverty: dreary public spaces, anonymous facades tediously replicated, smells of dollar store plastic and fast food. In such places the people who appeared from behind the chipboard doors were usually the girlfriends and baby mommas, hair drawn back in a scalp-punishing ponytail, their menacing stares mascara-spiked and kohl-rimmed, swaddled in velour to which there was almost always a child clinging and gazing with trained hostility. The other women were the older mothers, pouchy-eyed from worry and work, stooped and heavy-bosomed. Men rarely answered the doors. They'd all seen Wyn's type many times and hated him. Wyn couldn't blame them. He never knocked on their doors with good news.

On Wyn's command, Nick parked in front of a hydrant. They exited the vehicle together, and when Wyn took a moment to shut the ringer off his phone, Nick did the same. Then Wyn made his lugubrious way up the walk, his long black coat open and flapping like a large-winged bird in the stiff winter wind. The people on the other side of the lavender door were going to have their lives transformed today. Wyn's face and particularly his voice would be what they'd remember whenever they thought about their father, husband, son, whatever the relationship would reveal itself to be. There were dozens of people in the province whose internal playback mechanisms had Wyn as the narrator. He was like the friendly recording that gives you instructions on how to use a phone menu when calling the hydro company to complain about a bill. Except he wasn't very friendly, and he didn't give you options.

At the door Wyn said to Nick, "I'll do the talking," and Nick nodded assent. In order to not overwhelm vulnerable people, they had a rule about letting one investigator speak and the other simply observe, present only as a back-up in case things got difficult.

Wyn pressed the bell and after a pause almost long enough for them to concur that no one was home he detected the sound of footsteps, which paused on the other side of the door. He was sure he was being viewed through the small convex peephole, so he stepped back and took out his ID and held it up, then knocked again. "Open up, please," he ordered. A moment passed, then he heard the sound of something, or someone, sliding down. There was a mail slot. Wyn had had to use them to communicate with un-cooperative residents before. He lifted the flap and bent down and spoke again, more gently this time. "My name's Wyn Rhys. I'm an investigator with the Special Police Oversight Agency. I'm here about David. Could you let me in, please?" He could try getting a view through the mail slot but didn't want to be invasive, yet.

Then more sounds of scrambling, and through the flap emerged a small girl's hand, ragged nails daubed with turquoise nail polish that had been partially gnawed off. He interpreted the gesture as a demand for proof of who he was, so he placed his card, on which he had written his cell number during the drive over, into the upturned palm. The hand disappeared and the flap clattered shut. Snow started to fall, and Wyn pushed his hands deep in his pockets and stamped his feet. Looking at his watch, he mentally calculated how much time he realistically had to get through this part of the routine. It was 2:30pm. If he was to be on hand for the post-mortem and get to the airport, he had only about twenty more minutes left for this task. Less if the weather worsened. He looked at the sky. The clouds were low and choppy and moving fast, like waves on a windy lake.

After an interminable minute he heard the girl get to her feet and open the door slowly and only partway, to reveal just her face. A small, pointed face, with great eyes. Fearful eyes, oddly hopeful eyes, the fathomless colour of lakewater with rocks at the bottom. Wyn's heart dipped with dread; it was most definitely the daughter, Claire Drobac. In the blue light of winter her skin was milk white, almost translucent. She was a natural blonde, her hair so fair it was almost white, but parts of it had been dyed an intense shade of pink. She had it tied up, but Wyn could see it was very curly and one long tendril hung askew, almost in the centre of her forehead. She pushed it behind her ear. She wore a long white oxford shirt, a man's, that was much too big for her, over an ankle-length Indian-style patterned skirt with bells and sequins. Tiny, delicate. Wyn wished she had more guile. He had a sense immediately that she had been expecting him, maybe had been expecting someone like him to show up for a long time. "My dad's not here," she said quickly, before Wyn could inquire.

He held up his ID again, but the girl didn't examine it. "As I said, I'm Wyn Rhys, I work for the Special Police Oversight Agency. Is your dad David Drobac? Are you Claire?"

The girl looked down at the ground, where Wyn's galoshed feet faced her own small bare ones. "Uh-huh," she said, sounding regretful. The "uh-huh" followed the arc of an indrawn breath and ended on the exhalation, lending the syllables a sense of hopelessness.

"Can we come in?"

The girl merely turned and entered the apartment, which Wyn took to mean that he had permission to follow. He entered a cramped and dirty entranceway littered with different types of footwear: running shoes, ballet flats, a pair of red velvet boots. Wyn saw no men's shoes in the tumble. From the back of the flat a radio or stereo could be heard.

There was a living room to the right. Claire was there. It was large, with a huge desk with an Apple computer, a small battered sofa and, unaccountably, a dining room table pushed against the wall. There was no Christmas tree. On the mantel were photos and cards; Claire stood in front of it, her gaze on one black and white photo of a man. As Wyn approached he recognized her father. This photo was taken in his twenties, it appeared. Same blonde curly hair, but devastatingly beautiful, dreamy-eyed, a man with a future.

Wyn pocketed his ID. "Who else lives here?" he asked.

"Are you the police?" asked Claire, frowning.

"No, we're not police. We're investigators. I'm not here with a warrant; I just need to talk to an adult."

"There's nobody here right now," said Claire.

"Does your father live with you?" he enquired.

The child's face turned panicky. "Tell me where my dad is," she said. "Just tell me where he is. Is he okay?" High and girlish, with a feverish note. She looked back and forth at the two men, seeking in one of their faces the truth. She found it in both. "He's really sick," she said suddenly. "My dad's sick. He's in the hospital." She moved past Wyn and Nick and exited the room, jingling in her funny skirt, went down the hallway towards the kitchen.

Wyn closed his eyes for a moment. He was really too old to be doing this kind of work any longer. He had to be prepared for the possibility that she really was the only family the man had. If he had to talk to her in her agitated state he would need to employ some finely honed tools, which he feared had gone rusty from disuse. "Stay in here," he instructed Nick. Two men were too much for the child to handle. Nick nodded, looking pained. Not a good first encounter with a next of kin. He might resign after this experience.

Wyn followed the girl down the hallway past a very long line of bookcases, tidily organized. At least four hundred books, perhaps more. He entered a kitchen, however, that was rather bleak: the walls were cracked, faded peach paint had peeled away near the stove and the vinyl floor had sections held together with duct tape. The lighting was terrible, strips of comfort-leaching fluorescent that heightened the general friendlessness and made everyone in the room look too real. Wyn was careful to not appear obvious as he took in the details, seeking suspicious paraphernalia (burned pots, blackened spoons, chemical residue), but it was very tidy. There were no dirty dishes or grease splatters. The floor was clean. Near the window stood a Formica table and two vinyl chairs, both with split seats and the foam bulging out. On the table stood an eighties vintage boom box from which music could be heard – something classical.

Claire stood at the far end of the kitchen, near the stove, like a cornered animal. Wyn saw there was a door that likely led outside, and nonchalantly moved towards it, in case she decided to bolt.

He tried to make himself less imposing by taking a chair and sitting down. "As I said, we're not cops. Did you see your dad today?"

The girl looked at the floor, considering her answer. One bare foot slid over the other and remained there, protective. "I don't know," she said.

"I need a proper answer, please."

"What happened?" she said into the space where the collar of the buttoned shirt met her chin.

"Did you see him today, Claire?"

She nodded, still looking at the floor. "He went to the mall," she said.

"Were you with him?"

She shook her head. Wyn said, "Usually under these circumstances I would speak to an adult, a spouse or sibling. Do you have any family I can call or see? Where's your mother?"

She crossed her arms and closed her eyes, then opened them. "I'm his family. My mom died when I was little. There's no one else but me. Ever since I was seven it's been me and my daddy." Her voice cracked on her next words. "He's in the hospital, right? He's been to the hospital before. He's sick, really sick."

"What does he do for a living? Do you know any of his colleagues? Neighbours you trust?"

Claire's eyes opened wide, fearful. "You can't tell anyone what happened," she said. "If they find out he's sick he'll lose his grant money. He told me so."

"What illness? How often has he been in hospital?" If David Drobac had a pre-existing medical condition, especially a heart problem, it may have factored into his death.

Claire's face became blank, distressingly so. "I don't talk to people about my dad's business," she said.

"All right. You don't need to tell me about that. It's okay. But if there's no one else I can speak to then we need to talk. May I sit down? I think you should sit down too." He gestured to the table and chairs.

"I don't want to sit down. I want to know if my dad's okay." Knowing nothing really of their circumstances but reverting to the assumption, based on statistics, that David was either an addict, a criminal, or mentally ill (or all three), Wyn felt pity for the girl because of her history, more because of her present tragedy. Still, David could have been the only reliable adult in this girl's universe, and Wyn was highly sensitive to the fact that they could not take for granted that her father's permanent removal from her life would necessarily guarantee her a brighter future.

He cleared his throat, commenced his customary preamble. "The agency I work for investigates incidents where a member of the public is in a confrontation with officers that results in injury or–"

Suddenly agitated, the girl put her hands to her temples, then to her ears, then through her hair, rapidly untying it, loosing a scraggle of curls that fell over her shoulders. It looked as though it hadn't been washed or combed for a while. "I can't talk to you right now. I think you should come back later, when my dad's home."

Denial was the customary first response, either overt or implied, with anger swift on its heels, nipping and barking. It was incredibly rare that any investigator had to deliver tragic news to a lone minor. But he knew to use the same tactics with this girl as with all family members of victims: make no sudden moves, use neutral language, don't touch unless under threat of being attacked. Distract. De-escalate. Use first names frequently to engage and connect.

"Claire, do you want something to drink? A glass of water?"

She prowled back and forth between the back door and the table, shaking her head. The long pink curl was freed of its mooring behind her ear and skated across her white forehead, anxious.

Wyn went to the sink, drew a glass of water and made a careful approach on the girl, holding the glass at hip level and stopping about two feet away.

"Claire, I have a glass of water here. Come sit and have a sip. Then we can talk."

Wordlessly, she moved to the table and found a chair without looking, knowing it was there, as it had always been. She sat. Wyn handed her the glass of water and she automatically drank the entire contents in one long draught. A side effect of shock was dry mouth and sudden thirst. She put the glass on the table but kept her head down, picked at the crumbling nail polish on her hands. She seemed to be getting smaller and smaller.

Sliding a chair from the other side of the table, Wyn came closer to Claire and sat, his hands between his knees, limp and unthreatening. "Okay. Thanks for sitting down. Feel better after the water?"

A mute nod. Her hands spoke sign language to each other, fingers twiddling and stroking, picking and scratching. Wyn noticed a burn, a long line across her lowest knuckles, perhaps from an oven. It was recent.

She murmured something inaudible. "Beg pardon?" he asked, bending forward.

Claire cleared her throat slightly. "He's dead, right?"

Wyn allowed for a small pause before speaking, to show respect and ease her into the new reality she was about to enter, alone, unless there was some responsible adult in her life to fill the vacuum. "Yes, sweetheart." The "sweetheart" was unexpected. Maybe he'd said it because he had a daughter of his own, but he couldn't recollect ever calling her "sweetheart."

The child shook now, her knees twitching and her shoulders trembling: more of shock's effects. She could be weeping, Wyn couldn't tell. Cautiously, and with some trepidation, he placed a hand on her upper arm, breaking an ironclad rule, but she was a child. The last time he'd broken that rule was fifteen years ago, when he'd touched the third child. "I'm sorry," he said.

She did something unexpected, but not untoward. She put her free hand over his. It was half the size of his own hand, maybe even smaller. She clutched his index and middle finger and held on tightly. "He was at the mall. He wasn't doing anything wrong."

Wyn tried to see her face, but couldn't do so without touching her bright hair. "He was at the mall. Claire? Were you with him? Did you witness something?"

The girl shook her head vigorously. "No," she whispered. "I wasn't there. I was sleeping."

"Okay. This is what we know so far," he said and, measuring his words carefully, gave her a brief account of what happened, with very few details. He concluded by saying, "While under restraint he lost consciousness and couldn't be revived, I'm afraid."

Claire released Wyn's fingers, and he let go of her shoulder. She put her hands to her face, over her eyes. After a few moments she spoke through the screen of her hands, her voice a bit muffled but coherent.

"We can't afford to buy presents before Christmas, so we celebrate Boxing Day instead. I told Dad I wanted *Edward Scissorhands*. Ever see that movie?" Wyn was taken aback, but decided to let this tributary of conversation find its course back to the river of the larger situation. Such erratic changes in mood were to be expected from someone in shock.

"I don't think so," he said. "Is that a favourite movie of yours?" He hadn't watched a film from beginning to end since he was twenty. All he ever picked up were bits from TV when he couldn't sleep, usually dozing off.

The girl withdrew her hands and looked at the ceiling dreamily. Her eyes were dry. "I love all the Tim Burton movies. They're epic. Daddy and I watched them over and over together when I was little. In this one there's this boy made by a crazy scientist who's also, like, his dad, and he dies before he can finish Edward's hands. So he's got, like, these scissors instead and he makes awesome art with them, all kinds of crazy hedges and stuff." Wyn checked his watch. "A town adopts him and he falls in love with Winona Ryder and he–" She stopped and closed her eyes, and they roved beneath her lids, watching the film.

"He makes ice sculptures in California and it creates snow at Christmas time. But then the people all turn on him and make him run away. They can't handle him 'cause he's different – he scares them."

Wyn interrupted. "Claire, he didn't seem to be shopping. He built something, a kind of wall. Do you know why he would do that?"

Claire looked at her hands again. "He's an artist. He always says we're different, we see the world differently than everyone else. We see beauty in even the most boring and stupid things. He wants me to be a filmmaker. We were a team. It was going to be *so cool*." Wyn heard a funny sound and turned. Nick was in the hallway, just outside the door to the kitchen. Had he choked back some emotion?

He turned back to the girl. "Okay. We have to talk about what needs to happen next, Claire," Wyn said, pushing his chair back a few inches but not rising yet. He kept his gaze at her level. "I need the name of someone I can talk to about this situation. Do you have any friends? Would their parents be able to assist?"

Claire said, "There's Sasha. She's, like, my mom. I live with her when my dad's sick."

Thank God, Wyn thought. "Ok. We need to call her right away. Please give me her number."

The child looked past his shoulder, perhaps at Nick, who was in the hallway. She looked curiously detached. "Sasha doesn't like my dad. She's going to be mad at him."

Wyn sighed inwardly. Remember she's a child, he thought. A child who's just lost her only remaining parent. "Okay, we can call her in a minute. Can you provide me with some identification? Does your dad have a health card? All we have is his bank card."

The girl left the kitchen and Wyn followed. She entered a bedroom. Another bare room, bed without a frame but neatly made and a large table upon which art supplies had built a small, rich empire: brushes, sketchbooks, tubes, palettes. Above it was the only wall in the flat that had any decoration: an elaborate mural of the Toronto skyline overgrown with flowers and vines. "Did you make that?" Wyn asked. It had a naive quality.

"I helped," she whispered, and put her hands together in prayer mode, under her chin.

There was a very small desk with books and papers on it. Claire riffled through them. She turned, handed him a green card. "He, like, never carries it 'cause he's paranoid about someone stealing it. He doesn't even have a wallet," she said, calmer now than she'd been since they'd arrived.

A forty-seven-year-old man in North America without a wallet seemed absurd. Especially since he must have employment of some kind. Wyn examined the card. The living David Drobac stared back at him, his face bleached out by the camera's flash, his mouth a mere smudge, his eyes pale and vacant. It appeared that Death had already sniffed him out and commenced trailing him. "Thank you," he said to the girl.

She crossed her arms protectively over her chest and seemed more composed, though she swayed a little. "Tell me what to do now," she said, sniffling. Wyn reflexively reached in his pocket for tissues, but had none. She childishly wiped her nose on her hand.

"Now that we have confirmation of your father's identity we can proceed with our investigation. You don't have to identify him in person. There's nothing left for you to do. I just need you to give me Sasha's number so I can call her. You shouldn't be alone."

She turned and sat heavily on the end of the bed, then lay on it, stretched, crawled to the collection of pillows at the head, put her face to them. Was she weeping? She was very still. Wyn, in his long black coat, galoshes and suit, felt like a character from another movie who had accidentally wandered onto the set of this one. He sat on a nearby desk chair and waited. Sometimes it took a few minutes for the bereaved to collect themselves. But he was running out of minutes. He refrained from looking at his watch, but he knew it was almost three o'clock.

Finally she turned over, took a cushion and put it on her chest, clutched it. "I want to see him," she whispered.

Wyn's heart sank. "We don't recommend anyone under eighteen going to the morgue."

"I'm eighteen."

This statement made him weary. "I know how old you are, Claire. You're sixteen."

She sat up, edged forward by digging her heels in the bed. She touched his shoulder, gazed up at him steadily. "I'm eighteen today." She said it like she believed it; she had aged two years in the past twenty minutes.

"Claire…"

"You take me and tell whoever's in charge that I'm his daughter and I'm eighteen. They'll believe you. You look like someone people trust."

No one had ever said anything like that to him before. Trust wasn't something he had striven diligently to earn, which, he thought, was what perhaps made him inherently trustworthy. From her words, he knew that Claire would insist on him being the one to escort her. Before he could speak, Nick appeared in the doorway, his body only a silhouette against the bright snow-lit corridor. Wyn saw by the movement of his head that he wanted to confer with him outside the NoK's hearing. Wyn excused himself and left the girl on the bed.

Nick had been texted by Frank to say that he would pick him up and take him to the morgue. "Is that where I should be going now?" he asked, somberly. "I don't think there's much I can do here. I looked around the front room but didn't find anything particularly suspicious. I want to help, but … I'm not really that experienced with kids, especially kids in these circumstances. I don't want to do or say the wrong thing."

"No, it's fine. You were fine. Go to the morgue. I'll deal with the child."

Nick's phone beeped. "That's probably Frank," he said. He tilted his chin in the direction of the bedroom, where Claire remained. "Good luck. That must have been really hard. You were really good."

Wyn only shrugged, but was gratified, having demonstrated his level of finesse in even the most extraordinary of circumstances.

He went back to the bedroom. Claire had a cellphone, was busy texting someone. Wyn asked if it was Sasha and she nodded. "Give me the address," she said curtly. "She's going to meet us there." Suddenly capable, mature, unflinching. Wyn had a feeling that she had seen a great deal of mayhem in her short life.

Chapter Five

Claire put on a peculiar piece of clothing to go outside – a kind of cape, long, velvet, with a hood, something that one would wear as part of a Hallowe'en costume. Her father let her dress like this? Wyn's daughter wore the bland and tame uniform of most teenaged girls: jeans or leggings with long shirts and sweaters. But she said she and her dad were artists. Wyn had never met a bona fide artist before, but suspected that this one hadn't made a lot of money, in keeping with the stereotype. But at least this girl had boots and gloves.

It was getting colder and quite windy; Claire's cape swirled dramatically as she made her way down the block. Snow was falling more rapidly now, each centimetre adding at least ten minutes to his trip to the airport. It was after 3pm now and he had to get on the road by four in order to beat traffic and get his boarding pass. Wyn was used to scrambling to make flights, but Anna would be furious with him if he neglected to give himself ample time to make this one. God, how he dreaded it! He imagined telling her that he knew she'd been cheating on him, and her denying it or telling him that yes, she did have a lover, several in fact. Been fucking around on him for years. And he had never even coveted another woman in all the time they'd been married.

When the girl got in the vehicle, she dropped the hood and expelled a great breath of steam. Wyn took his phone out of his pocket but kept the ringer on vibrate. He would let calls go through to his voicemail until he was done at the morgue.

While careful to keep his eyes on the road, Wyn glanced at the girl a few times. She had the universal beauty of the young, but she was not beautiful. Her face and nose were long. Her eyes were disconcertingly pale in the winter light. Her pink hair made her forehead and neck glow. She slouched deep in her seat, pulled her knees up to her chest and wrapped her cape around them. Melting snow dripped on the leather, but Wyn didn't scold her.

She finally turned to him and asked, "Are you a cop?"

"No, I'm not a cop. I'm an investigator." Naturally, she'd forgotten much of their earlier conversation.

"Like CSI?"

"No, not like CSI."

"CSI is stupid. It's not real life. Nothing on TV is."

"You're right, it's not."

They drove in silence for several minutes, Claire frequently checking her phone, which beeped constantly. "Is that Sasha?" Wyn asked. She nodded curtly, her fingers busy on the screen's keyboard. "Can I speak to her?"

"No," said Claire. She had a harder edge to her suddenly, away from her home, and a disdain for him, the man who was supposedly trying to help her. But messengers were not frequently generously regarded. A part of her hated him, would always hate him, for being the one to have delivered such devastating news. And though he spent very little time in the company of his daughter, Wyn knew teenaged girls to be somewhat capricious and volatile. Such an extreme situation would no doubt exacerbate this. Still, he felt very self-conscious, which made him drive faster, even in the slippery weather. He wanted to get this over with as soon as possible.

Finally Claire put away her phone and said to him, "I just thought of a story my dad always tells me. Wanna hear it?"

Wyn waited a moment, then said, "Certainly."

"When he was a kid he had a dog. I don't know what kind of dog, except that it was small. He got it as a present from my grandma. I don't know what he called it. Anyway, when he was, like, eight he took that dog on a picnic with his mom to a place that had a river. It was spring, so the river was really strong from, like, the melted snow or something. They were having the picnic when his dog suddenly jumped into the river and couldn't get back to shore. The river was too fast, and it was being taken down the stream. Dad jumped in the river to save him, not even thinking whether or not he was in danger. He just had to save that dog, 'cause he loved it so much. Grandma didn't even see it coming – one second he was there with her and the next he was in the water and he wasn't a great swimmer, he was just a kid, you know? Somehow he got his hands on the dog and brought it back to shore. They both should've drowned."

"Really," said Wyn. "That's remarkable." He couldn't think of anything else to say.

"I know. But that's not the whole story. When he came out of the water my grandma was really, really mad at him for doing it. She didn't yell, though. She just asked him why he did it, and he told her he loved his dog more than anything in the world. You know what she said? She said, 'You know I love you more than anything in the world, right?' He said yes. Then she said, 'So how do you think I would feel if you drowned, saving a fucking dog?'"

Claire paused to let the impact of the story settle on Wyn, and he smiled, and as they were at a light, he looked over at her. "She probably didn't say 'fucking' – I bet Dad added that in to make it funnier. And he always, like, exaggerates everything. Do you think it's funny?"

"Not really funny. But interesting."

"I always thought it was funny." She paused and slumped again in her seat, staring through the windshield. She pulled up her hood, and Wyn could only see the tip of her nose. "Maybe I don't anymore. I mean, it's ironic, isn't it?"

Wyn recalled his public school education and his lexicon of literary terms. "The word 'irony' is frequently misused."

"I know what irony means. The dog died of starvation years later, when my dad was living in Budapest and was too broke to feed it because he was drinking all the time. He left it alone in his apartment for two weeks while staying at a friend's. That was before he met my mom and got clean for her. And had me. Then she died of cancer."

A moment to contemplate this statement, the pathos of the sacrifice. Finally Wyn said, "You're right. That is ironic."

"I know," she said. Claire leaned over in her seat and pushed in the button on the lighter next to the radio. "Why do you think he did that?" he asked. If there was one thing Wyn had learned from years of interviewing witnesses, it was to keep the dialogue as open-ended and interviewee-focused as possible.

She dropped her knees and let her feet settle on the floor, then put her hand in her cape pocket and drew out a pack of Rothman's King Size, which had been Wyn's brand. She couldn't have chosen a more mucus-producing, cough-inducing, macho cigarette. "Don't tell my dad that I smoke," she said offhandedly, unconsciously. "I think that booze is his dog," she said, sliding open the pack and coaxing a cigarette out with practiced fingers. She put it between her lips just as the lighter popped.

Wyn could taste the tobacco in his mouth and feel the smoke swirling in his lungs as he watched her light up and inhale. He inhaled with her. God, he missed smoking. He should have prohibited her, but he wanted the smell in his car again. He'd always smoked while driving – he hadn't been permitted to smoke at home, even before Rebecca's birth. His decision to quit had not been for health reasons but financial ones; he'd wanted to buy a new car and when he calculated what he spent a day on cigarettes he realized that he could afford a far nicer vehicle if he gave up the habit. Before going to buy the new car he bought a pack of Rothman's and parked in a secluded place, near the lake. Then he smoked as many cigarettes as he could in an hour (fifteen) and went to the dealership, traded in his old vehicle and drove away in the new, with the promise to himself that he would never smoke in it or anywhere else, and he never did.

Wyn considered asking Claire for a cigarette then checked himself. He hadn't smoked for so long, why did he want to now? He didn't feel the urge when he was around Frank anymore, and they had smoked together for years. Maybe it was the luxurious way she drew on the filter and so slowly exhaled, not blowing the smoke but letting it drift from between her lips, filling the small space between them with blue fog. Its acridity stung his nostrils, but delightfully. He took another deep breath, an audible one this time. Claire noticed and extended her little hand – a child's hand, it was so blasphemous – and offered her smoke to him. "Wanna drag?" she asked.

Wyn shook his head. "No," he said. "No," he said again, and opened his window. The outside reached in and tugged the smoke out on long phantom threads. It soon dissipated.

"Sorry," said Claire, looking abashed for the first time. "Guess I shouldn't smoke in your car."

"Not a problem. Go ahead. I'll just keep the window open."

"So, anyway, I told Dad that booze was his dog and he said it was true and that I was pretty smart for getting that. He quit drinking sometimes for a few weeks and sometimes just for a few days. He promised to keep trying. But he's promised before. He's sick. He's really, really sick." Wyn recalled that she had said this several times at her home. Her father doubtlessly had been saying it to her for years. To cover up his shame that he wasn't more present, that he couldn't provide her with better lodging, better food or clothing. Entreating her to pity him, instead of being man enough to get help, spare her this terrible shock and grief. But maybe she'd been expecting it for a very long time. No, he thought. Children don't expect their parents to die. They believe them when they tell them that everything will be okay.

Claire opened her window a little and tipped the cigarette out to flick the ash, then closed it again and took another drag, fingers trembling. "He joked that I was his dog now. That he loved me more than he loved booze. He's not perfect, but I'm all he's got. We were a team. Team Us, he always said." The girl lowered the window, threw her spent cigarette to the wind, closed it. Wyn saw that tears were creeping down her cheeks now.

"I'm sorry," he said again. And he was. He decided that he would be the one to interview her, once he got back from Mexico. Let her get through the funeral and some grieving and then he would draw her out in one of the office's small interview rooms. He wouldn't let anyone else do it. Even though he rarely conducted them anymore, he still had a reputation in the agency as being the most adroit and finessed interviewer, and not just because he'd done it for so many years.

The girl trembled violently and leaned forward, her hands braced on the dashboard, her head bent, breathing heavily. Wyn swiftly pulled onto a side street and whisked the car alongside a curb, shut off the engine. "Do you need to be sick?" he said, reaching over her to open her door. She shook her head violently, taking shallow breaths, quick in and out, and he feared she was having a panic attack. Wyn put his hand on the back of her neck, which was clammy. Her eyes were closed and now he thought she would faint. "Can you hear me, Claire? Claire, sweetheart, we don't have to go see your dad. Let me take you home."

The girl shook her head again and some sobs rose up, choking her. She coughed then turned in her seat and vomited onto the sidewalk, getting some of it on her cape. Then more tears, and her sobs were like a much younger child's. Wyn tried to draw her gently back into her seat and she suddenly turned on him like he had attacked her, so suddenly that he was ambushed. She lunged at his face with her hands, which he caught at the wrists, and screamed at him, then bit him on one of his wrists so hard that she broke the skin. Wyn feared someone passing by would see them and alert the police – assuming that he'd kidnapped the girl and she was fighting back. But then she stopped. Her head drooped and her hands, still caught at the wrist in his own, unflexed and went limp. Wyn let go and her whole body collapsed on him, which was awkward with the parking brake between them, but he did his best to support her, discreetly examining his wound while simultaneously patting her on the shoulder. It was not deep, but it would require antiseptic. The last thing he needed before leaving the country was blood poisoning. Human bites were dangerous.

Finally, she no longer shook, but her arms were wrapped tightly around his neck and he had to gently pry them apart and draw away from her to re-establish the necessary distance between them. Why him, and why today? He remembered another child's arms around him, a child that had trusted him. This girl was older than Justine Wolfe, had likely seen a lot of terrible things, but at least – thankfully – she had not had to witness her father die.

Her puffy eyes made her look drowsy and her lips were bright red. Wyn wanted to detach the pink tendril from her face, which had gotten caught in her mouth, but that seemed too intimate, so he simply set her against her seat, like placing a doll on a shelf, for she was just as unknowing and rigid. "I can take you home," he said as he restarted the car and pulled off the curb. "You don't have to do this. Just worry about yourself. Where does Sasha live?"

Her voice was trembling, but calm. "I have to see my dad. I have to see him, like, right away. I have to tell him something." She stared out the windshield, resolute. "I promised."

They were both silent as Wyn drove back to the main road and waited at the light. The girl roused herself, turned her head slowly to look at him, noticed his bloodstained shirt cuff. She leaned closer to examine it. "Cool cufflinks," she said.

They were cool. Cufflinks were Wyn's only concession to whimsy. He had several dozen sets. This pair was new; his daughter had given them to him for Christmas. They were a pair of blinking blue eyes complete with lashes. Claire touched the eye and it closed. "Wow," she said, then looked up at him as the light changed, and though he didn't meet her eyes, he knew they were apologetic. She withdrew to her side of the vehicle, took out her cigarettes again, heedless now whether or not smoking irritated him.

The girl knew what her choices were. This family friend would meet them, and if she wasn't able to handle seeing her dad she would take her home. Then he could make a break for the airport. The car clock said 3:15pm. He was really taking his chances, now. He'd had no choice but to go to the mall today. Nick was too new, Sylvia too rapacious. But Anna wouldn't see it that way. How many times had he broken promises to his wife, said he'd make it up to her, and never did. He should have stopped making promises long ago. After all, it seemed likely that she had broken her promise of fidelity to him.

Chapter Six

The Chief Coroner was on hand in the foyer to meet them. Fuck, Wyn thought. He had counted on Mike Quinn being home nursing a hangover or eating leftover turkey, but in high-profile cases he often made an appearance to see the body, ask questions, ensure that protocols were followed, and Wyn was most emphatically transgressing one.

"This is Claire Drobac," he said when Mike put out his hand. "She is the next of kin to David Drobac." There was no reason to give more information unless requested, and he kept his face impassive as he spoke. It was a bit like bringing an elephant to a party and challenging the other guests to question his assertion that it was his date. Then again, by her attire, especially the cape, it was difficult to ascertain her true age. She looked like a character out of a book, not a real person.

Mike very cordially introduced himself to Claire and assured her he would do everything in his power to assist her. Wyn thought she might act younger than her age, but she was surprisingly straight-backed and sedate. To the Chief's condolences she was silent, eyes wide and glowing. When

Mike commended Wyn, saying, "He's a great investigator, and the Director of the agency, you know. You're lucky to have his personal attention," he spoke like he was talking to an adult, though it must have been painfully obvious to him that she wasn't.

At that moment the door to the lobby opened and a woman entered. Claire turned, recognized her and ran to her. Sasha. She was tall but stocky with a great deal of blonde curly hair, like Claire's. She also wore a kind of cape, so the two of them were oddly well-matched. One might believe Sasha was Claire's mother. She gathered up the girl and he saw the gratitude on the child's face. She was safe. Wyn released a breath and noticed that he'd been holding it. The two women stood together for several seconds, while Wyn and Mike respectfully waited. Finally they came, together, towards them. Sasha extended her hand. She seemed strong and capable. "I came as fast as I could," she said. "I should have been there when you told Claire." There was some reproach in her voice, as if to say that Wyn had been negligent.

"We had no contact except her," he said.

Sasha sighed. "How many times had I told David to make me his power of attorney?" she said. "He has always been very troubled, and a severe alcoholic for many years. I've been afraid for a long time that something might happen to him. But nothing like this." She closed her eyes and took a deep breath, then opened them again.

"So you knew David well?" asked Wyn.

Sasha looked down at Claire, who had tucked herself under her arm, in her cape, which now resembled a mother bird's wing. The girl's eyes remained closed. "I know Claire well," she said, then looked up at Wyn again and she had a challenging expression. "She's been through a lot. Don't make her go through this."

"I am very sorry that she has chosen to come, but she did insist. She is in shock. After this I recommend that you get in touch with Victim's Services and speak to Maria Rosetti, who specializes in trauma among youth. She should be able to provide emergency counselling. In the meantime, I'm going to presume that you're her primary caregiver?"

Sasha Ginsberg nodded. "I have been looking after her off and on since her mother died a few years ago."

Stepping back a little, Mike Quinn said deferentially, "We are here to accommodate you any way we can. If you wish to see him, you may. But it's not necessary."

Sasha excused herself and the girl and led Claire away. There was a sofa in the lobby and they sat on it together, huddled in their capes, and conferred. Wyn observed Sasha stroking Claire's face and hair, there were tears again.

Finally Claire stood and came towards Wyn, Sasha close behind her. "I'm ready," she said.

"She says she's ready," said Sasha. "I can't go in with her. I can't see him." Her eyes were cold.

Wyn placed a hand on the small girl's shoulder. "Claire, I need you to know what to expect. If you don't think you can handle seeing him, we have a video camera in the room and a place for you to view him in privacy. That might be easier."

Claire frowned deeply and her mouth trembled, but she was fierce nonetheless. "What, watch my dad on *television*? No way. I need to see him. I need to talk to him. He promised he'd never leave me but I knew he would, and I have to tell him it's okay. I'm not afraid."

The two adults exchanged gazes, then Sasha shrugged, a very small, almost indiscernible shrug. A concession to the impulse of a distraught girl. Had she been around when the mother died? Wyn had the feeling that this person had been involved in the Drobac drama for a long time. She appeared weary, resigned.

Wyn said nothing as he accompanied the child to the viewing room. His mind felt blank. He couldn't imagine telling his own daughter he would never leave her. David Drobac may have made that promise, but his demons likely had broken it a long time ago. At least he hadn't left her to starve, like that poor dog. Even if he was not the most attentive father, Wyn provided security and comfort for his daughter, for all that she took it for granted, as her entitlement even. This girl would accept love from anyone, he could tell. He hoped she didn't end up with a boyfriend like her father.

At the viewing room, the forensic pathologist, Dr. Bilal Atik, had everything ready. He and Wyn had known each other for years, but Wyn hadn't seen him since he'd been made Director. Bilal appeared pleasantly surprised but was subdued in front of the next of kin. It was not polite to chat or gossip in times like these, so they exchanged only cursory greetings, and Bilal confirmed that Frank and Nick had been in to see the body and would be back shortly for the PM – shorthand for post-mortem.

Claire, more hesitant now, wasn't tall enough to see through the window into the viewing room, even on her tiptoes, so she whispered to Wyn, "Is he in there?"

Wyn nodded.

She touched the door with just her fingertips, then stepped back. A morgue employee in green scrubs intercepted and opened it for her.

Suddenly Claire turned to Wyn. "Do I go in alone?" she asked.

"It's up to you."

Her eyes rotated to take in all the strangeness around her and rested on him again. "You can come with me," she said.

They entered together. This anteroom to the autopsy bay shared the qualities of all the rooms of Wyn's profession: dispassionate sheens of steel and glass and ceramic tile, impervious to stains or memories. The blue-tinged flicker of the fluorescent ensured that Death had no shadows here in which to cower and tease.

He had never shared this room with a next of kin, and he thought he would feel something unusual when looking at

Drobac, but too many years of experience elided his compassion; it was a corpse no different than all the others he'd seen in his career. It was as rigid, as irretrievably lost to comfort and as friendless. Age, gender and mode of dispatch to the Other Side only heightened their sameness. Wyn made his usual observations about the man's physical state. He looked not unlike his health card. Frank had probably asked routine questions about the state of the body upon arrival, what bruises and contusions had bloomed under the man's tender surfaces in the hours after his demise. A body changes dramatically in a very short time; the process of decay is swift and irreversible, and the sooner a body is seen after death the more accurately the pathologists and investigators could evaluate the trauma. Dr. Atik, robed in the clerical whites, plastic apron and rubber gloves of his own office, had by now conducted his usual recitation of the catalogue of damages into his tiny recorder. The morgue attendant had only turned the sheet down to reveal the man's face and neck, which was quite bruised, but Wyn surreptitiously lifted it to look at his chest.

There were two Taser burns: one near his heart and one lower down, near his abdomen. His surprisingly strong, ropey arms were unblemished by tracks, though there were several tattoos, words. Poetry, by the looks of it. Having had taken some literature courses in university, Wyn thought he recognized some bits, Milton, perhaps Yeats, definitely Blake and Auden. He recalled that the apartment housed many books, so the man was well-educated, or at least well-read. He looked older than his forty-seven years, his face deeply lined, pouches around his eyes, but his hair was much like it was in the photo on the mantel, thick and curly. Probably drunk at the mall, though the wall had had an eerie beauty and symmetry to it. Claire said her dad was an artist. But regardless, even if he was under the influence, he was still likely no more than a nuisance, not a dangerous offender. The construction could have been the handiwork of a deranged imagination, but if he could prove the man had no weapon there was a strong case for charging the officers with negligence causing death.

He'd forgotten about Claire in his ruminations, and only recalled her when he looked up and saw her staring at him, her mouth slightly open. "What are you doing?" she asked.

He dropped the sheet. "Nothing," he said.

"He's still mine," she said.

He watched her now at the top of the gurney, looking into her father's blue eyes, open, as they must have been upon death, remaining contracted into the rigor mortis phase, which would have commenced within minutes of his passing. The eyes seemed to stare in disbelief through post-mortem miasma: that he was dead, that there was a God after all. Wyn had never had any strong feelings about something or someone on the other side of life, but the gaze of the dead always struck him as having an aspect of amazement.

Claire stood very still, gazing down at the catastrophe that was once her father. Her small hands rested on the edge of the trolley, near the sheet that covered him, waiting, it seemed, for permission to do something meaningful. Her eyes were lowered, but not closed, and her lips made small movements. She edged closer to the top of the trolley and she touched the man's hair, pulled taut one lock, right in the middle of his forehead, then placed her hand on his brow, as though testing for a fever. His temperature would have dropped at approximately 0.8 degrees per hour and would factor into determining the exact time he died, hopefully within minutes, which would be crucial in SPOA's investigation.

After withdrawing from the gurney, the girl swayed, closed her eyes again, and Wyn, sensing that she might faint, stepped over and put out his hand to steady her. She turned and placed her forehead against the wool of his coat. Having held her once, this didn't feel awkward now. She trusted him. Wyn didn't move. She then looked up at him with those lake-green eyes. "Tell me I'm alive," she said.

"You're alive," Wyn said, not reassuringly, not patronizingly. Just a fact. He hoped they could get out of here soon; it must be at least 3:30, even 3:45.

Claire turned to glance back at her dad a little hopefully, like he might tell her the truth. But he had only one truth remaining to him, and it was irreversible and comfortless. There were no more moments for him to contemplate, or decisions in his custody, or plans to be made. Claire had assumed all the burdens of his spent life onto her narrow shoulders. They would get heavier in the coming days and years, and she was still just a child. Most kids her age didn't know how to do their own laundry, yet she had a whole universe of responsibility before her. Soon she'd have to return to school and be among friends, whatever family there was beyond this Sasha person, and she would be different, fearless because she'd been in a room with Death. Bright lights couldn't completely dispel it; its claws were in everything.

Finally, she moved away from Wyn to the other side of the gurney and pulled out her cigarettes, put one in her mouth and lit it in such a fluid movement, and so quickly, that Wyn had no opportunity to stop her. She blew the smoke over David's face, and it was like she was sharing a sacrament reminiscent of a native burial. Still, her audacity shocked Wyn and he reached across the body to demand the cigarette from her hand. "You can't do that here," he said.

She sneered at him a little and took another drag, and Wyn snatched the cigarette from her fingers and held it awkwardly, like he'd never touched one before. It felt so strange, yet how many thousands of times had he smoked? He didn't know what to do with it – there was a bucket in the room, so he smothered it there. "I did you a big favour, letting you come here," he hissed. "I expect you to be respectful." Yes, she was in shock and yes, she was just a kid, but Wyn had put up with enough.

He was tired and wanted to get out of this cold room and cold city. It struck him suddenly that he might actually enjoy a holiday, cuckolding notwithstanding.

Claire turned and left the room and her father, slamming the door behind her. The tobacco smoke drifted lazily down and hovered over the dead body like a spirit.

***

Wyn followed Claire out of the room, saw her be intercepted by Bilal, who in his courteous, obliging way, drew her gently into his office and shut the door. Sasha would probably be the one signing the forms to release the body for the autopsy. The morgue attendant conferred with Wyn for a few moments. He wanted to know if Wyn would be in attendance for the post-mortem and Wyn, impatient, curtly informed him that he had a plane to catch. Frank came round a corner with Nick, who looked considerably more pale than he had at the Drobac house.

"So ya done with the girl now?" asked Frank.

"Not yet. She's with Bilal filling out forms. She wanted to see her dad. You've had a look at him as well, I understand."

Frank nodded vigorously. "Just a quick once-over, but we saw the Taser burns on his chest. Could factor into the death, but I'm pret'near sure there was drugs or booze involved."

Wyn looked at Nick as he spoke, to demonstrate that his next words were meant to be taken as a lesson. "Let's not make too many presumptions about substances. I found no track marks on his arms, but there is evidence of bruising on his neck."

Frank frowned. "Whaddaya thinking? Asphyxia?"

"With a baton, possibly."

Looking more doubtful, Frank said, "That'll be a tough one. We'll need the officers to confirm position."

"They are probably sorting that out amongst themselves as we speak. With Sylvia's assistance, naturally. I have a feeling that they'll offer some highly plausible excuse, such as accidental self-asphyxia with a roll of masking tape."

Frank snorted agreement. "Yeah, never know what they'll come up with. Still think toxicology'll tell us a' interesting tale. It's on the news, natur'ly, but I say we give it a day or two before we go chatting up the press." He sounded nonchalant, but Wyn knew that Frank was deeply suspicious of the media.

"A day or two is an eon in this age. A man has been killed by police in a public place with fifty witnesses. We're expected to be present and available," said Wyn. "You're the lead on this case, while I'm gone. Chantal will deal with the media, but you may have to release a statement."

Frank snorted. "Right. All I got to say is: 'we're investigating it.' They're not in charge of us. Keep that in mind."

Such moments as this one put Wyn in an awkward position. Because they'd worked so closely together in the past and he respected Frank, he hated to remind him that such decisions weren't to be challenged. "Word is going to spread quickly. There were people who filmed it on their cellphones. If the scene wasn't completely secured then something could have leaked. We have to be prepared for that. I need you to show leadership on this while I'm away."

"That's the problem," said Frank, ignoring Wyn's appeal, his hangdog jaw jutting as he spoke. "The whole fockin' world's got a fockin' camera now. Gets so the cops can't even write a fockin' parking ticket without it ending up on the internet – some loud-mouthed punk calling them bastards, arseholes, fockers. It's the fockin' opposite of a police state – it's a citizen state. It's not us watchin' them anymore, it's them watchin' *us*." Interesting, thought Wyn. You can take the man out of the force, but you can't take the force out of the man. "All the more reason that we keep the public appeased," he answered. "I have no intention of giving out any more information than is absolutely necessary. No names. But I want to put out an appeal for witnesses who may have left the scene before we arrived, or kept their cellphones. We need the public's cooperation."

"All's I'm sayin', you don't want to end up wishin' your cake dough."

"Cake's not dough, it's batter," Wyn answered automatically. It was a long-time joke between them, but Wyn had yet to admit to Frank that he had no idea what it meant.

In the lobby Wyn scanned for Claire and Sasha, but they were gone. He should have gotten Sasha's number, or given her his own. He should have advised the woman not to allow the girl to watch television or surf the net, because the story would be all over the news. Hopefully she had the wherewithal to figure that out on her own. But for the time being it didn't matter. The girl was safe.

He was grateful that he didn't have to be present for the autopsy. It would be difficult, observing the dead man's ribcage sawn apart with tools from Home Depot, his heart removed, his brain examined for evidence of oxygen depletion, having spent time in the company of the only person that he had probably ever loved.

And now, he had to catch a plane. Catch indeed. He pictured himself, coat flapping, suitcase dragging him down, galumphing down the runway, hand outstretched, fingers brushing the underbelly of the departing plane as it slid into the envelope of sky.

***

Toronto winters were capricious. Some years there was so much snow the city would shutter business for a day or two until it was cleaned up, and some years there was no snow at all. Sometimes the season couldn't make up its mind whether it wanted to be winter or not and the weather would be all over the map, so to speak, with bursts of intense precipitation ranging from rain to sleet to snow to ice pellets interspersed with lulls of eerie grey quietude, when one would wish something would happen, even a bad thing, just to dislodge the inertia. This December had been stonily immobile until Christmas Eve, when the Arctic dropped a coil of bitter wind, which, when greeted by the warm front approaching from the south, over Lake Ontario, generated a storm of messy wet snow. Now there were whiteouts along the highway to the airport and some cars in the ditch. Traffic, if it could even be called traffic, was creeping and idling, helpless under the enchantment of winter.

Wyn was not among the enthralled. Though he suspected that his flight would at least be delayed, if not cancelled entirely, he was resolute that he would get there on time to show Anna that he took her desire to vacation together seriously, and that the work crisis was not paramount. If he was to discover, tonight or at some other point in the next week in Mexico, that his wife indeed did have a lover, it was all the more imperative that his behaviour be unimpeachable, even if it had, heretofore, been anything but.

He had left a message half an hour ago assuring her that he was on his way, even though he had no real idea of when he would leave. Now, to catch up, he used driving tactics from his investigator days: honking his way past idle vehicles to get to the shoulder and then bolting along it at as fast as he could without putting himself or anyone else in danger. Or not much danger. The shoulder, untravelled, was more treacherous than the road, and Wyn's SUV skidded here and there, but he was a masterful driver and managed to keep the hulk in check. He even had managed to turn on the radio. He hadn't heard any reference to the Drobac incident yet. Chantal, he knew, wouldn't have issued a press release without running it by Frank first. She, like Nick Chirila, was still quite green, and probably had been waiting for Wyn or someone to call her since the incident had transpired, but Wyn was not in a hurry to release any information. He was grateful that she was available, however, to field all the calls that Wyn would never get around to answering, demonstrating to the public that SPOA was alert and in control.

He caught the 4:30pm newscast and it led with weather conditions and flights, stating that passengers should call their airlines to find out about delays. (Wyn knew from years of experience that this was pointless – one could never get through.) Then the story about Drobac was broadcast with only the basic facts. However, when the newscaster intoned that there had been an update on the story, he realized, cringingly, that he hadn't turned his phone back on when he'd been at the morgue with the girl. If there was an update, it was likely the investigators or Chantal had been trying to reach him.

When he heard the name Tony Lucci, the Toronto Police Chief, he knew he was in trouble. The newscaster stated that Lucci had released a statement at a press conference and played a snippet. "As you all know, at approximately 10am, police from 55 Division were called to the Gerrard Square Mall to deal with a hostile man who'd been threatening shoppers in a Staples store. Security called the police, who attempted to calm the man down, but he was unresponsive due to the fact he was suffering from excited delirium. When the suspect drew a weapon, officers had to use force to subdue him. The man continued to flail and be violent. The officers managed to handcuff him and after more struggle he was finally subdued and lost consciousness. His vital signs were monitored while waiting for emergency medical personnel, but the suspect did not regain consciousness and died on the way to hospital."

Furious, Wyn slammed his hurt hand on the steering wheel of the car, and it sang with pain. He skidded dangerously near the guardrail but managed to pull out of it and bring his vehicle to a stop. It was fortunate that he was still on the shoulder or he would have rear-ended someone, or been hit from behind. He fumbled to get his phone from its holster and looked at it, hands trembling. There were at least a hundred more texts and twenty-eight voicemail messages. He shouted "fuck" many times over in the snow-muffled silence of his car, then slumped in his seat and set the windshield wipers going to get the excess snow off the glass. Their repetitive swish had a meagre calming effect.

He plugged his phone into the hand's free device. He had to take care of his wrist. Instead of reviewing all the messages, he called Chantal on her cellphone.

"Oh thank god," she said, her high, perpetually breathless-sounding voice filling the close confines of his vehicle. She might know a lot about technology and social media, but she still looked and sounded like a prepubescent girl. He could never let her take his place in front of a camera or microphone. "It's you. I thought you must have left by now. Has your flight been cancelled?" She sounded hopeful.

"Had to contend with the next of kin. I just heard the news. What in bloody hell is going on?"

"Where are you? Are you near the office?"

Wyn looked out his windshield, where he could see the artful signage that had been posted on Highway 401 on Pearson land, which meant he was, for all intents and purposes, at the airport. Anna and Rebecca were in there, waiting for him, or not waiting for him. "It doesn't matter where I am," he said. "Is Frank back from the post-mortem yet?" Frank was the best person to deal with a crisis.

"No. But the other guys are here."

Based on what he heard on the news, Wyn said, "It's not unheard of for the Chief's office to make a statement for such things, but under no circumstances should he be making assertions about the cause of death. This business about 'excited delirium' is ridiculous."

Chantal said, "I didn't know what excited delirium was until one of the guys – I think it was Barry – told me about it."

Wyn had wrapped some gauze around his wrist, but it kept slipping. He'd forgotten to put antiseptic cream on it. Bugger it, he thought, pulling out a roll of tape. Just get it to stop bleeding.

"I hope he told you that excited delirium is not actually a medical condition. It's tantamount to saying he died of fright."

"People don't die of fright?"

"If you shot someone, then ran them over, do you think you could use the defense: 'not my fault, he was scared to death' in a court of law?"

Chantal sounded unsure, as though she feared the question was meant to trick her. "I – I suppose not."

"It's going to take us weeks to figure out what actually killed the man."

It was unclear how much of what Wyn said made sense to his communications assistant. "The media wants a statement, but I thought I should talk to you first," she said.

Wyn sighed. "Okay. Get ready to transcribe." He stared up at the utterly uninteresting roof of the interior of the car. The heat was on too high, making him sleepy. He opened the window and a swirl of bright ice crystals blew in, like magic dust. Wyn inhaled, wishing it would give him the power to make the weather, the media, his flight, and the entire Toronto police force disappear.

Sounds of Chantal moving about, then the clack of her fingers on her computer keyboard. Wyn turned his head to look at the giant blue sign with black letters spelling out STILL on the art installation that faced the highway. He'd noticed it before on his other trips to the airport, but never really contemplated why it was there. When he closed his eyes the word STILL burned white on an orange background on his eyelids. "Chantal, consider Lucci's statement as a lesson on how not to speak to the press. It's riddled with speculation. Lucci's blowing smoke. They don't even mention that they Tasered him." He regretted telling her this before it was out of his mouth, stupid of him to let it slip. Best to keep all information about the state of the body among the investigators. "Are you ready?"

Wyn recited the usual things that SPOA would state in a situation such as the one that had transpired, revealing little about what happened but only that SPOA was "following the usual procedures" to determine cause of death. In the meantime, any witnesses to the event who did not stay on the premises could call SPOA, or go to the website. When she read it back to him, Wyn told her it was fine to put on the wire, then halted her. "One more thing," he said, feeling his face grow warm, the way it often did when he was about to do or say something that might get him in trouble. "I want you to add this: 'The Chief's office did not observe the change in the mandate that stipulates that police officers who are involved in a death of a civilian remain on the scene. SPOA is expecting better cooperation from the Police Association as the case unfolds.'"

Chantal read it back to him again. If she thought there was anything reproachable in it, she did not say so to her boss. Wyn knew the statement would draw the Chief's ire. He didn't care. He was just about to ring off when Chantal said, hopefully, "So we just sit tight till you come into the office?"

Wyn did not want to go to the office. This was an unusual feeling for him. He tested his desire again to make sure it really was so lacking: pictured himself on the elevator, in the lobby, immersed in the hum and scurry of a breaking incident. Usually he felt a flutter of adrenalin, a small whoosh in his bloodstream. He'd felt it, briefly, at the office supply store, at the actual scene. But not now. The thought of being in the office proper made him sad and weary. "Look, I'm going on vacation. My first since I became Director. This is a fairly standard case; Frank is in charge. You can email me updates from the media. Lucci's press releases are not our problem. You'll be fine," he reassured her, and hung up before Chantal could express more anxiety. She'd get used to the pressure, or she wouldn't and he'd let her go when he got back.

The device rang again. An unknown caller. Deliberating whether or not he should let it go to his voicemail like all the other dozens of calls, Wyn flipped a coin in his mind, then took it. To his terse "Wyn Rhys" there was a silence almost long enough for him to think the connection was lost, or that the unknown person had the wrong number. Then a small, faraway voice said, "Hello?"

"Claire? Where are you?"

"I'm at Sasha's," said the girl, her voice tiny in his ear.

"Okay. Good," he said. Why she was calling him, he had no idea.

"I don't have my daddy. I don't know what to do. I'm scared."

Trying not to sound too rushed, Wyn measured his words carefully. "I know you're scared. Everything's going to be okay. You're at Sasha's. You can talk to her." He heard a beep. There was another call or message coming through. "Claire, I'm driving. I can't talk right now. If you could just–"

"I don't want them to take away my daddy. I want to be with him. I want to go home and sleep in his bed, but Sasha won't let me. We always hang out in his room on the cold days. He reads to me. I have to wait for him. He's in the hospital." She sounded so young. An orphaned girl wanting her daddy.

The post-mortem would have been done by now, the empty cavity in the man's chest sewn up, his body chilling in storage until the tests were completed on his organs. Wyn's heart should have gone out to the man's daughter, but he found compassion difficult to come by these days. Still, he hoped his deep voice would settle somewhere in her psyche and calm her. "Claire, sweetheart, you have to understand that there are people who can help you better than I can with this. My job is to find out what happened to your dad, and I must focus on that right now. I know this is terrible for you. Don't watch the news or go on the internet. You don't have to be brave, you just need to be safe." He couldn't remember talking to anyone like this, in all his years as an investigator. He had pity in him somewhere after all. She was quiet again and he wondered if he'd been soothing the ether, the connection on cellphones so often tenuous, especially in poor weather. "Claire?" he asked. "Are you there?" He started his car. He had to get off the shoulder, back into traffic, to the airport.

Silence, then: "Yeah." She was tear-snuffled. "Listen, I have to tell you something about the mall."

Wyn wasn't listening; his phone had beeped again. It was Anna. "I have a bit of an emergency to deal with, Claire. I need you to try to do what I requested. I need you to trust that I'm doing everything I can to help you." There was an exit just a half kilometre ahead; he had to get his vehicle into the right lane to get off the highway. "Can you hear me? Can you do that? Trust me?" There was no response. She'd hung up.

Through his rear-view mirror he could see the word STILL in the art installation had morphed into LIFE in red and yellow. He didn't get it. He felt guilty about letting Claire go. He just didn't know what to do with a child in her situation, but he had an unsettling feeling that he was abandoning her, and this feeling bloomed into the more familiar anxiety that if he left, everything at SPOA would fall apart. This had been what kept him from taking vacations for years.

"I've been calling you all afternoon," Anna said when he picked up, not sounding particularly angry, but it was hard to tell over the sound of his engine. "We're checked in but the flight's been delayed. They're saying 10pm. The storm is letting up, but I doubt we'll even get out then. Where are you?"

This was a tricky question to answer. If he told her that he was near the airport she would assume that he would continue on his way to meet her and Rebecca, which he hadn't decided to do yet. If he said that he was still at the office then she would think he had no intention of going to Mexico with them. He didn't know if she was even aware of the incident at Staples and its developments, but he decided not to bring it up and engage in an argument about his priorities. There was no time. He went with a vague version of the truth. "I was just getting on the highway when I saw how bad the weather was," he said. "I couldn't get through to the airline. Traffic's wretched. I'm … not sure I'll make it there for ten." He winced as he said this. He was only three kilometres away.

Anna sighed. "I heard about the death in custody incident on the way in," she said. "I'm assuming that you're knee deep in it? Are you really on the highway or at the office?"

"On the highway. It's just ... there've been some developments. Lucci issued a press release that I swear is calculated to make us look like fuckwits, full of bloody hearsay and..." he trailed off, feeling like he was talking to himself in the clinging silence of the car's interior.

A short silence, then Anna said, "I need to know whether or not to expect you on this flight."

Wyn wished he could simply remain in this no-man's land between heaven and earth, neither fleeing to paradise nor stalwartly remaining in the purgatory of his office. Here on the highway he was neither captive nor free. He could keep driving to the airport and leave the case in Frank's hands, and Chantal could muddle through her first really big PR responsibility with some long-distance guidance. The child had a caregiver, access to counselling. But he saw the condom packet, so innocently concealing a ridiculously simple bit of prophylactic technology, a tiny thing, but a momentous thing. Finally he said, "Most likely the flight's going to be cancelled. You should just go home."

"Wyn, this isn't working."

"What are you talking about?"

"Us. This was your last chance. And you blew it."

Struggling to get into a lane, Wyn couldn't quite register what his wife was saying. "My last chance to do what?"

"To be a husband. To be a father. To be a human being in this fucking marriage." The words sounded practiced, like she'd said them to him in her head, many times.

Sweat bloomed on Wyn's brow and his eyes filmed over. His fury was mounting as steadily as his speed as he nudged rather belligerently into traffic. "Last chance for me? Really? Seems like you made up your mind a long time ago," he said, growled, really.

"Oh, how so?" She sounded level, but cautious.

"Well, the condoms in the vanity, for one thing."

"Yes, you left one on the counter. What do you want me to say?"

Wyn thought for a moment. Maybe he'd been mistaken. "That you bought them for Rebecca?" His daughter having sex – it hadn't even occurred to him until now.

"They're not for Rebecca. The flight's just been cancelled. We're going home. I suggest you stay at the hotel you go to every Saturday." Anna hung up.

Wyn had to get back into the city now. He should never have left. It had been so outrageously idiotic that he had gone to Gerrard Square Mall, gone to the house of the next of kin, then tried to get to the airport for a trip he never wanted to take, to save a marriage that was beyond all repair. Eyes blurred with tears, he manoeuvred between lanes, seeking an exit. But nothing was moving. It was completely dark now. He would die of old age on this fucking highway.

He wondered briefly if Anna might call him back and say she wanted to talk things over, work things out. But he knew she wouldn't. She'd said all she wanted to say, and, like him, she was a logical person and unsentimental. Had he made her that way in the course of their twenty-one-year marriage? Would she regain some sentiment now with a new partner?

He tried, for a moment, to imagine what a life without his wife and child would be like, but all ideas attached to this thought slipped off the edges, pooling somewhere inconveniently distant. What woman would Anna be now, without him? What man suited her? Someone who wasn't obsessed with work, probably, and with a more expansive mind. Wyn's world had shrunk to the extent that he couldn't offer opinions on world events or culture or politics anymore. He didn't share the interests of his peers; he didn't golf or watch Canadian sports, he didn't play the stock market, he didn't have affairs. He'd rarely socialized with Anna's friends;

he didn't even know most of them anymore. Another man would give her long walks on the beach. He'd lean his head to one side and thoughtfully listen to her talk about the garden. He'd tell her she was beautiful every single day. It was no less than she deserved; she'd worked hard to be beautiful and deserved to live a long time with someone who enjoyed life as much as she did. She was still young, had never really been old, which was what he had loved most about her, perhaps because he was old, had been since he was about twenty-four.

But whatever man stepped in to replace him, that man would never know what it was like, seeing tired and dry-lipped Anna cup her hands to receive her newborn child after forty-two hours of labour. Another man's love couldn't erase the toll years of keeping a fragile family together had taken on her. She may be young, but her very best years were still behind her and she had given them to her daughter, to her job, to a man who didn't deserve them. Wyn wished now that she'd left him sooner, or he'd left her. It would have been an act of kindness, ending this marriage ten years ago. But he supposed she'd stayed so long because of Rebecca. Or because she'd hoped he'd change, but she must have known that he'd work until it killed him.

His phone blinked at him and started ringing, the screen blazing with the name "Justine Lyons." It wasn't possible. Hands trembling, he swiped the screen, tentatively. Hearing his own voice say "Justine Wolfe" was frankly bizarre. He'd thought it so many times, but never spoke of her to anyone, except her lawyer.

"Wyn Rhys," came the reply. A young woman's voice, not a child's. Assertive. "I saw you on television today. My lawyer gave me your number."

"Where are you?" Wyn asked, but it wasn't quite a question.

A pause. "I think you know where I live."

Part II

Chapter Seven

Old City Hall, Toronto
June 18, 2002

Nestled behind Old City Hall and in front of Wyn's office on Bay Street was a square, and in that square a labyrinth had been laid a few years before. Wyn had never walked it but had observed others meandering it during his smoke breaks, or on his way to get a coffee. Mostly he didn't pay attention to the activity, having assimilated it into the landscape of the everyday. He had never been exceptionally attuned to the ordinary, quotidian events that unfolded around him, preoccupied as he almost always was with cases he was working on, reconstructions of past events and following their reverberations into the present. The future was mercilessly caged in the boxes in his electronic calendar, usually months in advance, but his personal future was scarcely reflected upon except in some abstract, generalized way. Work, advancement, retirement at some point. Beyond that, a blue-tinted rest and ultimately a demise. But that seemed mercifully very far off. He was only thirty-eight.

He'd been in court all morning and this was his first break. The first drag on his cigarette was always like a first kiss. Each subsequent drag was a progression through a love affair that resolved itself, invariably, with burnout and rejection. Then the whole cycle would repeat itself twice a day, at this location. He carefully calibrated his schedule around a free ten minutes at exactly 10:30am and 2pm to go outside for his rendezvous. Usually he smoked more, but since this trial commenced he'd been careful not to miss much of the proceedings. Today was going to be very stressful, so when he lit up he took a deeper breath than usual, to push the endorphin rush, the calming effect. He let his gaze rest placidly on the beautiful day in front of him. June in Toronto can be absolutely lovely, and today was one of the beautiful days, even in the crush and hum of Bay Street. Golden light passed through the coin-shaped leaves of the young trees in the square, reflected blindingly off the glass façade of the mall. A day for picnics, walks down at the lake (he'd been there less than ten times in as many years) for a pint on a patio.

A girl stepped into his peripheral vision. She was about twelve, not very tall, wearing rather formal attire: a skirt and short-sleeved blouse, ankle socks, low-heeled Mary Janes. Something a kid would be forced to wear to church. Her black hair was long and very curly. The child commenced walking the labyrinth, determination in her step, like she was prepared for a long journey, had her bags packed, food and water in case she got stranded along the way. For some reason she captivated Wyn. Everyone else in the busy square disappeared.

Her hair bounced in accord with her walk, like girls skip-roping, and swung away from her body every time she made one of the many hairpin turns. Her long legs were brown, unscraped, and her white socks looked whiter against the tan. She let her arms swing, but did not march and kept her head down to ensure she didn't stray from the path's narrow command. The rhythm: stride, stride, stride, quick turn, stride, stride, stride, quick turn. Wyn wanted to see her face, but her hair obscured it. Sounds: some birds, a breeze, traffic. The Old City Hall clock intoned the quarter hour. To her (and him, vicariously) belonged her preordained destination: the flower in the centre of the labyrinth, in the centre of the square, in the centre of a glass city, on a Tuesday in June. On the path there were other people and sometimes she passed them, or they walked along parallel lines, never intersecting.

At the centre the child stepped onto the flower and looked up at the sky, as though she expected the world would look different from this special place. She had her back to him, but he could imagine her closing her eyes against the glare of the sun. What was one supposed to find at the centre? Enlightenment? Death? Or was the journey the whole point of the exercise, the denouement meant to be anticlimactic? Someone called to her and she turned and abandoned the game, ran to meet a woman at the side of the square. Wyn had a sudden memory of walking the same labyrinth years ago at Chartres with Anna on one of their first dates. One was supposed to retrace the path, it was the only way back out to the world.

Wyn's cigarette had burned to the filter. He hadn't taken more than the first drag.

***

The courtroom in Old City Hall where the Jameson trial was held was one of the most beautiful in the city, well-lit by large windows, accented by bright blonde wood and tasteful green upholstery. Still, it was not a place one wanted to spend countless hours, especially hours organized around the horrific events of one particular night. The press had been coming regularly to sit in the gallery and take notes during the proceedings. Wyn had been there every day, getting someone to cover his shift at SPOA. He did not want to miss one moment. Especially today, when Justine Wolfe was to give her testimony regarding what had happened on June 28, 2000, two years before.

It had taken a year for the forensics team to complete its analysis of all the evidence: the bodies of the victims, the house, in which they had spent weeks, in every room, collecting hundreds of samples of fingerprints, blood, hair. Then another year for SPOA to organize the evidence and integrate it with the testimonies of the officers to create the most accurate reproduction of the events of that night.

The Crown had accepted SPOA's recommendation (submitted by Wyn) that Constable Jameson, who had fired the shot that killed Kevin Wolfe, be charged with manslaughter. The rationale: the officer had killed the man in a fit of passion, rather than talking him down. Kevin Wolfe had been unarmed. There was another person in the room whose life had been jeopardized by the policeman's negligence. What if it had been the girl who opened the door?

Wyn was not a lawyer, but he was more well-versed in the law than the average SPOA investigator. He had worked closely with the Crown preparing the case against the officer. They had relied mostly on the recollection of the subject officers (the ones who confronted Wolfe) and the witness officers, who arrived shortly after the man was killed. There was the forensic evidence as well. But the prosecution was still insecure about getting a conviction. It needed the testimony of a witness who wasn't an officer. Justine Wolfe, who had been ten at the time, was the only living witness, and a crucial one.

The child was living with relatives, the sister of her mother and her family. Her name had been legally changed to Doyle, her mother's maiden name, presumably to detach her from any connection to her notorious father. Upon being subpoenaed, she had to undergo a process called *voir dire*, which would determine her capability to testify. Wyn was not in attendance for this but understood it to mean that the girl had to prove that she was competent and compellable. She needed to understand what it meant to make a promise to tell the truth, and understand what the truth actually meant.

SPOA kept its machinations very quiet, releasing little information to the public and deflecting the Police Association when it put in requests for information. So when the charge was laid, the Police Association under Bill Watson was deeply chagrined. Bill was a very decent man but weak-willed. He had given SPOA the officers without complaint and had cooperated fully with the investigation in the hopes that the result would be a demand that Constable Jameson be dismissed only (he had been suspended with pay) and make a public apology. He had also worked diligently to improve training for officers in dealing with people in crisis. Upon being informed of the charge by the Crown, he had called SPOA's then-Director Gaston Tremblay and begged him to reconsider, to save the association the ignominy and the officer the shame of having such a stain on his record. Tremblay, at Wyn's behest, did not back down. Justice had to be served and Jameson made an example to other officers. The association had subsequently learned of SPOA's decision to compel a minor to testify and appealed to the public to condemn the agency for making a traumatized victim, a child, take the stand. There had been some debate among experts in the media and the consensus had been that SPOA was operating within the ethical boundaries of the law. Justine Wolfe was not a character witness but integral to the case; no jury could recommend a conviction beyond a reasonable doubt without her testimony.

The girl had easily passed the *voir dire*, and the Crown decided to reserve her testimony to near the end of the trial when it would have the most emotional impact. The Crown lawyers used questions Wyn submitted and kept SPOA in the loop. As the trial progressed, Wyn felt all the more confident that a conviction would result from Justine Wolfe's testimony. He couldn't wait to see her on the stand, telling the world (the case had been high-profile enough to attract international attention) what really happened that night.

So when the girl who walked into the courtroom turned out to be the girl he saw on the labyrinth only an hour before and a few yards away, Wyn was strangely not surprised. Likely a part of his mind had recognized her, thus his intrigue. When she had walked the labyrinth, what was she thinking? Upon reflection, she had seemed somber, perhaps making a wish as she walked that everything would be okay and hoping it would come true when she got to the centre. Is that the way twelve-year-old girls think? His daughter was only four years old, so he had no clue about the ways of children of that age. While he had thought about her importance to the case many times over the past two years, he had forgotten the particulars of that night, until now.

Now he recalled how she had felt so light in his arms when he lifted her, how she had smelled of blood but also of buttered toast. She had appeared in his dreams for several weeks after the event, always surrounded by horror in different guises and always serenely above it, inviolate, but he did not reflect on these dreams upon waking. Yet all along he had imagined her as incapable of feeling traumatized, that in the intervening time she had never had nightmares of her own nor wept, but had just carried on with her childhood existence. Now something deep in him quailed, observed how she walked through the courtroom, her stride sedate, nothing like her bounding progress on the labyrinth only a short time before. He sat in the front row so he had a good look at her face as she mounted the stand. He couldn't remember, did she look older?

She looked around the room without turning her head, and it was with no little fear and trepidation, then her eyes rested on Wyn and remained there for what seemed to him an eternity. He felt his face grow hot. He presumed that she would have forgotten him in all the chaos. But there was no doubt she knew him now, and stared at him so disconcertingly he wanted to rise and flee, suddenly feeling guilty, even ashamed, for bringing her before this circus of reporters, the curious, the faceless jury, the stern face of Sylvia Hughes, who was representing Mike Jameson. Jameson himself. Wyn could not look over at the officer, who most certainly would be deeply perturbed, seeing the child whose life he had so needlessly endangered. Wyn kept his face neutral but smiled a tiny bit at Justine Wolfe, encouragingly. Her face was impassive, but he was sure he saw something in her eyes that reproached him.

She made an oath that she would tell the truth, her little hand on the Bible. The Crown was the first to cross-examine her. She looked very nervous, even though she had spent quite a lot of time with Sam Butler, the Crown lawyer who had counselled her on how to testify (with a psychologist present, to assure that she wasn't in any way manipulated). His first question was simple enough: what did she remember of the night of June 28, 2000?

Justine looked down at her hands, silent for a few moments. When she lifted her head she seemed older all of a sudden. She said, in a clear voice deeper than her years seemed to belie, that she remembered a few things, but not everything. Sam Butler nodded, said it was okay, she only had to tell the court what she recalled. She spoke slowly and clearly, beginning with the start of the evening, how her mother had been out for dinner with her Aunt Valerie and left her dad in charge of her and her brothers. He had been in a bad mood all day, she said.

"Did he often lose his temper?" asked Sam.

Justine nodded. "They fought a lot. He sometimes scared my mom, and we would go for long drives or stay at Aunt Valerie's or Grandma's until he was okay."

"We have evidence that your dad had been drinking that day, and used drugs. Did he often get drunk?"

Justine shrugged. "I don't know," she said. Wyn thought: how would a ten-year-old child know that their parent was high or intoxicated? They would see the behaviour but not likely know the cause.

"Were you scared of him?" asked the prosecution.

Justine was still for a time, then shrugged, looked at her folded hands. "Sometimes. But sometimes he was good, he was nice. He used to read me stories in the big bed and fall asleep with me. He liked pretty music. We had a lot of music playing in the house."

"Did he play music on this day?"

Justine nodded. "Really loud. Like, super loud."

Wyn hadn't heard this detail. Did Kevin Wolfe play music loudly to drown out the noise of his actions?

As the prosecution asked questions, the story unfolded. Kevin had put her in charge of watching her brothers in the bath and got angry when she filled the tub too high and put the small boys at risk. They were two years old, able to stand and walk, but they could slip underwater easily. When caught in her error, her father had become enflamed with fury, and set about drowning Liam, to show her how easy it was to drown in a bathtub. "He told me that if the boys drownded – I mean drowned – he would tell Mommy that it was all my fault. He held Liam's head for a long time. I didn't know how long it takes to drown someone. It seemed like a long time. Sean started screaming, but I couldn't move."

"You thought your dad was going to stop and that everything would be okay?"

The defense interrupted at this point and said the prosecution was leading on the witness. Sam rephrased his question. "Did you understand how much danger your brothers were in?"

Justine shook her head. She looked mournful. Wyn suddenly remembered the droop of her mother's head as she hung in that garage, the serene capitulation to the overwhelming power of death. How many times had this girl thought about what happened? "I jumped up and ran out of the room. I didn't make any noise. I knew if I made noise Daddy would come after me. All I thought was that I wanted my mom to come home and make Dad stop hurting the boys. I went into my room and hid in the closet."

"How long were you in the closet?" asked Sam.

Justine shrugged again, looked up at one of the large windows. "I stayed in there for a long time. I think I fell asleep."

This gap in the narrative was revealing, thought Wyn, and not uncommon. The child may very well have had a narcoleptic seizure at that time. The body had an exquisite capacity to avoid trauma. Justine couldn't flee because there was nowhere to go – home was the only safe place in her universe. She didn't fight because she had no power. Playing dead was the only option left to her, and sleep its most effective manifestation.

She went on: "When I woke up, it was dark in my room so I guess it was late, because the sun sets later in the summer. Everything was quiet. I was scared of leaving my room, of even moving, but I really needed to pee. So I crawled out, and crawled down the hall to the bathroom, scared that Daddy would see me. I don't know where he was, maybe in the basement."

"This is the same bathroom where your brothers had their bath?"

Justine nodded, slowly. "We had a bathroom in the basement, but I didn't want to go there and see my dad. And I thought … I thought that what happened was just a bad dream. Or maybe that Liam and Sean were okay, Dad was just being weird, but not wanting to hurt anybody. I didn't turn on the light. I didn't want to see."

"It's all right. The court knows what was in the bathroom. So when you came out, what happened next?"

"I went back to my room, on my hands and knees. I put on my PJs, decided to just go to bed. Then I heard sounds. My mom was home. I heard her shoes, which were high heels. Then I heard Dad's footsteps coming up from the basement. My door was shut, but I knew he would be mad at my mom for coming home so late. I don't know why, but I was sure it was really late." Justine Wolfe paused, rubbed the side of her nose with the edge of her hand, artlessly. "Then they started shouting. Then Mom went down the hall to the bathroom." The girl stared at the ceiling, squinting, as she had done when standing in the middle of the labyrinth. Did she believe in God? Wyn wondered. Who would believe in God after such a thing happened to you? Or perhaps that was all the more reason to believe. Being an atheist himself, and a rather committed one, he saw no obligation to be grateful to, or to entreat, a higher power for anything. Everyone makes their own fate, he thought. Character is much more the determinant of how our lives play out than circumstance.

The court was silent, waiting for Adele Wolfe to find her sons. Justine finally said, "She screamed a really long scream, a scream that was like it started on the first day of the world and would only end on the last day." She blinked rapidly for a few seconds, like she might cry, but her face remained passive.

If the court was silent before, it had now become something else. Wyn couldn't think of what it was except that it might be that time actually stopped when the child said those words. Sam Butler, who had the practiced expression of mildly compassionate active listening, frowned. Justine Wolfe was to follow an agreed-upon script, and this was clearly not in the script. "I see. That must have been very frightening for you."

The girl frowned. She suddenly seemed a lot older, and resented being talked down to. Her voice changed as well. "Yeah, you could say it was really frightening. But finding your twin babies drowned in a bathtub is a lot more frightening, in my opinion."

The court gasped, and someone up in the press gallery actually let out a short bark – a laugh.

Sam Butler was discomfited. He had prosecuted many important cases in Canada, including one where a child had been kidnapped and raped by a relative. "We're not here to discuss opinions, only facts," he said.

"Okay." Derisive.

"What do you remember from what happened next?"

Wyn had read over some of Sam's notes on the events that had unfolded after Adele found the twins; Justine had claimed to remember little, almost nothing. She recalled faintly that she was in the basement playroom when the cops broke the door and killed her dad. That would be enough to secure a conviction of Constable Jameson; irrefutable proof that a vulnerable person had been needlessly put at outrageous risk. Butler assured SPOA that there was enough detail in her recollection to corroborate its findings.

Imagine his alarm, and Butler's, when Justine flicked her black eyes towards Wyn again, then said, "I remember everything."

The lawyer put his hands in his suit pockets, rattled some change in there. Wyn had a feeling this was a nervous tic; it gave away his lack of preparedness for what might happen next. But he said smoothly, "If you want to tell the court–"

Justine Wolfe interrupted, leaned forward in her seat, her face pinkening, her eyes wide. "You said to tell the truth, right? Tell you what I remember? This is what I remember." She looked at Wyn again, and for the duration of the monologue, delivered in a queer monotone, and staccato, at a breathless pace, she did not once take her gaze off him. Wyn, mystified and not a little petrified, did not look away.

"I did see my brothers, in the dark. They were like white plastic dolls, one on top of the other. Daddy didn't take them out of the bath. He just left them there. I remember my mom screaming and screaming and screaming and I put a pillow over my head to block out the sound, but it didn't work; I could hear everything they said. If anything it was louder. I could feel Daddy coming down the hall and then Mom said he was a monster, she was calling the police, where was Justine? 'Where is my little girl?' she said over and over. 'What have you done with my little girl?' Daddy tried to say things in a quieter voice, but she just got madder and madder. Then Daddy got mad and started calling her names: bitch, cunt, whore. He said he could smell another man on her, that she fucked every man she met, he knew them all. He followed her, he said, to the places where she fucked men. Mom told him he was crazy. She sounded scared, not angry. She told him that everything would be okay, just tell her where her little girl was. She started walking towards my bedroom and I think Dad stopped her and said he had called the police. The paramedics were coming and the boys would be fine. They just got scared, that's all. Mom started crying. I could see the shadow of her feet in the light coming in under my bedroom door. She could have come in my room any second, any second, but she didn't. I think she was too scared, that she'd find me dead. I wanted to yell something, tell her I was okay but I couldn't make a sound.

"Then Daddy was doing something to my mom but I don't know what it was. He dragged her, and 'cause she was screaming I think he must have been really hurting her. Maybe pulled her hair, which hurts a lot." Justine gathered some of her ringlets in her hand and tugged them down. "I held onto the pillow as hard as I could, and asked over and over to make them stop. I wanted Grandma or Aunt Valerie to come and make them stop being crazy. They were both crazy – sometimes when they fought they would be so mean to each other, call each other names. I laid down and tried to just go to sleep, that was the only way to make it all go away. I think I did sleep, for a little while. I don't know how long. I don't know what happened to my mom except that he killed her."

The court remained silent, a reverent, almost religious silence. Justine could have suspended her testimony indefinitely, stayed on that stand with her last words hanging in the air above the crowd, and they would wait, and wait, until she found her voice again. Or until she walked off the stand, taking all the memories of that night with her. Maybe she was telling them – him – now because it was too hard to keep it all to herself anymore. The only person who knew exactly what happened to her mom and her brothers that night. SPOA and the Crown had thousands of pages of documents, of interviews, test results, and each one failed to tell the whole story, or the real one.

She leaned back in her seat, calmer. Her voice slowed, but it still had a queerness to it, a detached quality. She paced her words at precise intervals. "Anyway, I was asleep when my dad came in my room. All the lights in the house were off and he had put music on again – I don't know when. He said I needed to come with him, he had to show me something. I said I was really, really tired, could we do it tomorrow? He said no, tomorrow would be too late. I didn't move or say anything so he came up and pulled my arm, then pulled harder, and I got out of bed. His hand felt sticky. I was scared. I asked where Mom was and he said she was sleeping. I asked if the boys were okay and he said sure, they were fine. I followed him out of the room in the dark and down the hall to the living room. The curtains were closed; I couldn't see hardly anything. We sat on the couch. Dad said that he needed to call the police because he did a bad thing and he was sorry. 'You want to say sorry to the police?' I said. And he said no, he wanted to say sorry to Mom, and to Liam and Sean. 'Do you think they'll forgive me?' he asked in the dark. All there was was his voice in the dark. 'Yes,' I said. 'They'll forgive you.'"

Sam Butler had been standing near the jury, one hand on the bar. Wyn could see him in his peripheral vision. He had his other hand on his forehead, shielding his eyes. Was he trying to convey sympathy for Justine to the courtroom? Or was he perturbed by what he was hearing, and disappointed that the girl had not heretofore trusted him enough to disclose this information in the privacy of his office? Wyn had requested permission to interview the girl for the SPOA investigation but the girl's family would not give him access, and he didn't have the legal capacity to subpoena her. He was certain, judging by the way she seemed to be addressing him in particular, that she had intended this story only for him, but unfortunately, the entire courtroom and the media would hear it too.

Justine went on, "Daddy asked me to bring him the phone so I went in the kitchen and got it for him. I had to turn on the light to see where I was going. There was blood everywhere, all over the floor and the sink. I pretended it wasn't there. I came back and gave it to him, and he called 911. He told the police to come quick, someone had been hurt. His voice sounded really scared, like someone had come to our house and hurt us, even though that wasn't true. Then he hung up and took my hand and said we had to go to the basement – it was safest down there. I asked if someone had broken into our house and hurt Mom and he said yes, someone had hurt Mom. We had to go to the basement to be safe. So I went down with him.

"He kept the lights off but held my hand so I wouldn't fall down the stairs or bump into anything. We went to the playroom. He told me to sit on the couch and be as quiet as a mouse; even if the police came downstairs and wanted to talk to me I had to say nothing. Just be quiet and we would be safe. I thought about a mouse that came out from under the fridge once and ran along the edge of the wall. I remembered how scared that mouse looked, and the little squeaking noises it made. I didn't make a sound. It was really dark down there; there's only one tiny window. I asked Daddy to turn on the light and he said it wasn't safe. He held me on his lap, even though he hadn't done that since I was really little. He held me and rocked me and said he was sorry over and over. I heard sirens, and they sounded so worried. I thought of them being like a voice saying, 'We're coming we're coming we're coming.' Closer and closer, until the lights came through the window: blue and red and white. I got scareder and scareder but was quiet as a mouse.

"Then a lot of things happened all at once, so I'm not sure what order to put them in. The police or somebody banged on the door, and yelled something. Not angry yelling, but like, 'Is there anybody home?' yelling. They banged some more and then they came in, because Dad left the door open, and walked around upstairs in their heavy boots. It seemed like there were hundreds of them everywhere at once. I held on tight to my dad, and he was shaking. I didn't know if the police were there to help us or arrest us. Then the heavy boots came down the stairs and Dad pushed me off him and told me to hide behind the couch. I asked why and he got mad, whisper-yelled to just do as you're told. So I hid behind the couch. The police banged on the door and there were lots of words but I don't remember any of them, because everyone was talking at the same time. I just hid and wished I had my pillow so I didn't have to hear anything. Then the door opened and a man said, 'Freeze!' just like in TV shows and then an extremely loud bang. And then there was quiet. The men said things to each other but I don't remember them, and then someone upstairs called them and they left the room really fast and ran upstairs.

"I sat in my hiding spot for a really long time. Or maybe it was a super-short time. I don't remember. But the room was really quiet and I thought that maybe my dad was scared and needed me so I came out on my hands and knees and crawled around. The room was dark dark still. I crawled until I felt something: my dad's hand. I felt around and touched him in a few places, asked if he was okay. He didn't say anything, and I had this weird feeling you get when you know you're alone in a room. Like: when someone is in a room you know they're there, even when you can't see or hear them. But even though my dad was there, he wasn't. I put my hand on his chest but he wasn't breathing. I could smell something weird, and then there was something wet under my knees, wet and hot and spreading. I thought: I peed my pants, or Daddy did. I checked and it wasn't me. I touched my dad again and then thought of when my grandma Betty died and they put her in a casket with her hands over her chest, like she was protecting her heart, or maybe praying, and I thought maybe the hands are put that way to let God know that you're ready to go to heaven, like a signal. So I put my dad's hands in that position. Then I laid down beside him. I put my hands in that position too because I wasn't sure totally if I was alive or dead, and maybe I should give heaven the signal just in case. I was just a little kid then. I guess I thought weird things.

"We laid there for a long time in that quiet room and there was so much noise all around us, but we were safe. I waited for an angel or something to come and get us. I almost fell asleep or maybe I did fall asleep for a while. Then I opened my eyes and the light was on and there was someone there and he picked me up and took me away. I never saw my dad dead."

Justine took her eyes off Wyn finally and slumped forward, shoulders hunched, and looked down at her hands. There was silence for some time, the courtroom tense, waiting for more, but there was no more. The child had come to the end of her extraordinary recollection. In Wyn's mind the entire night had taken on the hallucinatory quality of the old Technicolor films he used to watch on TV as a kid: the intense scarlets, lemon yellows and turquoise. It was as though he'd been examining mathematical formulas to explain the existence of the cosmos and had then been presented with photos from the Hubble telescope of the Horsehead Nebula.

Sam Butler cleared his throat. "Someone took you away? Can you tell me who?"

Justine's head dropped further, suddenly very shy and withdrawn. Her hair completely obscured her face. "I don't know his name," she said in a small voice.

Sam Butler walked to where Wyn was sitting and put his hand on his shoulder. "Was it this man?" he asked.

Justine looked up and her eyes flickered from one man to the other. "Yes."

Sam said, "His name is Wyn Rhys. He's an investigator for the Special Police Oversight Agency. He came after the police arrived. He found you."

Even though Justine had her eyes on Wyn the entire time she'd been recounting her story, it was only now that she seemed to actually see him, once he had a name. She may have heard his name on other occasions but had no idea that it referred to the man who had found her in that basement room, lying next to her dead father. No one would have shown her a picture of him.

Wyn was not the kind of man to draw attention to himself. He had chosen to be an investigator because he preferred to be behind the scenes, solving problems, not in the limelight, making announcements or proclamations. So when Sam singled him out he felt a deep ambivalence. But he offered Justine what he hoped would bring her some comfort and peace: he smiled at her, the way he imagined he would smile at his own daughter someday, when she was of an age and did a remarkable thing, a thing he would be proud of and amazed by. Justine did not smile back. Did she think she imagined him, and seeing him again, feel elation, fear or dread? Whatever it was she felt, she had been compelled to tell him everything, only him, as though she'd been waiting all this time for him to appear. She'd unburdened herself to him, knowing perhaps that he was strong enough and resilient enough to carry the weight, just as he had carried her out of the wreckage of that night. She didn't seem to care if SPOA and the Crown prosecuted the constable who killed her father; she did not look at Constable Jameson, not once.

The judge called for a recess, but no one moved, or they moved slowly. A court aide came and escorted Justine Wolfe off the stand and she walked past Wyn, her eyes on him the entire time, her head turning more and more as she got farther away, until she got to the door, and then she turned around completely and stopped in her tracks, like she was waiting for him. Wyn's whole body wanted to approach her, thank her, tell her everything would be okay, touch her hair, her face – *alive* – but he couldn't move.

***

Later that afternoon, when the court had recessed for the day and he had had his smoke break, Wyn took the elevator to the ninth floor of 330 Bay Street, where his office was located. The elevator's outer glass wall afforded a view onto the square, and the labyrinth suddenly resolved itself in Wyn's mind as a cross-section of the human brain. He had looked down at it countless times, and never made the connection. The coils and sharp volutes of the cerebrum, organized around the floret of the hypothalamus. The organ that thinks about itself. Cells organized to store and retrieve experiences in the material and spiritual world. What Justine Wolfe had locked away for these past two years. What she had likely never shared with anyone. How did she stand it? Why hadn't it driven her mad? Because she was a child, and children have the capacity, with their fluid, still-developing brains, to find hiding spots to tuck bad thoughts: under pillows and mattresses, behind bookshelves, in an attachment to a toy or blanket. But what kind of woman would this experience make her? Would she ever be able to love anyone, feel safe in a man's embrace? Or would she always be fearful and mistrusting, retreat into booze or drugs or some other vice, end up on the street? Wyn closed his eyes and did something he'd never done before: he prayed to God that she would turn out all right, and that what he and SPOA had done – in compelling her to testify – would not have a deleterious effect on her maturity and future well-being.

What did Justine Wolfe's testimony do to enhance the Crown's case against Mike Jameson? Sam Butler conferred with Wyn and the Director, who had been sitting a few rows back in the courtroom so as to not draw undue attention away from the witness, and told them there were no bad consequences to what Justine did, except perhaps the media castigating the system for exploiting the trauma of a minor, but that burden would be distributed evenly among SPOA, the

Crown and the Police Association, which was being sued by the sister of Adele Wolfe. On the positive side: there would likely be an outpouring of sympathy from the public for the pretty little preteen who witnessed horror and survived, only to lose her admittedly batshit crazy father to the impulse of a trigger-happy cop. Kevin Wolfe had felt remorse, which the child emphasized very adequately, and most importantly, he hadn't killed her. Whether or not he had been suicidal was a point of conjecture; there was no real case to be made that he had provoked the police into killing him, though Wyn had virtually no doubt that this was in fact a blue suicide. He asked if there had been any indication that the girl was going to say what she said on the stand during prep for the trial, and Sam shook his head slowly. The child had been compliant, but not very communicative. There was a chance, he said, that she may have only suddenly remembered what happened once she took the stand. "I'm no psychologist, but there are instances of instantaneous retrieval of long-dormant memories, in particular circumstances," he said.

Wyn didn't think so. For the twenty minutes she was recounting the events of that night it had been only the two of them in that courtroom. He was convinced that she'd been waiting for two years to see him again and tell him what happened. She had no idea the impact her testimony would have on Jameson's future, or the future of police training, nor how it would affect Wyn's career.

Sam Butler had been partly right. The media had been enchanted by Justine Wolfe, but did not criticize SPOA for putting her on the stand. Her testimony had been too compelling, and the urgency she had demonstrated indicated that she wanted to see the police pay for what they did to her troubled father, whom she had no doubt loved, perhaps even forgiven. In the coming weeks, Constable Jameson's defense insisted vociferously that the officer had only been doing his job, had followed his training, and brought pedantic expert witnesses to the stand to support what had always been the standard defense in such cases, but the public remained unconvinced. The jury was in accordance, and found the officer guilty of manslaughter and endangering the life of a minor, sentencing him to nine years in prison with eligibility for parole after four years, as he had killed Kevin Wolfe with a firearm.

Every media outlet described the moment the child pointed to the tall, diffident English investigator in the front row of the courtroom who had, to her mind, rescued her. Wyn's office was flooded with calls from the press, asking him to give an interview. He refused, and even when he was asked about that extraordinary moment several years later, when he had put in his name for consideration for the role of Director of SPOA, he remained adamantly opposed to using it as leverage.

Chapter Eight

December 26, 2014

Justine Wolfe lived in a loft on King Street near Bathurst, in one of the newer hip neighbourhoods in Toronto. Ten years ago the landscape was somnolent and regretful – beautiful brick warehouses, built to service the garment district at the end of the nineteenth century, had been abandoned for decades when manufacturing moved to Asia. Around them the indifferent housing, built for workers, deteriorated further when broken down into boarding houses, and the nearby insane asylum did nothing to improve property values. But in the late nineties all that changed; Queen Street stopped being the hangout for hippies and punks and was now chain-store savvy, transformed by the baby boomers who'd eschewed alternative lifestyles for alligator shirts and Polo cologne, but saw an opportunity to resell the esthetic in sanitized form to their privileged offspring. The old warehouses had their facades scrubbed and powerwashed, their Douglas fir boards buffed and polished, and twenty-first-century pipes, cables and Wi-Fi installed. At first, mostly older artists resided there, but in time these grand spaces were partitioned, lofted and inhabited by people born after 1980, more often than not from another country than Canada, and then, even later, cubicled and emblazoned with the brands of software designers, telecommunications companies, high-end clothing outfitters, upscale bars, with the odd art gallery or two to lend the street the old authenticity it still coveted.

That Justine Wolfe would live here didn't surprise Wyn. He knew that she had been awarded five million dollars when she turned twenty-three. Her extended family had won a civil suit against the Police Association. It hadn't been enough to see the man who killed her murderous father put behind bars; there had to be some monetary compensation for the loss of Justine Wolfe's last close relative, whether he was a killer or not.

She had given him the unit number of her flat, but she had been right, Wyn knew the address, had memorized it when her lawyer informed him she'd moved there last year. Once in a while he had taken a detour when on his way to some appointment in the west end; she lived right downtown. He would never go into the lobby and look her up in the directory or ring her. He had not once contacted her or seen her in person since that day in the courtroom, when she'd turned at the door and stood waiting for him. He imagined her having not moved from that spot since; she was still that little girl. And now she'd contacted him. She couldn't know that he'd searched for her on the internet just the week before, but he had the peculiar feeling that he'd been caught.

She was less obsessed with social media than most women of her generation, with their semi-nude selfies, up-to-the-second Instagram posts, Snapchats and so on, but she still had a presence. He had found thirty or so photos of her: her grad picture from high school, a couple from events in which she had partaken, some profile pictures on a popular social media account. In some she looked ordinary and just part of a crowd, but in one or two she'd been luminous. There was a likelihood that she used other pseudonyms on the web – available only to those who knew her well, or whom she wanted to know her well. Had he wanted to, Wyn could have probed deeper, but even the little information he had gleaned had made him feel furtive and clandestine.

Seeing her in the flesh was something he had never pondered, believing it impossible. But here he was on a snowbound night, standing in the foyer of her condo and punching in the code to ring her loft. And she answered, and her voice was a woman's voice, not the child's. And she let him in and he bounded up the stairs (there were only four floors, no elevators) and had to stop at the top of the last staircase, catch his breath. He hadn't smoked in years, but he still was in terrible shape. He had to not seem too anxious. He ran his hands through his hair; it was damp, his forehead a bit clammy. He realized he hadn't eaten all day and felt dizzy.

The doors were all metal, set in the exposed brick of the corridors. His galoshes made a heavy sound on the floorboards. He heard a door open and her face peered around its edge, a tiny smile. As he drew up to meet her, he saw that it was a face that had been touched by more wind and rain, her hair would have grown out and been cut many times. Now it was short short, an ingenue cut *à la* Audrey Hepburn but curlier. Her eyes were as black as he remembered, her skin still golden with rose tint high on her cheekbones. Her lips ridiculously small and precise. From her photos, he knew something of what to expect, but he was breathtaken nonetheless. She couldn't be the kind of beautiful he encountered on June 28, 2000, because that beauty was irretrievably momentary and stood out against a backdrop of unspeakable horror. She couldn't be the kind of beautiful that traversed the Road to Paradise behind Old City Hall on the day she testified. So he had to content himself with the beauty of Boxing Day 2014 and it was enough. She was beautiful enough.

"It's you," she said.

"Yes, it's me."

Her mouth curled upwards like a smile, but her eyes were soft, a bit sad. "Let me take your coat," she said.

Wyn knew it was too much coat for her to handle. "I'll hang it," he offered, shrugging it off. He'd been wearing it for so long that removing it was like shedding a skin, a very heavy skin.

She watched him. He hung it on a nearby hook. He was wearing, of course, the same suit he had donned so early this morning. This morning. He realized now how tired he was, how unprepared for this experience. He was in the presence of Justine Wolfe. Even on his white-knuckled, two-hour ride over he hadn't let his mind really settle on what he was doing. It had been an automatic, reflexive response, not unlike the response he had to the call to go to the shopping centre this morning. He was needed, urgently, but perhaps he was the one in need, of what, he had no idea. As he drove his phone bleated and snarled, wanting his attention and, feeling hateful towards Toronto, SPOA, his wife, he'd disregarded it. When he exited his car, he'd put it in his coat pocket, and there it remained.

He turned now and Justine hadn't moved, just stood, very still, very cautious, like he was wildlife she had come upon and didn't want to disturb. She wore a black dress that covered her from neck to knee, asymmetrically cut, above black stockings, and it accentuated her girlish form: subtle slopes from shoulder to breast to hip, insouciant in their disregard for the boundaries between child and woman. The proportions that Wyn had observed on the night he found her foretold a longer, leaner woman but were seized in childhood; she was scarcely five and a half feet tall. He could lift and carry her as easily now as he had at thirty-six. Well, not quite so easily, though the thought of lifting her and taking her somewhere – Mexico, England, a bedroom – suffused his imagination with a complex thrill that made his teeth, of all things, ache.

The girl blinked at him. "I honestly didn't think I'd actually see you, tonight or ever." Her voice was low and lustrous, a sheet of metal that vibrated when shaken slightly.

"By sheer coincidence, an opening suddenly appeared in my schedule," Wyn said.

She tilted her head to one side, blinked at him slowly, then turned and led him, small hips swaying, from the entryway into the living space, and it was like emerging from a tunnel into the wider world. The loft was one room and was huge, at least the size of the entire main floor of Wyn's house, and along the far wall ranged windows that were the largest he had ever seen, around twenty feet high and multi-paned. They had no curtains, and afforded a view of the CN Tower, at least, the bottom of the CN Tower, as it was only twenty blocks away. The walls were all exposed brick but nonetheless hung with many prints and mirrors, even carpets. There were also many carpets on the floor and an eclectic range of seating: some antique, some modern, all of varying sizes to accommodate a large range of human dimensions and assembled into small clusters. Instead of one big social convention, there was allowance for several small ones. To one side was an open kitchen with contemporary fixtures and a very large dining table with benches instead of chairs. Near the windows, the loft had been subdivided horizontally and a spiral staircase led to the second level, where Justine's bedroom presumably was. It was among the few indoor spaces Wyn had ever entered where he didn't feel like he overpowered it. So this was what five million dollars looked like, he thought.

Justine was at the fridge, removing a bottle of wine. "I have this," she said. "And any other kind of liquor you might want. Whiskey, scotch, gin, whatever."

"Scotch. But only if it's good."

She bent and drew a bottle out of a lower cupboard. "It's very good." He watched as she poured him a far too generous tumblerful of the tobacco-brown liquid. If he consumed that, in his already exhausted state, he wouldn't be able to drive home. Not home – to a hotel. She topped up her already rather full glass of wine and raised it, but not to toast. As Wyn approached, it seemed like she was looking at him through the filter of the golden liquid, through the lens of nostalgia. When he lifted his glass to his lips, she set hers down and pointed to his bloodstained shirt cuff and the clumsy bandage beneath. "What happened?" she asked, her eyebrows coming together like two birds landing on a wire.

"Cut myself shaving." Wyn took a tentative sip of the scotch. It was extraordinary, or perhaps he just needed a drink now more than he ever had in his life. He took a braver draw, savoured it.

Justine put out her hand across the counter that divided them, and Wyn permitted her to examine the injury more closely. "It's no big deal," he said. She surprised him by peeling away the tape and unwrapping the wound.

The wad of gauze stuck because Wyn had put no ointment on it, and its removal now made him wince and take another swallow of scotch to dull the pain. The wound looked upset to have been so poorly tended. The sign of a serious infection, he knew, would be if the red blazed streaks up his arm. It wasn't that bad, yet.

"Let me take care of this," said Justine, leaving Wyn and going to a door he hadn't noticed before, where presumably the bathroom was. While she was gone, he made a discreet tour of the art on her walls: all original works, drawings and etchings mostly. He wondered if they were made by Justine. They were good, insofar as Wyn knew what good looked like. He thought again of Anna, how she had given up studying for her Master's degree to marry him and bear their child. In the ensuing years, though they had plenty of money, it never occurred to her to collect art. Everything in their house was faux: faux art, faux period furniture. Even the architecture of their house was called Mock Tudor.

There were no personal photos. He looked at the custom-built shelves attached to one part of the wall and all the objects on them, some valuable, such as vases and sculptures, some ephemera, presumably from the travels he knew from her lawyer that she had taken before going to medical school: Europe, South America, Australia. There was birch bark that still held the shape of the tree from which it was peeled, palm leaves dried to ash delicacy, some rocks that had nothing exceptional about them beyond the fact that they'd been selected for display, even a couple of napkins with drunkenly scrawled phone numbers and sketches on them. These objects were given as much space and reverence as the decorative boxes and vials.

When he turned away from the shelves, Justine was again at the counter, busy with a collection of bandages and unguents. "Come back," she said, the tone of her voice curt and brooking no resistance. He returned and Justine told him to remove his jacket and roll up his sleeve, and he obeyed, setting the cufflink – the penetrating blue eye – on the counter. "You're a doctor," said Wyn.

Concentrating on swabbing the wound with stinging alcohol (Wyn took another bracing swallow of his drink) Justine answered, "I'm in med school. At U of T. But you knew that." She glanced up at him, one eyebrow arched.

"Yes, I did," he admitted. Why keep it a secret? Her lawyer probably told her everything. His most secret secret, how much he had thought about her over the years. But perhaps she'd thought about him too.

Deftly, Justine daubed antibacterial ointment on another swab and applied it to his wrist. This was more soothing. He noticed that her left hand had a pale blue butterfly tattoo in the crotch between her index finger and thumb; the wings opened and closed with her fingers' movements. "Mostly ER stuff – car accidents, gunshot wounds." She'd been focusing on her work but now looked up at him. "The kind of stuff you see all the time."

"Not so much, anymore."

"That's right. You're the Director now." With her small teeth Justine tore a packet of gauze and slid the square onto Wyn's wound and pressed. He winced. She unrolled some medical tape and passed it over and under his wrist. It was snug, not tight. She smoothed her fingers over her handiwork and now it felt to Wyn more like a caress. "We are so fragile," she remarked.

"Nice tattoo."

Justine looked at her hand. "One of Nabokov's blues," she said. Wyn knew of Nabokov, but the association with butterflies was lost on him.

"Have you more?" Wyn realized he'd made a kind of insinuation, completely unintended.

"Yes," she answered neutrally.

He took a sip from his glass and saw it was the last. Justine refilled it. The warmth from the first drink had penetrated every blood cell in his body. He attempted to re-affix the cufflink, but the alcohol had dulled his fingertips. Justine did it for him. She put her butterfly hand in his palm, so capable now, tapered and long with rounded-off nails, and all the nerve endings in Wyn's hand leapt to meet her. Finally, Justine slid her hand away, and trembling a little, raised her glass to her lips. "That's a human bite. You could have been in serious trouble." Still official, she set down her glass and squinted at him. "How did it happen?"

"Accidentally."

Justine looked skeptical. She scanned him from neck to waistband. "There aren't any more, I hope."

"No." Her face changed, became softer in the soft yellow light. The doctor retreated and the ten-year-old girl peeked out. "Funny, the first time we met I was the one with blood on my clothes."

Wyn felt his young investigator self emerge to meet the child, but cautiously. The quiet room seemed to hold its breath.

"You got your compensation two years ago. Enough to buy all of this, presumably." Wyn indicated the room with his hand, which, under the whiskey's influence, felt heavy.

Justine's mouth twitched dismissively. "I don't care about money."

"Easy to do when you've got lots of it." This was something he'd said to his daughter, many times. Then he realized to whom he was talking. "You got what you were entitled to. It doesn't make up for the loss of your family, but that's the only compensation available."

Turning her wineglass in the small pool of condensation on the counter, Justine said, "That, and justice."

"Do you think justice was served?"

Still staring at her glass, Justine nodded, a small, unwilling nod. "They shouldn't have killed him. Even if he was a killer, even if he was evil, he didn't deserve to die like that."

Wyn leaned over the counter and braced himself on his elbows. "He wasn't evil."

The glass moved more quickly, tracing a figure eight. "That's what you think," she said. "I've often wondered which half of me is the evil half, the part I got from him."

"'Evil' is too grandiose a word for the ridiculous things people do to one another, and to themselves."

"Ridiculous."

"Absurd, misguided, impetuous, desperate, crazed, terrified. But not evil." While Wyn had long harboured this belief, he had never expressed it to anyone.

"I kind of think that that is exactly the definition of evil."

"Evil is when people deliberately do things to serve their own ends, with the mistaken belief that it is for the greater good," said Wyn. He had studied some philosophy back in university, and had contemplated the concept of evil before. It was inevitable, in a profession like his.

"So, then, why did Kevin Wolfe kill his family?" Justine was cool, reserved, clinical.

Wyn remembered what Allan Guthrie said on that terrible day and repeated it. "We don't know what goes on in the mind of a killer," he said. "But the why doesn't matter, ultimately. *Why* doesn't get anything done."

Justine blinked slowly, and Wyn wondered how much alcohol she had consumed before his arrival. "I want to believe you ... Wyn." This was the first time she'd said his name, and it emerged reluctantly. "I suppose then I shouldn't ask why you came over to see me right away."

"I suppose that I've been waiting all these years to hear from you," he said now, trying to sound casual. "And there was a chance that perhaps you would change your mind about seeing me. A mad impulse perhaps, borne out of Christmas ennui."

Justine shook her head, clasped the edge of the counter more tightly, like it was holding her up. "I wouldn't do that," she said. The image he had of her as a capable young intern had completely dissipated. Wyn experienced a desire to protect, but more than that. The whiskey had slipped velvet gloves over his hands, and his mouth felt soft, yet numb. He wanted to touch her, to slide one hand along her face and neck, feel the pulses: temporal, maxillary, capillary, the brachiocephalic one at the hollow of her throat. He put a hand to his eyes to gather himself inward for a moment, to get some control over these troubling sensations.

"Are you all right?" asked Justine. The counter seemed like an ocean, and her place across from him another shore.

"Just ... a bit tired."

"Why don't we sit down?" Finally, Justine came around from her side of the counter and approached Wyn, then touched him, placing her hand on his chest, on the paper-white expanse of his shirt, over his heart. He should not have come here. He was exhausted, achingly so. Justine stepped away from him and went to the sofa and sat on it, or rather, lowered herself on her knees and tucked her legs under her. Wyn remained standing.

"Why did you never try to contact me directly?" she said suddenly. "Were you afraid I wouldn't speak to you?"

The ache in his heart came out in his voice, he was quite certain. "I wanted to, very much. I couldn't. That goes against the ethics of our organization. We consider all victims of police misconduct to be vulnerable people, regardless of age or circumstances."

"My lawyer told me that you'd kept tabs on me. It was … comforting, to know someone cares. But I'm sure no one would have cared if you'd called me," said Justine, gazing at him levelly.

Wyn poured himself some more whiskey (he was experiencing that recklessness when the alcohol in the body commandeers it, and insists on company) and returned to the girl. In her small corner of the large sofa, Justine had been sitting quietly, fingering the silky fabric of her skirt. The decision between the spindly antique chair and sharing the sofa with her was not difficult to make. Wyn sat on the sofa. "You were raised by an aunt and uncle, I understand," he said.

Justine looked into some middle distance, past his shoulder. "Yes," she said. "Funny thing about being an orphan, you don't really get attached to many things, or to people. It's hard to trust anyone."

Wyn thought about Claire Drobac. What would her adulthood look like, parentless, adrift? He wondered if someday he would see her body in a morgue. He shuddered involuntarily.

"Are you cold?" asked Justine.

"No," he replied. "Just thinking."

"About the man who died today?"

"Hmm."

"Did he have any children?"

"I'd rather not discuss it. It's confidential."

"Of course," said the young woman, sipping her drink. It seemed that she would never make much headway in it, her sips were so delicate, so measured.

"I assumed you contacted me to talk about you."

"I contacted you because I saw you on television and I wanted to see you. I've seen you on TV before of course, but this time, I made the leap. Impulse. I don't know why I didn't do it sooner ... I suppose I was afraid that you wouldn't want to meet me. That you were keeping tabs on me for purely professional reasons. Unless, of course, you did some of your own detective work?" She never took her eyes off him.

Had she asked him a week ago he wouldn't have had to lie. "No."

"Too bad."

"That day in the courtroom, I confess it affected me." He paused. "Your presence was so ... powerful. The fact that the defense chose not to cross-examine ... they basically lost the case the moment you stepped off the stand. Sylvia Hughes–"

Justine put up a hand, flat, palm up: stop. "I don't want to talk about that experience," she said, and her voice sounded a bit halting. Wyn wondered if the alcohol was affecting her. "It was the Longest Day after the Red Night." Wyn could hear the title case in her words. "Mostly, I just try to be present in the moment, follow my truth or whatever. Growing up without parents, a real family, makes a person ... carefree. No obligations to anyone. I guess I don't do commitments well. I'm suspicious of people who can't understand where I come from, and most people never know, will never know."

Wyn thought about why he married Anna.

"You're young," he said. "You have lots of time to think about what you want and when."

"I don't know," Justine said, sipping again, and Wyn saw now that her glass was nearly empty. "I've wondered for a long time if I have inherited my father's inability to really care about people. His psychotic break didn't really come out of nowhere, you know."

The way she spoke was chilling. Wyn knew that victims of trauma often became distressingly detached from their feelings, but it was disconcerting seeing it in Justine.

"It's pointless to think about your life that way. Very particular circumstances led to that night. You are not your father's ghost. You are your own person."

Their knees now touched and Wyn thought, this is maddening. He should silence her with his mouth over hers, press her against the armrest and find a way into the space behind the black barrier of her dress. Did it have a zipper or buttons?

"I've had so many conversations with you in my head over the years. Hundreds probably. I told you my story in many places: sometimes we're in an office. Sometimes we're in a bar, surrounded by people. Once or twice I told you in a bedroom, after making love." She suddenly put her hand in his hair, above his forehead, and let her fingers sink right to the scalp. Casual ownership. Wyn had a sudden flash of recollection: Claire's hand in her father's hair as he lay on the gurney.

Justine picked up her glass of wine and tipped its contents down her throat. Wyn, quite intoxicated now, watched the sternohyoid and omohyoid muscles flex as she swallowed. Justine's glass lolled between her loose fingers, and Wyn plucked it away from her and set it on the floor, clumsily. She draped her legs over his knees, the black-stockinged feet dainty and alert. It touched and troubled him, because it was a tacit acquiescence to a power he didn't want this girl to presume he possessed.

He accidentally dropped his glass off the back of the sofa and it fell on the carpet below but didn't break. With both hands he pulled Justine as close to him as he could without hurting her, and felt her small shoulders quake under his hands. Such fragility and need. He had forgotten the things that mattered in favour of pieces of paper. Endless flocks of it swirling in his mind, their formations like cages around his life. He had to beat them away to see horizons, possibilities.

Her feet twitched a little and Justine tucked her head under Wyn's chin. "I guess I sound pretty okay with it, now," she resumed, each word a puff against his neck. He presumed she meant she was okay with what happened, like it was no big deal. "I see it as the space between two magnets when their poles are held together. There's this pillow of resistance, where they are fighting to unite, but can't. I don't feel like I'm detached from it as much as that I can't quite reach it somehow. I always wondered though, why he didn't come after me. I should have died too."

"But you didn't." Wyn's voice sounded strange to him, faraway and belonging to someone else.

"No. Wyn saved me."

When he heard his name, Wyn blinked and moved. Justine drew away now and shifted to get a better look at him. Her eyes struggled to focus, from drunkenness or from being too close, Wyn couldn't tell. He was having trouble focusing himself.

"You," she said. "Well, a version of you. A you-like person. Actually, a you-lion person. Your amber eyes. Like a lion."

Wyn couldn't grasp what the girl was talking about. "I'm not a lion," he said stupidly.

"Well, I know that now." Justine scrambled a little to remove her legs from Wyn's lap and become more upright, so she could look at him fully, face to face. "But then! What I knew then was that, in all the horror, you came to save me. But you weren't a person – how can I explain it? Nothing in my head was working anymore. The world was allowed to do whatever it wanted and I wouldn't be surprised. So you could have appeared with wings, or in a chariot. Two plus two could equal five. The colour red could disappear. Something in my kid brain turned you into a lion. That's why I changed my name to Lyons when I was old enough."

Wyn's mouth felt thick and numb, and when he spoke, it disconcertingly sounded like he was talking in his own ear. "Children have ... remarkable capacity ... for protecting themselves from trauma."

She smirked. Could she tell that he was getting drunker? "Of course, this time I didn't wish for a lion. I wished for a man. The tall man I saw in photos and in videos on the internet with the beautiful English voice and the black and white suits. The man who never ever gives up on justice." Her eyes dropped from Wyn's and her fingers, the ones who'd lately dressed his wound and still smelled of antiseptic, touched his lips. "Do you remember what you thought, when you found me that night?"

Her fingers were still on his mouth. "You were – you were a miracle," he said against them.

"A miracle," she repeated. "I am, aren't I?"

Wyn touched her face. It was warm. He fingered the upcurled hair near her ear, swooped his thumb over the plush of her lips, marvelled at how her mouth opened slightly when he pressed, like he'd found a secret button, showing her bottom teeth, her tongue. In that second or two that he was distracted she put her hands on each side of his face and kissed him.

He'd been kissed, probably not enough, by women he knew cared about him and for whom he cared in return. But never had he so intensely poured himself into a kiss. His need was a vessel filled to brimming, and he had carried it over stones and through fires without spilling scarcely a drop. But now he tipped it, sent its cascade into the mouth of this girl, and the water was imbued with a lifetime of sorrows and regrets, but also with all the beauty he had known (and sometimes, though he'd never allowed it to rise to consciousness, he found the catastrophes of the dead deeply beautiful). And even while he gave it so freely, he knew that it would undo him. Alive, he thought.

The room's boundaries seemed fluid. Justine broke the kiss, but did not resume her story. She reached to pull off her dress. Wyn leaned forward and moved her hands away so he could do it himself, drawing it up and over her head, and it was like the unveiling of a statue. She was completely naked beneath, and the completeness of the transformation took Wyn's breath away. She'd prepared for this moment, planned for it. All that remained were the black mid-thigh stockings. And the most startling thing of all – she was completely covered in tattoos; or rather, one incredible tattoo.

Feeling more drunk than ever, Wyn leaned back and away from the young woman, in awe.

"I know. Pretty awesome, huh?" Justine crossed her arms over her bare chest, then unfolded them, relaxed them at her sides. Let him see her.

Her entire body, at least from her hips up, was anatomically mapped. Precise as a textbook, drawn in the finest detail with the lightest touch, muscles, organs, veins and bone, but not everything, not all at once. One arm depicted only muscle. The other, only veins. Near her neck were the clavicle bones. A heart hovered to the left of her sternum. Lacy bronchioli traced over one breast, the other was left tantalizingly blank and white. She had ribs, she had a uterus and fallopian tubes. An artery wound its way down from her left ear to her groin. "Turn around," said Wyn, breathless.

Justine turned and there were the scapula, tendons holding them in place, her spine, the back of her hip bones. A delicate masterpiece, the touch like a da Vinci drawing.

"It took over a year," said Justine. "I found all the drawings in old anatomical textbooks and a really great artist. I haven't done my legs yet. I thought about shaving my head and doing my brain but decided that was going too far."

Wyn hadn't touched her yet. She took his hand and put it against her neck, in the hollow above the clavicle. Her pulse beat exactly where the artery was located. She slid his hand down, over her heart, her left breast. She then released it, drew his head towards her. Wyn kissed her sternum, moved to each breast reverently. Pressing scarcely at all, only roving, grazing. He felt as though he had penetrated her skin and was inside her body.

There was no sound in the room but the sound of his lips on her skin and her breath quickening, catching in her throat.

She drew away finally, and in the rose-gold light of the room, he could see she was blooming and lush with desire, her mouth parted, her eyes glazed, fearful even. She looked suddenly so young that Wyn's own breath caught and he faltered, thinking that he should stop. With purpose, Justine moved forward and he reclined, letting her dictate the geography and geometry of their bodies on the sofa. She leaned in more and pressed her pelvis, hard, into his belt buckle, and it jabbed him in the abdomen. "Ow," he said.

She pulled back, but only slightly, her lips puffy and very red from kissing. "What?" she whispered.

Wyn was embarrassed suddenly by the proximity of certain parts of their anatomy. Without the beam cast by her kisses, he felt he was languishing back into his former grey self, his careful self, the man who didn't take risks. "If we're going to … if we're going to do this, we need protection," he said, thinking of Anna, of the condom in the vanity. Anna was like him, thorough, businesslike.

Justine levered herself up, her elbow resting on the back of the red sofa. Her other hand was on his chest, over his heart. "I don't have anything," she said frankly. "Can you make me pregnant?" She tilted her head in that way she had of assessing him, a bit crafty, a bit calculating.

"No," Wyn admitted.

"Then don't worry," said Justine, sounding again like the doctor who'd dressed his wound. "I won't give you any diseases." She shifted, bent like a willow branch against him, supple and supine. Wyn felt overwhelmed by her, by the way she had affixed herself to his body. How would it feel, to let someone else be in charge for a change?

As he lay back, a febrile laxity travelled down his arms and torso, and Justine leaned away from him, knowing, perhaps, what he was letting her do. She ground her hips more firmly against him and, sighing inwardly, Wyn placed both his hands on the creamy skin just above where the stocking's elastic indented her leg and stroked the even softer inner thigh with his thumbs; his first time touching that part of a woman, other than Anna, in more than twenty years. The blackness and the line where the stockings stopped was almost unbearable in its contrariness, like a border between the sacred and profane. Tilting forward, she put her forehead on Wyn's and their noses touched. There was nowhere to look but in her eyes now. They were all pupil, no iris, no whites, just black tunnels into which Wyn believed his very thoughts could fall and be lost forever. "Tell me what you want, Wyn," she whispered, and the words were in her eyes and in her breath.

The command lowered the drawbridge from the tower in his mind that, for decades, had been sealed, windowless in that lonely thicket and overgrown with moss and thorns.

"I want to forget," said Wyn.

She unbuckled his belt and removed it, then unbuttoned his trousers and slid them off. She murmured and sighed and said a couple of things he couldn't hear but eventually lowered herself on him and placed her head under his chin and braced her hands on his shoulders, pressing him into the sofa's armrest. She then slowly stroked him with that inner extension of her body, and he let her control the rhythm, though he did put his hands on her hips and then around her buttocks to guide her. They said nothing, just exchanged breath with the room.

After several minutes of being pinned to the sofa, Wyn sat up. He needed more control and more of her body against him. He forced her upward on the rock of his hips, and leashed to this new power, Justine's abandon unspooled from her more rapidly on extended breaths, then culminated in tremors and a cupped moan. She shuddered and fell against him, gasping, and, still clutching her to him, Wyn rode on exquisite rolling waves that crashed against an inner shore and released something in the core of him that dissolved and entered his bloodstream and touched every cell of his being. He had inked the needle of his desire and need and driven it into Justine Wolfe.

They lay in the emptiness and darkness for several minutes, the only sound and movement coming from their rapidly slowing breath. Wyn touched her head and the dampness at the back of her skull, where hair clung to skin. She, in turn, ran one hand up and down the paper of his shirt, then along his arm from shoulder to fingertips, and he took her hand and their fingers interlaced. The room had retreated somewhere to mull over what it had witnessed. Everything dropped away in soft clumps, like melting snow from a rooftop.

Then Justine spoke, and for Wyn, it was like the woof of a siren on a faraway street on a summer night, even though it was only a whisper. "Did it work?" she asked, conspiratorial, like they'd built a fantastic machine with the potential for either wreaking outrageous havoc or saving all of humanity.

"For now," Wyn answered.

Chapter Nine

December 27, 2014

The storm had passed and left Toronto transfixed in winter's diamond grip under a staring blue sky. Snowplows had churned through the night to clear the main thoroughfares but the side streets remained serenely untraversed, inhabitants choosing to hunker down with Christmas turkey casserole and a good book rather than break the uncharacteristic quiet.

The loft on King Street was twenty blocks away from SPOA, and even though he had driven to Justine's, Wyn decided to leave his car parked on the street and walk instead. A snowplow had partially buried his vehicle, and he had no inclination to dig it out. If he got a ticket, so be it.

There was no wind, but it was cold, the kind of cold that took one's breath away. Wyn pulled his collar up to his ears and switched hands frequently as he checked messages on his phone. The voicemail he ignored; that took too much time. He looked only at text and email messages, of which there were scores, updates mostly on the events of the previous day. A few missed calls, but none from Anna or Claire. His methodology was to go back in time and move forward so that he didn't miss anything;

he realized that he had neglected his phone for almost twelve hours, which, save the day he had accidentally left it at home, was utterly unprecedented for him. A testimony to how much a woman had beguiled him.

From what he could gather, the team had determined that the cellphone evidence, so far, had been decidedly unhelpful. Because David Drobac had built a barrier between himself and the curious and their phones, no one had been able to film the actual confrontation with police. All that had been captured was the building of the wall and the arrival of the cops. When they'd disappeared behind the construction, other officers had shouted at the crowd to step back and stop filming. Frank had written, *Goes to show it don't matter how many cameras people got, you can't film what you can't see.* He then warned Wyn that the collected eyewitness accounts were no more helpful; no one had seen behind the wall. *Pretty near impossible to pin a misconduct on these guys without reliable witness testimony,* he'd tersely written. He never used "fuck" in his emails, but Wyn could hear it nonetheless.

He scanned the remaining messages for urgencies and then, feeling bored and noncommittal, turned off the ringer and thrust it back in his pocket. His mind felt as empty, as blue and as white as the day. He could not remember ever being in a moment so utterly. For the duration of the walk he was nowhere, had no past nor future. The glass towers along King Street had a frozen grandeur, and their desertion in the wake of the storm was eerie yet soothing. Wyn saw his tall black-coated self reflected infinitely in their mirrored facades, one lone man, over and over.

Chilled through and ears stinging from the walk, but his hangover somewhat frozen into submission, Wyn felt a strange otherworldliness, entering the elevator. Everything looked exactly the same, cool and grey and transparent and ungiving, but the edges were a little blurred, like a 3-D movie without the special glasses. He needed his desk, a phone, the comforting scroll of email and a strong coffee. But it was not going to be that easy.

The elevator doors opened on what could only be called a mob of some of the strangest looking people Wyn had ever seen. Hipsters, some young, some older, tattooed, pierced, some dressed outlandishly, others in scruffy clothes. One guy had dyed his bushy beard and eyebrows blue. There were a couple of transvestites. They were all angry.

As soon as someone saw him and said, "That's the guy! The Director!" he knew that it had something to do with David Drobac; they must have seen Wyn on television the day before.

"What's going on? Who are you?" he demanded.

The blue-bearded man stepped forward, his chin raised to make him seem taller. "We're friends of David Drobac," he said. "Do you have any idea who he is?"

"He died in a violent confrontation, and that's all that concerns me," said Wyn.

"He is also an artist, man. A really great fucking artist. What he made in that store, it was art, his last masterpiece. And the cops fucking killed him over it." As he spoke, several of the people in the crowd murmured epithets, made appreciative and disparaging noises.

Claire had said her dad was an artist, but Wyn hadn't paid much attention at the time. But that was not the primary concern. "Were you there?" he asked. He definitely would have remembered these people during the canvass of witnesses at the store.

Bluebeard's eyes shifted away, then down. "No. None of us were there. It was, like, *spontaneous*, man."

"Perhaps had he let the proprietor know what he was going to be doing with his merchandise, the police wouldn't have been called in and the whole debacle could have prevented."

Bluebeard sneered. "That's not how he operates. He is, like, an *art criminal*, he goes into the bastions of capitalism and perverts them. He's done it in New York, Paris,

Budapest. He's fucking famous for them. And now you're saying it's his own fucking fault he got killed?"

"Absolutely not." Wyn tried to push past the man, but he held firm.

"What are you going to do about it?" he demanded.

Wyn stepped closer, close enough that the man had no choice but to tilt his head quite far back to bridge the disparity in their heights. "I'm just as upset about this as you are. That's why I'm investigating it. You barring me from my office is preventing me from doing my job."

"You don't get it, man. We're going to the press, we're spreading the word. David wasn't just some dumb asshole high on crack. He's a respected member of a community. And we're not letting you assholes in your suits try to cover it up."

"You're not making any sense," said Wyn, irritably. "I have no intention of covering anything up. We're an investigative agency that uncovers the truth. Perhaps you're in the wrong building. Why don't you go to the Police Association? No one in my office killed that man." He nudged his way forward, to get to the door to his office, but a girl, scarcely twenty with blonde hair in pigtails, stepped up. "We were there, too," she said. "We're gonna be everywhere. There's going to be a demonstration at City Hall. Word is getting out because of the videos. We're talking *thousands* of people."

Luckily, Wyn was experienced enough to not ever demonstrate when he was surprised, or taken aback. Videos? he thought. He said, "Good luck with that. You're making my job that much easier. I'm on your side." He took out his card, handed it to Bluebeard. "Put me on your email lists, keep me in the loop," he said. "Anyone who wants to come into the office and give a statement about David Drobac can set up an appointment with my assistant. If you want real justice, you have to cooperate with the system. That's how it's done."

Mollified, Bluebeard pocketed the card, nodded to the group, giving them permission to disperse. They had got what they wanted, the ear of a powerful man. "We don't want David to die in vain, man," he said, in a softer voice. "He was really fucking amazing. A total shithead when drunk, but otherwise, a genius." The group moved, herd-like, towards the elevators. No one had mentioned Claire. Presumably they knew who she was, but their connection to the dead man was professional, not personal.

The lobby had large glass doors that could only be opened by magnetic key passes. Wyn swiped his key to gain entry to the dimly lit entrance, which, on both sides, afforded a view into the large open workspaces through more glass walls and doors. At the time he'd been hired, the office was rather dingy and dark, with long corridors of anonymous-looking doors, wood panelling, covert blinds and grey carpet. Within a few months of becoming Director, Wyn had the blinds removed and the panelling chipped off. Walls were demolished to create large open spaces for cubicles, and new lines were drawn, nearly all in glass. Not the frosted kind either, but crack-your-nose-if-you're-not-watching-where-you're-going kind of transparent. A bird would be dead of a broken neck within moments. During business hours, great rhombuses of light fell across the bent heads and busy fingers of industrious administrative staff in their tidy cubicles. Now the only enclosed spaces were the interviewing rooms and offices of the management, including Wyn's own, but they too were glass-formed. The carpet was patterned in multicoloured and cheerful blocks, and there were sofas placed in discreet corners, though no one was expected to actually relax on them. The office was often virtually deserted during a large incident requiring all available hands; other times it was jumpy with men making calls, checking locations, setting up interviews. There was a syncopation to it all, a repetition in what looked random; everyone moved seamlessly around everyone else, each in his orbit and obeying its laws and boundaries.

His assistant, Barb, was at her desk of course, and rose to meet him as soon as he came within her range of vision. A tiny woman, usually unassuming in her pale suits, today appeared quite anxious. "I've been calling you," she said. "Anna let me know that the flight was cancelled and you weren't going to Mexico."

"I was ambushed in the lobby by mad artists. Why didn't anyone take care of that?"

"Barry and Frank talked to them. They said they wanted to see you. They told them to wait quietly. They probably tried to call you as well, to warn you."

"Where are they?" asked Wyn.

"In the Safehouse. But Chantal wants to talk to you. It's quite urgent. Can I call her over?"

Shrugging off his coat, Wyn said, "Give me ten minutes."

Barb nodded, returned to her desk.

He went to his private bathroom, something he'd requested during the renovations. It wasn't that he was that averse to sharing a toilet with his staff, it was simply that he not unfrequently came into the office from overseas travel and needed some privacy to wash up and change. Today in particular it came in handy, as he hadn't shaved yet and still wore a bloodstained shirt. There was always a fresh suit and several shirts in the closet in the bath, along with a toiletry bag. So before confronting all the demons of his day, Wyn betook himself to the toilet to recalibrate.

At the washbasin he tried to sneak up on his reflection in the mirror – to see if he had the self-satisfied appearance of a confident man who'd slept with a lovely girl half his age. But all he saw was a middle-aged man who looked haggard and a bit confused. Under his eyes were puffy pouches, his unshaven face lent him a shifty appearance, and his hair, which needed cutting badly and had been subjected to restless sleep and poor weather, looked quite wild. He took off his shirt and put his head under the faucet, let the warm water trickle over his scalp, over his eyes and face, into his dry mouth. He changed his vest, slipped into a clean, fresh shirt, rolled up his sleeves and commenced shaving. He saw the nick from the day before, when he'd been shaving in his bathroom at home. If he hadn't found the condom, would he have so impulsively risked his plans with his family to attend a scene? Would he have persevered to the airport even after Anna had told him the marriage was over, tried to reason with her, or rather, appeal to her gentler self, apologize, book a hotel room at the airport and taken the first flight out of Canada in the morning, going anywhere? Could a small piece of prophylactic technology be blamed for unleashing the cascade of events that changed him from honest man to adulterer, from steadfastly married to imminently divorced?

Earlier, he had hoped to take himself away before Justine awoke, but she stirred, then sat up suddenly just as he was buckling his belt. She was even more beautiful in the morning, her curly hair a sweet mess, her lips flushed, the etched line of the tattooed artery glowing blue below her ear. The duvet hid everything else, but he remembered how her nakedness had molded itself to his own as they slept. All those bones and tendons and veins over the surface of her, the parts of the human machine that were meant to remain mysterious because they were too shocking to contemplate. He had seen the insides of so many people, but they had to cease being people in order for him to withstand the exposure.

She had asked if he would stay for breakfast, and he said no, that wasn't possible, but promised they would have dinner together later in the evening. He didn't think to ask if that was all right with her, just presumed that she would want to see him again. Indeed, she didn't protest, though she did tilt her head in a funny way and raise her eyebrows at his presumptuousness, he later realized.

Lastly, before leaving the bathroom Wyn worked off his wedding ring with lots of soap, feeling savage, wanting it separated from him. When he finally got it off, leaving his knuckle burning red and swollen, he was surprised how soft and pale the skin was where it had once been. Protected from the elements, the band on his finger seemed younger than the rest of him, and more innocent.

Clean and moderately more in control, Wyn returned to his office and sat down heavily in his very large, very executive chair. He gazed glumly at the stacks of paper on his desk, reports mostly, submitted by his investigative team about other incidents on other days, all over the province, incidents that never ceased unfolding, almost every week of the year. Intermingled with them was supporting documentation on cases, ministry briefs, conference papers on oversight practices around the world. In the past few years oversight had become more prevalent in developing countries, and as his office was one its earliest practitioners, he was called on frequently to present at these events. He was an adequate presenter and highly respected, if a bit didactic. Several troubled nations, among them South Africa and Haiti, had requested that he provide specialized training for their fledgling agencies, but he had no time. He could scarcely keep up with the operations of his own agency, even with the hours he worked.

Still, that was no excuse for the catastrophe that was his office. When he'd had SPOA's offices renovated four years ago, he'd thought it a good idea to show his staff that the Director was just like everyone else, so, like everyone else, he had his own office made with transparent walls. It had been a terrible idea. Not only was there no privacy to be had in it, he stupidly neglected to consider his slovenliness. Every time he neared the Director's office, he winced a little at his own dereliction. What should have been a handsome room, with its high-quality furnishings and intriguing view of the gargoyles scowling on the ramparts of Old City Hall, was diminished by the stacks of binders and paper that had taken up residence on the antique cherrywood desk, the dark green leather sofa, the windowsill, the floor.

He noticed, for the first time in months, the rather neglected-looking school photo of Rebecca that he'd tucked behind his computer monitor and forgotten. He extracted the cardboard frame from its dusty exile. It was different than the photo that Anna had placed on the stairs; this one was taken at least two years ago, when her hair was its natural black, and there was a tranquility and hope in her face that it no longer possessed. Soon she'd be living with her mother in a condo downtown, her precious attic loft sold along with the rest of the house in the spring. It would fetch a very good price; the market was hot right now. He had to think about where he would live. Right now, he couldn't contemplate anything except getting Barb to pick up a coffee for him.

In his peripheral vision Wyn noticed Chantal LaPierre approaching his door. She knocked, a pointless gesture, seeing as there was no way he could pretend he wasn't present, or too busy. Wearily, Wyn signalled her to enter as he opened a desk drawer and slipped the photo into its black depths and closed it.

Though the young woman had been with his agency for almost six months, Wyn still wasn't convinced that Chantal was the most suitable person for the role of communications manager. She was too young, a twenty-something graduate from the communications program at Ryerson University. She came equipped with lots of theory and enthusiasm but virtually no practical experience. She spoke French, which Wyn believed was a purely ornamental attribute in a city that had far more Chinese, Urdu, Portuguese, Italian, Russian, Polish and Greek speakers, but as a public agency his office was obligated to give preference to bilingual applicants. Upon meeting the new hire, Wyn had stormed into his HR manager's office demanding just what the fuck she was thinking, hiring a girl barely past puberty to manage the delicate reputation of an oversight agency? Agnes had just smiled mysteriously. "She will do fine," she assured him. "A woman in this role, and a young woman, shows the public that SPOA is in touch with a highly politicized demographic – twenty- to thirty-year-olds – and promoting gender equality. Besides me, she is the only woman in this agency in a non-support role." By "non-support," Agnes meant that all the other women were secretaries. There were no female investigators, despite Wyn's attempts to lure women to the profession from other government agencies. Police investigating was not conducive to the priorities of any woman who had a family or was adverse to extreme violence. Even lawyerly Nick, he was coming to understand, struggled with certain dimensions of the job.

"I understand you wanted to see me? Make it quick, I have to meet with the team as soon as possible," he said mildly. Chantal frowned, dismayed.

"Haven't you seen them?" she asked.

Wyn vaguely remembered being perplexed by something in the corridor, with the gang of misfits. "Seen what?"

"The videos. They're all over the web."

He recalled now what Bluebeard had said. "Videos of what?"

"Of the confrontation." Chantal was annoyed, which didn't please Wyn. He moved to turn on his computer.

"We have the videos. The team has been reviewing them," he said.

"Not all of them. Several people left the scene with evidence, and now there's a channel on MeWeb dedicated to them. They've gone totally viral."

"Fuck," he said automatically.

While his computer was firing up, Chantal gave him a summary. Seventeen clips, some only a few seconds, others several minutes. Wyn remembered what Frank had said, that the collected evidence hadn't shown much. "Tell me that one of them shows the man being Tasered," he said.

Chantal shook her head. "No. They're all of the wall, and you can hear a little bit of what's going on behind it, but it's mostly obscured by ambient noise, or the cameraperson's commentary, or officers yelling at the crowd to step back. But it doesn't matter what they show. They left the scene. And I've been on the phone with Brad at the Chief's office, and they're having a complete meltdown about it." Chantal had an air of competence, even a tiny bit of self-importance. Her first real test as a communications manager, with a whopper of an incident. Wyn considered his options.

"Come with me," he finally said.

***

SPOA had twenty full-time investigators and many more part-timers – on-call men – spread out all over Ontario, and several of the men who'd assisted with yesterday's canvass of witnesses at the shopping centre had stayed in town overnight, partly because of the unpredictable weather, but also because they knew that Wyn would hold a planning meeting. They were in the Safehouse now, and any casual observer couldn't help but notice that they all shared certain characteristics that had come to signify the SPOA investigator: they were all white men over 50 with police heft that had grown soft, but they retained the police swagger and authority. Rail-thin Frank and lanky Wyn and now, young, handsome Nick were the only exceptions.

The Safehouse was the only room at SPOA not reconstituted in glass, because it was structural, part of a cylinder of concrete that formed the core of the building. As such, its walls were the opposite of transparent; not only were they half a foot thick, they were carpeted and panelled in wood for extra noise absorbency – to what original purpose, no one could fathom, as the building had only ever housed benign government offices (Infrastructure, Northern Development, Tourism and Culture), but it was built in the 1960s so it was not unreasonable to presume that it was engineered to double as a shelter in the event of a nuclear attack. Indeed, its resemblance to a fortress was reinforced by the twelve-foot-high doors, which opened like a castle gate, and a majestic table that seemed to wish it had a loftier purpose.

Most of the guys had been there since early morning. Indeed, Wyn knew that some of them had been up most of the night in this room, putting together an investigative plan based on a template he himself had developed in his early days as an investigator. While the Safehouse was very large, it had poor ventilation and was by now close and stuffy from long exposure to body odour and exhalations. Frank stood over a seated Nick, watching him as he laboured over a computer. If anyone looked like he didn't need to be in a room that stank of ex-cop, it was Nick. Barry, who with a few other investigators stood in police fashion, in a huddle, all holding cans of soda and talking. The day supervisor, Stuart, sat at the head of the table where Wyn usually presided, but when the Director entered he rose and gave him his seat. Chantal seated herself a few feet away from him. Frank noticed her and said, "We've not told the papers nothing, right?"

"Of course not. We've only responded to Lucci's ridiculous statement. But I've given Chantal permission to attend this meeting. Let's watch the videos." He didn't want to give away the fact that he hadn't seen any of them yet, nor looked at virtually any of his correspondence since last night. The website was projected on the large screen, and there were quite a few videos on the playlist, more than a dozen altogether. The title: "David Drobac's Death by Dirty Cops." They had been watched, so far, a rather astonishing 10,341 times. 10,342. 10,343. The counter was going up steadily, in real time. Wyn was told there was no chronological order to the videos, as far as anyone could tell, so they started at the beginning of the list.

As Chantal had warned, the videos were virtually all the same, distinguished from one another only by small shifts in vantage point, length, and sound quality. They were all scenes of a man who appeared under the influence doing something weird with the merchandise in a Staples outlet. Seeing David

Drobac alive, after yesterday's surreal events, should have made an impact on him, but strangely, it didn't. The man – tall, thin, with wild curly hair, in a tight t-shirt and jeans with a large buckle, covered in the literary tattoos Wyn recognized at the morgue – looked like many people he'd seen in crisis. Perhaps more clever, and more articulate, but with the familiar fevered gaze and disconnectedness. The man was talking to his audience, spouting some fairly coherent rhetoric about capitalism, quoting, Wyn was sure, Marx and maybe Hegel. For all that he seemed to be rather drunk, he negotiated space adequately and his dexterity as he built the wall was quite remarkable. Maybe he wasn't drunk. Claire Drobac kept saying her dad was sick. Wyn wondered if he'd been hospitalized for mental illness. The team would have put in requests for his medical records and his criminal record, if he had one.

In each of the videos Wyn saw the story progress in the same way: the police arrived and the vantage point changed, everyone was forced to step back, step back, some right out of the store, and the noise of the police and the general hubbub of the crowd, murmuring, expressing anxiety and excitement, dominated. Some shouting from behind the wall but far off and indistinguishable from the ambient noise. By the tenth video Wyn became impatient. He said, "Tell me: are they all like this?"

Frank said, "Yep, they're pret'near mostly all the same. Once the wall is up, the cops come in and ever'thing takes place behind the barrier, like I told you."

Chantal said, "There could be someone who filmed it behind the wall and is holding on to the evidence, perhaps will try to sell it. With only this evidence, you're in a good position, however, because the victim has public sympathy. You can leverage it to make the police cooperate."

More silence, but not from discomfort, as far as Wyn could tell from his surreptitious canvassing of the men's expressions. Save Frank, most of the guys, thus far, had been affable enough around his communications manager, treating her like she might be one of their daughters, teasing, but never coy. Frank extended his mistrust of the media to include SPOA's in-house expert and was usually brusque and dismissive of her, when he spoke to her at all.

Like now: "Meself, I'm not too particular about what the public thinks, or about 'leverage' with the police. I'm particular about the evidence and such. You know, facts." Out of deference to the girl's youth, perhaps, Frank kept his swearing in check.

Ignoring him, Wyn said to Chantal, "I understand what you're saying. We absolutely want the public on our side. However, your first priority will be to reassure everyone that we're in control."

"We're not in fockin' control," grumbled Frank. "Stupid kids with fockin' cellphones are in charge."

"Right," Wyn said, and he stood up, removed his jacket, and commenced rolling up his sleeves. "Let's get some things straight here. The police were the first on the scene, naturally, not us. It was their responsibility to secure it until we arrived. The delay, however, was unconscionable. Superintendents are to call SPOA before ringing up lawyers.

"But remember, no witness is obligated to hand over personal property or be searched without a warrant. It's in the Charter. The people who took the videos could have been there the entire time, and decided to exercise their right to privacy and, later, their right to freedom of expression."

"We should make it mandatory that witnesses submit evidence like that, on the scene, not go to all the trouble of getting search warrants," Stuart said. "And have them charged with obstructing justice if they go public. I agree with Frank – the world's turning into a goddamn circus, with everyone filming everything in sight."

Wyn said, "Did those officers – the ones doing crowd control – seize any phones? Was that caught on any of the cameras?"

"Nope," said Barry. "I watched all of them yesterday a few times."

"But it could have happened." While it was uncommon in Ontario, because people knew their rights regarding their property, there had been incidents over the past several years where the police had snatched phones from curious bystanders under the guise of protecting the public. The G20 Summit in 2010 had precipitated a number of hostile encounters between cops and civilians that had been captured on video and uploaded, much in the same manner as people had taken action in this latest incident. Toronto, Canada, was one of the most liberal, progressive cities on earth, with a diverse population that was on the whole highly educated, affluent, and very demonstrative. Wyn wouldn't put it past the cops managing the crowd to try to seize any documentation of misconduct, but if they did, it would only be a matter of time before the public backlash began.

"Make sure that the witness testimonies don't have any complaints about property being seized. And we'll put out a call for witnesses to contact our office if indeed that happened, even if they left the scene before it was secured." Chantal was busy taking notes, but Frank and the other investigators merely watched him solemnly. Wyn felt suddenly anxious and uncomfortable. "It would be divine if we could control every person under every circumstance," he said, "but if we did we'd all be living in a police state, and this agency was created to ensure that we don't." Wyn needed to move, to speak, to pontificate, which, as his team knew, was his wont. He stood up. "It is obvious that this death was completely pointless and preventable. We've seen the body of David Drobac," he said, gesturing to Nick and Frank. "There's bruising on the neck where a baton was held. Frank saw two Taser burns. We're talking possible positional asphyxia and ventricular fibrillation." Ventricular fibrillation was a disturbance in the heart that can occur when a Taser has been deployed in between heartbeats, resulting, in weak subjects, in a heart attack. The phenomenon had been studied using pigs, but the data was inconclusive because the pigs hadn't been meth or coke addicts whose bodies had undergone the stress of poor diet, homelessness, or exposure to extreme weather.

"Wait a sec," said Frank, putting up one of his dog-chewed bone hands. "We don't know nothing yet. At the post-mortem we didn't see gross evidence of a heart attack."

Barry spoke up. "We won't know for sure 'til bloodwork's done. If the guy had Hep C from intravenous drug use or a recent flu, it could be viral myocarditis. Enzymes'll show if it was a heart attack."

Wyn put up a hand. "Wait a bloody minute. If they hadn't Tasered him *twice* – a civilian merely making a nuisance of himself in an office supply shop – we wouldn't be having this conversation in the first place. I don't care if he died of a heart attack or a stroke or bloody *drowning*, he should not have died at all. They should have talked him down, cuffed him, and led him away. Charge: public mischief. Sentence: three months' probation, unless he has a sizable criminal record, then it would be – at most – sixty days in jail. Case closed. Those cops saw that wall as protection from public scrutiny. The equivalent of the back alleys of yore. But the body has its own story to tell."

"You're being a wee bit dramatic, wouldn't you say?" asked Frank. "I've not seen all the forensics yet but was told there was a weapon. A box cutter near the body, prob'ly from the store itself."

"We'd need to have more proof that he made threats with it. He could have used it while making the wall. What about the other evidence? From security cameras? The ambulance?" asked Wyn.

Stuart said, "We don't have footage from the EMS, but we interviewed them at the hospital. They said the cops were monitoring vitals and told them they performed CPR and resuscitation. Suspect was DOA at the hospital."

Looking around at the circumspect but suspicious faces at the table, Wyn felt singled out, like a maverick, not the trusted expert he knew himself to be. Why had he allowed Chantal to sit in on this meeting? He should have predicted that it would become divisive. "I agree that these men weren't planning to kill David Drobac. I agree it was a perfect storm. But even if he had some kind of weapon, it is highly unlikely that he would've gotten close enough to the officers to inflict any injury. Mental health and addiction experts will be all over this. And now we have a strong arts community weighing in as well. They will perceive extreme prejudice in the cops' conduct."

Some of the men looked down at the boardroom table, Barry and Stuart made unmistakable disapproving sounds as they leaned back in their large comfy chairs. Retired cops, yes, but cops all the same. It wasn't as though they thought a police state was a grand idea, but what clung to them still was the solidarity of cop culture. Wyn pulled out his heaviest ammunition. "The friends of David Drobac are out for blood, I can tell you. Their outrage combined with the leaked evidence is going to create a great deal of bias against the police in the eyes of the public. Not to mention, he was the parent of a teenaged daughter who is very photogenic, and an orphan. Mother died when she was seven."

Stuart groaned outright, flipping his pen across the table.

Wyn indicated Nick. "We had to break the news to her. Not pleasant. But we have to keep her under wraps until the present furor winds down a bit. We may not even need her. At the rate things are going, we won't have to do a bloody thing. Those three cops will arrest themselves out of sheer remorse."

Frank rose at this remark. His jaw seemed longer and protruded more than usual. Perhaps because he'd been up all night with the other investigators, and hadn't shaved, he looked gaunt and every moment of his sixty-odd years. "I got work to do," he said.

"Let me know when the involved officers arrive to be questioned," Wyn told him. "I want to be present for that."

Frank looked up and his eyes, small and bloodshot, were fierce. "That's not how we do things." What he meant was that the SPOA Director did not generally participate in any investigative work, only reviews reports and approves recommendations.

"These are extraordinary circumstances, I think you would agree," said Wyn levelly.

At that moment, Barb came in. "Chief Lucci's on the phone. He says it's urgent."

Of course it is, thought Wyn.

Chapter Ten

Tony Lucci was appointed Toronto's Chief of Police in 2002, the same year as the verdict indicting Constable Jameson for manslaughter in the Wolfe case. The previous Chief, Bill Watson, who had cooperated so thoroughly with SPOA during the trial, had not been liked by the union or the Police Association, and would have been fired had it not been for the prevailing public sentiment at the time, that the police force was a monolith that needed dismantling. It was a kind of antebellum period in SPOA's relations with the police, but it had lasted only three years. After Watson retired and Lucci took over, the relationship began to deteriorate.

The current Chief was very adept at responding to media furor around high-profile incidents by reminding everyone that the city's "blue boys" (he always said "boys," an artless but effective hearkening to simpler times) were unfailingly committed to serve and protect, then, when the heat subsided, reverting to his usual way of dealing with SPOA, which was to casually ignore the agency's requests for better transparency and cooperation. He had been an active duty officer during the years of the Wolfe case and naturally had taken the side of the charged officers. When he heard of Wyn Rhys's appointment, he had been quite damning: "While I appreciate that Mr. Rhys was a cop once himself for two years, a couple of decades ago back in England, his investigation into two of our best boys was a travesty and the court case a damn circus. Rhys thinks he's the face of the future of oversight; okay, then I'm the poster boy for police chiefs who won't let Bay Street lawyers put good men behind bars for doing their job." To which Wyn had replied: "The last I checked, the Police Association's law firm is on Bay Street."

Lucci looked very different from his nemesis. He was short and quite overweight, with skin the colour of a boiled ham, and like a ham, his face always glistened with an oily sheen. His features were daubs on its surface, his eyes like currants in dough, and his sparse blonde hair was always damp and slicked back. Like so many ex-police officers, he had a large circumference and spindly legs and arms, his great gut hanging like an awning over the belt of his pants.

Lucci was sly and knew how to make deals, something Wyn, who deplored compromise and nepotism, refused to do. The suits at City Hall and Queen's Park admired Director Rhys's incorruptibility, but did not invite him to many parties or rounds of golf. Lucci, on the other hand, was part of several clubs, philanthropic associations, charities. He was present for photo ops with the Mayor and the Premier. Wyn only seldom forsook his intense schedule to attend a Christmas party or fundraising event. He always had the excuse of work and that famous quote: "Eternal vigilance is the price of liberty."

While Wyn considered himself superior to Lucci in bearing and speech, he did not underestimate his rival's intelligence, nor did he think the man would back down or retreat when threatened. One couldn't push Lucci too far and not expect retaliation. Already Wyn had perhaps alienated him too much. Besides having secured the first-ever manslaughter conviction against a police officer twelve years ago, he had gotten the important change made to the Police Service's Act and SPOA's mandate that was supposed to prevent fuck-ups like what had happened at the Staples store. Lucci's statement the previous day indicated that, in fabricating a plausible excuse for his men's extraordinary use of force, he had decided he had nothing to lose. What was that saying? The man who is soaking wet is not afraid of the rain.

***

Back in his office, Wyn sat down heavily on his chair and stared at the red blinking light on his desk phone. Could he just leave Lucci on hold forever, put the universe on hold so he could catch his breath? He turned in his chair to take in the view of the city – the city towards which he had felt nothing but ambivalence in the hotel room only a week ago seemed to be on its tiptoes, peeking in this window, waiting for him to triumph, or to be sent packing back to the UK, where Lucci had said more than once was where he belonged.

He picked up the phone and Lucci commenced speaking immediately. "Hey, Llewellyn, how are you?" Lucci always called Wyn by his full Christian name, knowing Wyn hated it, because he always mispronounced it. "I was just thinking, one of my people who just retired might consider joining your outfit. 'Cause they're Metro I guess you'd send them up to Bumfuck Ontario to investigate missing pets. Am I right?"

Wyn said, "As you may be aware, we can't hire ex-cops as investigators in their former jurisdictions. But then, I'm not really interested in hiring any of your men. Ex-cops aren't very *de rigueur* in the oversight world anymore. Civilians are far less biased."

"I'll let Elizabeth know," said Lucci.

Wyn was chagrined. Lucci knew how desperate he was for female investigators, but it could all be a bluff. "Why did you put out a statement yesterday before calling my office? Excited delirium? Give me a break. I saw the body. Two Taser hits, perhaps simultaneously. And he was likely asphyxiated. That statement was an utter hash of speculation and hyperbole."

"You know what I always liked about you, Rhys? How you can cram so many goddamn big words into a sentence. You've been sounding a lot like all them lawyers who used to do your job. Anyways, I didn't see no harm in letting the media know we're on top of things. They were calling your office and some fourteen-year-old girl was working the phones."

Chantal. He really needed to do something about her, or her voice.

"She kept saying that you were coming out with a statement. But no statement came 'til practically the end of the day, and what did it say? That we didn't follow the mandate. Such bureaucratic bullshit – no one cares about that kinda thing, Rhys. They care about *people*."

"Yes, apparently we're all supposed to care about the involved officers. How traumatized they are and so on. Not give a shit about a man who was killed for building a fairy castle in a department store."

Lucci said laconically, "I spoke to the officers personally, and what was in my statement was from the horses' mouths. They are really traumatized. Maybe you don't remember what it was like to be a cop, but when someone dies on your watch, it fucks you up."

"I remember. I do sympathize, but the mandate is the mandate. Your men should have been telling *me* what happened, as this is my investigation, not yours."

"Telling you? You mean your investigators, right? 'Cause since when does the Director show up at scenes? You think I wanted to subject my guys to a grilling from you? What kinda message are you trying to send? That your men are incompetent and need their hands held? Or that my guys are outta control and not cooperating? Whichever it is, it makes you look bad, Rhys. Stay in that glass office of yours where you belong."

"So that's what this is about? Me being on the scene? The weather was wretched. Frank was delayed. I had only one investigator in the east end. Circumstances dictated. But if you pull another stunt like yesterday, calling Sylvia before calling our office in order to sneak away the subject officers, then I will be showing up at scenes, absolutely. I will brook no opposition to the mandate. I want those men at SPOA immediately, or I'll file a complaint against you for failing to comply with our investigation."

"They were doing their jobs, following their training. There is nothing different about this incident than any other except that witnesses put it all over the web." There was heat in Lucci's voice now, which Wyn found gratifying. Anything was better than his oily disdain.

"You know David Drobac is some kind of artist? There's hue and cry all over the city from the art community over this. I presume you've seen a few of them at your office? Hard to miss – they all have blue hair and tattoos."

Silence for a moment, which meant Lucci knew about the protesters. "I heard that David Drobac has a reputation among certain of our citizens, sure," he said, and by his tone Wyn knew that he thought them hardly reputable. "So what? I don't care if the guy worked for the circus, or ran an animal shelter. He was armed and dangerous. My men did what they had to do."

"Are you also aware that the man has a child, whose mother is also dead? While Sylva was coaching your men on what to say to save their arses, I was telling a sixteen-year-old girl that her dad was killed because he built a wall of file folders."

Another silence. "You can't release that information." Lucci's voice was cold. He didn't give a fuck about the tiny girl with the chipped nail polish, who'd blown smoke in Death's face.

"Not yet, but I want you to know just how very, very much in trouble the association is going to be over this. Artists have a way of attracting attention to themselves, just like Mr. Drobac. They're planning a demonstration at City Hall. If you're lucky, the weather will remain subzero for a short while yet, but the moment they don't risk frostbite you can be assured they'll be all over town."

"You don't scare me, Llewellyn. You get the subject officers when you admit that SPOA neglected to retrieve important evidence at the scene. I know you had a guy there with no experience, as a cop or as an investigator. I'd say that's a sign of incompetent hiring practices. You were at the scene 'cause you knew that kid couldn't handle it."

"You know, Lucci, if cops resisted the urge to use excessive force, my office wouldn't even need to exist. Such a pity that you routinely fail to learn from past mistakes." Wyn hung up. The tips of his fingers were tingling, as was his scalp. He thought about Justine Wolfe, naked, sinuous, etched everywhere with fine needle lines. To have her here, now, on his lap, hands on his shoulders, her back arching as he slid his hands over her.

Just then another call came through from Barb, telling him that Sasha Ginsberg was on the line. It took a few moments for Wyn to recollect who that was. "She says it's urgent," Barb said.

Phantom Justine slid off his lap, but he was still intensely aroused. Wyn allowed Barb to transfer the call. "Wyn Rhys," he said automatically.

"Mr. Rhys, this is Sasha Ginsberg. From the morgue yesterday. I have Claire staying with me."

"Yes, that's great. You've been in touch with Maria Rosetti? If you have any questions about counselling, you should address them to her. She's really the main contact with regard to victim's services."

"I understand that. That's not why I'm calling. Well, not the only reason."

Wyn looked at his computer screen. There were at least fifty emails in his inbox and more appearing, every thirty seconds or so. "What do you want to discuss?" he asked.

"It has to do with the media and these videos. They are very upsetting. I want them taken off the web. Claire is extremely fragile right now."

"I understand your concern, but we don't have the power to do that. They don't depict anything egregious. Perhaps you can take her out of town for a few days, until things settle down? The press hasn't found out where you live, have they?"

"No, but they've been to David's. I don't think you understand the situation, Director. I don't exactly have a lot of money, and there's no one else to help her. David's friends are, well, not the kind of people a grieving teenager should spend time with. I'm worried about Claire's state of mind. This Maria person has been in touch, but they're really busy this time of year – she said she'd get back to me in a couple of days. Basically, I have to handle all of it." She sighed. "Claire had a difficult relationship with her father."

"How do you know him?" asked Wyn.

"I curated a few of his shows in my art gallery, when Claire was little. I was also friends with his wife, Isabelle. I took her when he was too messed up to look after her. David was brilliant but incredibly difficult. That stunt in the Staples store was just the last in a series of crazy things. Things that you might not want to be made public if you want to depict him as a victim in this incident."

"I'm not sure what you're insinuating. Please tell me what you want and I will do my best to assist you, within reason."

"Other people have information about him that they will almost definitely go public with if they think they can profit from it. I'm a strong member of the arts community. I'm using all the influence I have to prevent it from happening. I need you to promise to keep the media away from Claire."

"That is not as easy as you think. As long as they are on public property, we can't bar them from being near her house. Make sure she doesn't go back."

Sasha Ginsberg sighed deeply. "I really hope that your office will put those cops in jail for what they did."

"Would you be willing to come into our office at some point and provide some details about David's life, his character and so on? You can set up an appointment through my assistant, Barb." He had to get this woman off the phone. He had far more important things to be doing. "My hands are very full at the moment, but I can assure you, we do care about Claire. We appreciate everything you're doing to keep her safe." Now please go away, he thought.

Sasha was silent for a moment. "I don't want Claire to be more messed up by this than she already is. I'm just barely hanging onto her."

"We have worked assiduously to keep her out of the picture. Keep David's friends away from the press if possible, explain to them that it will harm our case against the officers if he is depicted in an unfavourable light."

"I will do my best," said Sasha coolly. "I expect that his body will be released shortly?"

"In a few days, yes. I really must go, Ms. Ginsberg. We will be in touch, I assure you," said Wyn. Before Sasha Ginsberg could respond, he hung up. He needed to create a position in his office, a permanent one, for an on-site counsellor. The Director should not have to deal with such matters. He wasn't even good at it.

Grabbing his coat, he made his way to Frank's office and was told that his senior investigator was, unsurprisingly, outside having a smoke. There was nothing Wyn wanted more than a cigarette; pity Frank smoked those wretched Old Ports. But there was no one else with whom he could vent his frustration about what had just transpired. No one understood these things as well as Frank. They'd been in the trenches together, to use the old cliché. And Frank never withheld his opinions.

As in the parking lot the day before, Frank had his hands deep in his peacoat pockets and wore his trademark fisherman's cap, looking for all the world like the vista before his wind-watered eyes was the tempestuous Atlantic, not the austere and immobile glass tower of the Eaton Centre. When he saw Wyn he did little more than shrug in his coat and stamp his feet, plastic-tipped cigarillo clamped in the side of his mouth. The cigarillo smoke rode high on the acrid wind, tinting it a sweet grey.

"I talked to Lucci. He is not giving up the subject officers," said Wyn. "He likes you. Would you call him and see if you can get him to cooperate?"

Frank turned his head a little and squinted. "Maybe."

"It has to be as soon as possible. The longer the delay, the more time they have to collude."

"What difference does it make? What was it you said in the Safehouse? 'The body has its own story to tell.'"

"Well, it does. I saw the body, I saw the scene. Maybe he was holding a box cutter, but that doesn't mean he should have been Tasered twice and suffocated."

Frank took his hand out of his jacket pocket and removed the cigarillo from between his brown teeth. "You shouldn't've been there," he said. "You're giving Lucci rope. He's had to roll over on the mandate and then you go poking up like the watchdog off his chain. You gotta give the man his space, for fock's sake. Let him take care of his men. Give him 'til tomorrow with no hassles, he'll come 'round. As for the team, well, they were none too impressed that you said the cops was acting with impunity and whatnot. You know better'n that, Rhys."

"Can I help it if I find their actions to be beyond the pale? That man was an artist, with a reputation, apparently, in this city. He had a daughter who is now an orphan. This has to stop happening, Frank. It's on the rise everywhere."

"What's on the rise is people filming it. Cops aren't doing their jobs any differently than they was before."

"Then they have to change. There are too many people needlessly dying. You know as well as I do that emergency workers deal with people in crisis all the time. Someone can walk into an ER room brandishing a pair of scissors and trained staff know how to subdue them. They're not wearing bulletproof vests or carrying guns and Tasers. How many police are killed in the line of duty by the mentally ill or addicts? Almost none. The risk is ten times higher that the ill person will die when confronted by police."

"What're you saying? That this is another Wolfe? Decent white guy with a family? Admit it, Rhys, people like Wolfe and this Drobac guy attract attention 'cause they're not hoods from Regent or Jane and Finch. How many black guys have had run-ins with the cops and been injured and killed? How much press does that get?"

Wyn considered this. "I think there's a difference between a man making an artistic statement in a public place and a man packing heat in an alley."

"Tell that to his mother."

Frank moved back to the entrance, just as an excitable gust of wind entered the courtyard and devilishly skipped around it, trapped among the buildings and kicking up snow. "You gotta make a statement about those videos, admit that we didn't fully secure the scene. Rookie investigator. And don't let those wacko friends of the victim railroad the investigation. Try easing up on the police brutality angle and show Lucci that you're not gonna come down hard on his boys."

Wyn wasn't comfortable with compromise at the best of times. "I wish just one of those videos showed what happened behind the wall. Proof he was unarmed, not making threats. Something like that would bury Lucci."

"Or it could show that they was doing their job. No worse to scrape off extra butter than to spread it too thin." Frank threw away his cigar. "Fockin' freezing," he said, as though the weather had only just declared its hostile intentions to him. He went inside, leaving Wyn to ponder another one of his cryptic Newfoundland expressions.

Chapter Eleven

His house didn't welcome Wyn home. It never had. Tonight it seemed particularly resentful, and mutely resisted him when he put the key in the lock, hands half frozen, and struggled his way in. As he set down his briefcase in the foyer, he remembered the moment, thirty-six hours earlier, when he'd picked it up to leave and saw Anna at the top of the stairs. He recalled that he had taken the pink iPod and it was still in his pocket, waiting for him. There was nothing else in this house he would actually covet, if he were to be given a choice of its furnishings when he moved out. All those boxes of records could be discarded. The tiny pink device was all he needed.

He had spent the rest of the day dealing with the press and the media with Chantal. He had given a press conference in the afternoon. It was quite brief – even though the videos were all over the web, it was still Christmastime and not a lot of reporters were around to attend, especially at the last minute. And sadly, in recent years such incidents and their recordings had become more and more common. Wyn recalled the furor around the death of a Polish man by police in the Vancouver airport in 2007. A bystander's cellphone footage had been confiscated by the RCMP. When the phone was returned to him after filing a complaint, the footage disseminated on the internet. It showed something not dissimilar to what had happened at Staples, and provoked national and international outrage. Now the public had grown accustomed to seeing police brutality. Even the G20 debacle had failed to change police procedure in any meaningful way. Wyn had waited for the artists who had been so vocal this morning to be all over town, but they seemed to have gone underground. Were they planning something? Or were they prone to the same apathy?

It was midnight, but Wyn thought there was a chance, albeit a faint one, that Anna had waited up for him. But the house was silent. He could have gone to the basement, where his office and cot were, but tonight he wanted to feel like the man of the house. He tiptoed into the front parlour, a room almost never used but decorated for show, like a furniture shop display. Compared to Justine's eclectic and unconventional abode, this room with its beige walls, beige sofas, beige curtains and timidly less beige cushions was flaccid and sterile.

After turning on a side table lamp, he fiddled with the liquor cabinet and was shocked to find it locked. Since when had they been securing their booze? Had Rebecca been messing around in it and been caught? Or was it a preventative measure, to ensure that she wasn't tempted? And where was the fucking key? Feeling reckless in his need, he rattled the flimsy doors, then braced himself to give a good yank. He could hear wood splintering as it gave way and popped open with enough force to almost knock him over. Anna would be furious, but he didn't care. He'd buy another cabinet with a padlock, and next time he'd have the only key.

He drew out a crystal carafe and with a trembling hand – from exhaustion, he reckoned – poured a tumbler full of caramel-coloured liquid. He thought maybe it was cognac. He sniffed it. Alcoholic brown drink was all that came to mind. He then settled into a not-very-comfortable armchair he couldn't recall ever having sat in before, turned off the light, and took the biggest gulp he could without choking and settled back, tried to relax. He closed his eyes.

But his mind, tireless, questing, kept returning to the conversation he had had an hour ago with Justine Wolfe from his car, which he drove down to the lake, through crunching snow, and parked near Harbourfront. He had needed to see some sky, even if it was black and lowering. As soon as she picked up she said, "It's late. When are you coming over?"

"I can't come tonight," he answered.

A long pause. "Didn't I give you what you wanted?"

"Yes." Yes, yes and yes, he thought. Then, no.

Another long pause, and he thought he heard her pouring something, wine maybe. He wondered if she had a drinking problem. "I want you, Wyn," she said.

"I want you, too," he heard himself say in the deep silence of his parked car. He'd shut off the engine, but he would have to restart it soon to put on the heat. In front of him he knew the lake was moving, it was too early in the season for it to freeze.

"Then come over," said the girl.

"I can't," he replied. "Not yet."

Justine had sighed then, and he thought he could feel her warm breath in his ear. "All right," she said. "Call me tomorrow." She hung up.

Now, in the comfort of his own home, Wyn could reflect on the interaction in its entirety and, through the clouding warmth of the brown drink, let his feelings assimilate themselves to his thoughts. It was like watching dawn break and twilight settle, moments that, if one took the time to analyze them, were like a suspended eternity, simultaneously of the moment and beyond it. Such was love, in a way, and the troubling question dominating his mind was: did his fascination with Justine Wolfe amount to love? Would he be a different man if he loved Justine Wolfe? Would she in turn be transformed, loving him?

Into Wyn's ruminations stole the stealthy creak of floorboards, and when he opened his eyes he saw Anna in the archway from the dining room. She leaned on the edge of the frame, arms folded, head touching the wall, like she was tired, like she didn't really want to see Wyn or talk to him, but the inevitable moment had arrived. There was something familiar about this scenario, even though they had never actually played it through. Or perhaps they had been, in stages, and he only noticed it now. If only she knew what he'd been up to since last they saw one another.

"I broke the liquor cabinet," he said by way of announcing himself.

"I heard." Anna entered the room, went to one of the beige sofas and sat on it, very erect, very formal, as if this room demanded nothing less. She turned on another table side lamp. Though its wattage was low, it hurt Wyn's eyes. He felt like a raccoon, caught in the curious flashlight of an intrepid homeowner. He leaned back in the shadow of the armchair and took another sip of the brown drink. "You could've given me a key. I'm sure it isn't locked to keep me out of it."

"No, it's not. I only lock up the very good stuff. You're drinking twenty-five-year-old brandy."

Wyn held the glass up to his eyes, as if he could tell its age by looking at it. "It's good," he said, taking another deep swallow. It made him feel sick. He had drunk more in the past couple of days than he had in months. "I needed to pick up some things," he said. Anna merely nodded, and when Wyn asked about Rebecca's whereabouts, she said only that the girl was at a friend's house for the night.

"Have you rebooked the flight?" he asked. Best to get this part over with.

Anna shook her head. "I've decided to wait until after the New Year and go on my own. I imagine I'll need it more then."

Wyn said nothing. Obviously, he was not going to be welcome to join her. A day ago he would have said something brittle and sarcastic, perhaps picked a fight. But after everything he'd done he had no right, no right at all. And he wasn't even sure he cared.

Anna rose and went to the cabinet, took out the carafe of brandy he'd been pilfering and a glass. She set the glass next to his and poured herself a rather large tumblerful, then replaced the bottle. She examined the door of the cabinet. Wyn looked at it too, the splintered wood near the tiny lock. "I guess that will cost a lot to fix," he said, not unapologetically.

Flicking her free hand Anna said, "Who cares. It's not an heirloom," and went back to her island of sofa. There was nothing to indicate she was suspicious about his whereabouts the previous night, which, for some unaccountable reason, annoyed him.

After she settled and took a sip from her drink, she said, "Tell me, Wyn. When did you stop wanting to be in this marriage?"

He was grateful that she initiated the topic; he really had no idea how to go about it himself. He looked at his hands, the place where his wedding ring had once been. He felt old and tired. "I never stopped wanting to be in this marriage," he said, the words sounding unconvincing. He poured himself more brandy.

"Really. I couldn't tell by the way you've been acting. When you walked out on Boxing Day to go to work, on a holiday, on the day we were to go away, I thought, 'he couldn't give a fuck if he never saw us again as long as he lived.' Rather harsh, don't you think? That I would think that of you? This is not what I believed our life would look like when I met you at that party in Montmartre."

Their first encounter in the summer of 1992 hadn't been among the memories he'd tried to scavenge that curious day with the iPod, but it had been waiting, perhaps for this moment, to reveal itself to Wyn in all its touching splendour. He pictured the candles stuck in Chianti bottles in that flat in Paris, the dome of the Sacre Coeur in floodlights just a couple of hundred metres away, looming, moonlike, in the open window. "I thought you were the smartest woman in the room," he said. "I could hear you talking to a group of students about the painting of *Olympia* and how you admired that woman, Manet's model – can't recollect her name–"

"Victorine Meurent," said Anna. She had been in Paris studying Impressionist art for her Master's thesis at the University of Toronto. After meeting Wyn she never completed it.

"'Cause she was so shameless. The men at the party wanted you to take off your clothes and show them the pose, show them you had the same white skin as that girl, and you almost did it. You unbuttoned your blouse–"

"It was a cardigan. I had a camisole underneath."

"And the men, mostly French, were smugly impressed. I was just gobsmacked. I thought you'd do it. I would have cut off my right arm to see you do it." Anna's white neck as she threw back her head to laugh at the men who tugged at her slip and the loops of her jeans. Of course she wasn't the kind of woman to let loose that way. That's why she admired Manet's model; she didn't have the audacity to do such things herself.

"I remember, when I first met you I thought you looked like Peter Gabriel." Anna smiled a little at herself, saying this. "When you opened your mouth and weren't French – when you were *English* – that did it for me. I wanted to take you home with me that night." In the moment of silence before her next words, Wyn sensed clouds gathering again, blocking out the watery sun of that memory. "And now, I don't believe for a second that you want to be married to me, or to anyone, probably. I don't think you even know what the word marriage means."

Indeed, she was more correct in that assumption than she knew. There was no point in telling Anna about Justine. How could she possibly comprehend what had happened to him, after years and years of repression and self-denial? And what did he owe her, after what she had done to him?

"Oh, I know you want to believe in this marriage. Because you expect yourself to do the 'right' thing. That's what you do at the agency, right? You're a paragon of virtue there." There was no mocking element in her tone. "I can say almost definitively that, today, in doing your job to the best of your ability, and being that splendid example to your colleagues, you never thought once about me and Rebecca. You weren't going to show up at the airport. I know how your brain works, Wyn. For the last ten years or so I accepted that I had traded intimacy for security. This," she glanced around the beige room with its tasteful anonymous prints and mathematically precise cushion placements, "was good enough. I actually believed it was good enough." A small moue of disgust curled her upper lip. "I was okay to make this home and raise our child on my own." When Wyn moved a little in his chair, Anna interpreted this as an objection and said, "Please don't insist that you played a part when we both know better. That beautiful young woman – a woman, now, Wyn – has never had a father. What saddens me is that neither of you knows what you're missing. Did you know she sometimes sneaks out in your overcoat to sit on the back patio and listen to music? Her iPod has all your old music on it because she listened to your records in the basement when she was thirteen." She paused, and Wyn wondered what she saw on his face. He felt numb. Did he look numb? "Do you remember the last time we made love?" She said "made love" very quietly, almost reverently. This may be because they so rarely talked about sex, even when they were having it regularly. Sex simply happened between them, like weather happened.

Wyn was silent for so long Anna spoke again. "So you don't remember."

He knew it had been a long time. So long he couldn't – wait. It had been in the summer. After the wedding of one of Anna's nieces. They'd both had quite a bit of champagne. "Samantha's wedding," he said. Rebecca had been a bridesmaid in a wretched little pink dress that made her look, he told Anna, like a Disney princess moonlighting as a stripper.

Anna nodded, looking a little surprised that he remembered. "That's right. That was two and a half years ago."

Everything they were talking about had years attached to it. Twenty-five-year-old cognac. Twenty-one years of marriage. Two and a half years of no sex. "Oh," he said.

"I had tried to bring it up in other conversations," said Anna, "but you're very good at deflecting things you don't want to talk about, or think about, or accept responsibility for. Anyway, it doesn't matter now. It hasn't mattered for a long time."

"Why did you even ask me along on this holiday?" he said. "Unless you thought it would be amusing, dumping me over margaritas. You could have asked your lover instead." Wyn picked up his drink again and sipped it.

Silence for a moment, then Anna said, "For an investigator you are incredibly thick." She shook her head unbelievingly. "There were so many others. I tried to cover it up then realized it didn't matter, you wouldn't even bother to look. And I think we can agree that you aren't entitled to know what I've been doing with my time, as you've always done what you wanted with yours. Like every Saturday."

Wyn knew that his decision to take time for himself on Saturdays would eventually come back to chastise him. He should have at least discussed it with her, asked her opinion or explained the need to her. Trusted her to understand. Instead he acted like a sneak, like a cheat. "It's not what you think," he said, trying not to sound defensive.

Anna tilted her head to one side. "What do I think?"

"That I'm having an affair. I'm not." And technically, what he was doing with Justine was not an affair because his wife had declared their marriage over before he went to the girl's home.

His wife snorted a little. "I didn't think you were having an affair. You wouldn't make the time in your busy schedule to go to all the trouble of wooing a woman. But there are other ways to get satisfaction." She looked a little satisfied herself, saying this, like she knew all about the vicissitudes of men.

At first, Wyn thought she was hinting that he was homosexual, but then he realized what she actually meant. "You think I visit prostitutes?" he asked.

"Aren't they called 'escorts' now?" asked Anna, and though Wyn was angry, he could see that she was hurt, too. "You're a man, you have needs. Obviously I don't meet them any longer."

How could he tell her that, until last night, his needs, such as they were, had been adequately served by occasional dates with his hand, usually late at night, in the basement? That in fact he had been spending his Saturdays working? No doubt she'd feel even more pity for him than she did now. He didn't want her pity. "It is a two-way street, you know," he said. "I haven't exactly had the impression you were terribly interested in me, especially after you put a bed in the basement."

She let the Saturdays and her part in their sexual problems go with a flick of her hand, as if it were all inconsequential now. "It wasn't the sex that I wanted or missed, it was the intimacy. We were intimate once, Wyn, though it feels like such a long time ago. Rebecca was born and it was over. You had your job, I had my child. Now she's grown and I've decided to focus on myself. I plan to move out in the spring."

As Anna talked logistics, Wyn paid scant attention; he felt like he was underwater, the current thumping against his ears, distorting everything she said.

"I suppose you'd think it brazen of me to ask you to reconsider," he said. "To give me another chance." He knew he sounded unconvincing. But for years he'd had some vague, fuzzy idea of a future with more vacations (all right, a vacation) and more time to do things like go to the cinema or out for dinner. An indeterminate date when he would quit working and get to know his wife again. Superstitiously, he wondered if he'd somehow brought this all on his own head, just for even thinking about another woman, the first in decades.

Anna looked pained, then shook her head. "I kept thinking that maybe if you slowed down a bit then we could figure out a way to be together. But you're not going to slow down, and I just don't think you really care enough about me. Or maybe you do," she added, shaking her head, flustered. "But you can only really care about one thing at a time, and it's always work. I know – god knows I know – that you consider the people you help at SPOA as more deserving of your attention than me and Rebecca, or your parents, or friends. We're not victims of police abuse, or grieving lost loved ones. Although, ironically, I guess we've been grieving the loss of you."

He decided, out of cowardice perhaps, to not discuss this further. "When are you moving out?" he asked. Practical things he could manage.

Anna drew herself up straighter, to show that she didn't care that her husband hadn't apologized or even conceded what she'd said was true. "I've looked at a few condos and will probably buy one in the spring. We need to get the house ready for sale. We'll split the proceeds. You should be able to find something convenient. You always said you hated the commute from Lawrence Park." There was something smug in these words, like her leaving him was a favour, to assist him yet again with his top priority: his job.

"And money? Do you want money from me?" Wyn knew she didn't care that much about money, but he wanted to make a last assertion that, in the family dynamic, he'd always been the higher earner. He wanted her to still need him for something.

"No, no money," said Anna quietly. She spoke then about pensions, and RRSP's and the like. Wyn knew that neither of them had anything to worry about from a financial point of view. Funny, he'd justified for years his hard work because of the money he perceived they needed, the security. Truth was that he could have worked half the number of hours and would still have earned the same. He was a public sector worker, after all.

"I don't want to hurt you, believe me," came Anna's disembodied voice. Already, she seemed distant and uncoupled from him. "And Rebecca ... Rebecca is sad about it too."

"I imagine she doesn't give a shit about whether or not I'm happy, as long as she has lots of toys and pretty clothes." He knew he was being unfair to the girl, but at this moment he hated her. He recalled the photo on the staircase, but didn't mention it.

"I believe she thinks you already are. You've always done precisely what you wanted." Anna paused, then said, "Remember the nickname you gave her when she was small?"

"Bex," said Wyn automatically. "But she hates it now."

"Well, she'd probably prefer it over 'Child Rhys,' or 'The Heiress.'" Wyn had, of late, taken to mocking his daughter's sense of entitlement.

Anna went on, "Whatever. I'd ask you not to mention any of this to Rebecca, but then, you don't see her much anyway."

Wyn closed his eyes, thinking of Christmas night, when he'd sat so close to his daughter and had no way of conversing with her. She was his blood, she had his hair colour and his mouth and the same arch in her brow, but she was otherwise an utter stranger to him. If he died today, what would she recollect of him besides his adolescent appreciation for punk music, or the heft of his long coat on her slim shoulders?

Anna walked over to him, her footsteps so muffled by the carpet that Wyn didn't know she was near him until she put one hand on his head, on his thick hair; just the flat of her palm, not letting her fingers sink in. It wasn't an unloving gesture, but he knew she was thinking: this is the last time I will do this. Everything they were to do in the coming weeks would have the same finality to it: eating together, driving together, talking to Rebecca together. They would never sleep together again. That distant night after the wedding – it had been in Boston and they'd stayed in a hotel – he could hardly remember anything about it, but that was the last time he'd been inside her, felt her mouth on him, her arms wrapped around his neck. Her scent – a tendril of it uncurled above him now. She wore a very citrusy perfume, fresh and young, because she said she never wanted to smell like her mother. "Wyn," she said, in a voice that still sounded like his wife, not like the stranger she was about to become. "I'm sorry."

"I know," he said, lifting his head. He couldn't let her see him weak and emasculated. "I know you're sorry." It didn't occur to him to apologize to her.

Chapter Twelve

December 28, 2014

There had never been a time in his entire adult life that Wyn had wondered if he'd taken the right course of action, or doubted himself after the fact. Should he have done things differently? He knew he had always done what was most expedient, most logical, and almost invariably it had been the correct decision. His colleagues had come to expect it from him; his authority at SPOA even before he became Director had never been challenged.

So when he decided it was a perfectly good idea to get into his car in poor weather at night, having had a quantity of brandy and not enough sleep, it did not occur to him to reflect on it, or question it, certainly not rescind it. He had thought everything he'd done heretofore had been a good idea: working hard towards retirement, paying his bills, financing his daughter's education, procuring promotions, defending the rights of the indigent, the poor, the addled, the addicted, being so responsible, only to have his wife fucking random strangers in hotel rooms, lounging in bed with them, laughing, eating room-service breakfast, showering with them, giving them head, letting them fuck her in every conceivable position, maybe more than one at a time. Maybe women. Maybe orgies. His blonde fifty-year-old wife, surrounded by beautiful strangers, pleasuring them, having them pleasure her. Paid for on his credit cards. The cuckold, locked in the basement, sleeping on a cot, unworthy of even having access to his own bed.

He drove slowly and took side streets; he knew how to avoid being a target for random police checks. It was Christmastime, but with the terrible weather there weren't many cars on the road; he reckoned the cops were taking it easy. The city had been so still, so truly frozen, the past couple of days, it was as though time had stopped. No wind. Bone-chilling cold. Sky unchanging grey. In another universe he had decided to not go to Gerrard Square Mall, had not even taken the call from Stuart, and he was asleep in a queen-sized bed in front of open French doors leading to a balcony overlooking the ocean, having had a wonderful meal with his wife and daughter after a day of whale-watching or hiking or whatnot. In that universe David Drobac was dead, yes, but Wyn wouldn't care. It would be Frank's investigation; there would have been an uproar and so on, but his office could have handled it. Wyn showing up at the scene: that's what turned it into a shitshow. Inviting the ire of the Chief so soon after the mandate had been changed. Had he not gone to Staples he would not have been on television, Justine Wolfe would not have seen him, he would not have gone to her loft, drank with her, fucked her. He'd have come back from Mexico with a tan. More relaxed. Anna would have kept her dalliances secret, at least a little bit longer.

He had no idea what time it was when he finally parked the car (probably illegally) on King Street, buzzed and asked, as calmly as he could, to be let in and made his stumbling way up the stairs to Justine's loft and knocked on the metal door. When she opened it, her face puckered with a frown, worried. He immediately apologized for the late hour, haltingly, careful suddenly because he realized his madness now, a moment too late. But she let him in. She wore flannel pyjamas in a leopard-print pattern and socks.

"You should have called," she said.

"Yes, I should have called," he agreed.

"What's going on?" The girl had a studied calm. The doctor, but not only that. The child who'd had erratic parents who fought, a father who drank and did drugs.

"Nothing's going on. I'm just … here. Like I said I would be." He had promised to come over, hadn't he?

Justine crossed her arms over her small chest. "You said you couldn't come."

Wyn took off his coat and laid it on the back of the sofa. He removed his jacket and placed it on top of that. "I'd love a drink, if you could manage that. I've had a fucking insane day."

The girl shrugged and went to the island counter in the kitchen, took out some of the lovely whiskey he'd had – when? yesterday? That night was at the end of a long, dark tunnel in his mind; it had happened an age ago. Or perhaps in a different universe. Which one was he in currently? Oh right. The one where his wife admitted to having fucked around behind his back for years, told him she was leaving him.

Justine poured a small quantity in a tumbler and handed it to Wyn. Her eyes looked a bit red; had she been crying at some point? Wyn raised his glass in a small toast and drank from it.

Justine said, "Is this something you do?"

Taking his glass with him to the sofa and settling heavily on it, Wyn said, "Something I do? What something? What am I doing?"

"I told you I wanted you, and you chose to put me aside. I'm assuming it's for work. Or someone else." She sat on one of the small, uncomfortable chairs. Even in her pyjamas she appeared older, more restrained. Or maybe she appeared so because he was so unrestrained, so flagrantly transgressing his own boundaries. The room seemed smaller than he remembered it.

"I have a family, you know," he said.

"That doesn't usually matter to most men," she replied.

Wyn huffed. "I'm not most men," he said.

"Indeed. You definitely aren't to me. I said things I have never said to anyone in my entire life, and it seemed to have no impact on you whatsoever."

"They did. They absolutely did. I just don't know what to do with that information right now. I'm in the middle of my biggest case since–"

"Since the Wolfe case? How appropriate, that we should meet at another watershed. But I'm not in crisis anymore, so I'm not important."

Wyn took a long pull on his drink, finishing it inadvertently. "I'm not even going to dignify that with a response," he said. He set his glass on the floor and leaned his head on the back of the sofa, closed his eyes for a few moments, then opened them. "I really don't know how I can be what you want. You don't even know me."

Justine leaned forward in her chair, her elbows on her knees, cupped her face in her hands. "Tell me what he did to my mother."

"What he did to your mother? You mean, Kevin?"

She blinked slowly. "No one ever told me what he did. I could have found out, but I have never read about my case, not ever. I needed to hear it from you. You saw her. Tell me."

Through the miasma of his exhaustion, an image emerged, of Adele Wolfe, lit bizarrely from below by the lights from the ambulance, her limp body, her upturned hands. He saw photos of her face after the post-mortem, but she was so mutilated he couldn't tell if her daughter resembled her. But her eyes– "She had your eyes," he said involuntarily.

Her own eyes opening wider, Justine said, "Really."

Picking up his glass from the floor and sipping from it, even though it was empty, Wyn said, "I only saw her for a few moments. You don't need to know. It doesn't make any difference to your life, or to your future."

"I have seen lots of death in the ER. I've attended post-mortems. You can't shock me."

"It's not the same when it's someone you love." He had no experience of this. His parents were still alive, and he had no close friends.

"I have a right to know. I know there was a lot of blood. Stabbing? Disarticulation?" The girl stood now and came to the sofa, sat down near him, but did not make any intimate advances.

"Stabbing, yes. She was stabbed eleven times."

"Where?"

Wyn looked at the ceiling, and pictures of the post-mortem flashed through his mind. "Mostly to her legs and torso. No further mutilation."

"Then she died of something else. Unless she lost a lot of blood."

Sighing, Wyn said, "She was hanged. In the garage. That was what the cops who shot your father saw when they first arrived on the scene."

Justine let out a long breath. Now she knew. Did it matter? "They saw her, and when they found him, they shot him in the face."

"Yes."

Justine drew her legs up to her chest and put her arms around them. "God," she said, and bent her head to her knees. Was she crying? "No wonder they killed him. Finding that and then–" She was silent but Wyn heard her breathing. He remembered her breath as he held her all those years ago, the quick breath of a child. He wanted to feel tenderness for her, but he was strangely detached and numb.

He hadn't realized it, but he had closed his eyes when she asked her question, and they now refused to open. A hand on his nose, sliding down to his mouth. He kissed the fingertips, which travelled over his chin, to his shirt collar, to the buttons. Deftly the woman undid his shirt and then her mouth was under his jaw, at his throat, her tongue darting in small flicking motions. Though his hands felt heavy he smoothed them up her flannel sleeves, took her head in both hands, drew her to kiss him. Her mouth was luminous, and its light penetrated a thicket in Wyn's mind, sending blades that cut into the dark places and exposed feelings long concealed there: loneliness, yearning, desire, terror, joy. It was like the pause between heartbeats, like the fluid in the ear that calculates balance: so minute but encompassing magnitudes, the brink over which lay uncertainty, even death.

But now. Justine broke the kiss and nuzzled his cheek, her fingers in his hair. She whispered in his ear and her breath felt hot. "When I was twelve I started masturbating, thinking of you. You were my first lover. You held me on your lap that day covered in blood – I got blood on your shirt, I remember. In my fantasy you hold me on your lap then take off my pyjamas, put your fingers deep in my cunt and it feels perfect, exactly where your fingers should be. I kissed you and you wanted me so badly you were sweating and delirious. The wrongest place at the wrongest time. Anyone could walk in, but they never do. I kneel between your legs, and unbuckle your belt–"

Wyn gasped, "Stop. For fuck's sake – stop." But he didn't move.

She continued, "It wasn't about sex. It was life in a room full of death. Making something instead of destroying it. Intimacy like that never existed between two people in the history of the world. I have fucked dozens of men. I travelled all over Europe, picking up strangers for an entire summer. But every one of them was you." She drew away and Wyn, afraid to open his eyes, for all this to be real, said only, "You're mad."

"Of course I'm mad," she replied, and he heard a catch of mirth. "So are you. Look at me."

He looked. Her face filled his vision, her black eyes deeper than anything he'd gazed into. "There's so much more in the world, Wyn Rhys, than just police doing stupid things to people. There are other colours, not just black and white.

Colours for all the confusion and thrills in the world. You can't go back to black and white so soon, can you?" She smiled a small cat's smile, suggestive but also taunting.

Red, he thought. He wanted red. Splashes of it, streams and rivers of it, oceans. Without really knowing what he was doing, he grabbed the girl round the shoulders, hooked his arm under her knees, as he had done that terrible day. She instinctively wrapped her arms around his neck. He stood, lifting her, and carried her to the other end of the loft, where the staircase to the bedroom led. A spiral, tricky. But he negotiated it. Justine held the rail to keep them both from falling. It was vertiginous, the ascent. He kept his eyes focused on the top and the bed waiting for them. His heart beat madly, his breath came in ragged gasps.

Angry sex was almost as good as tender sex. He'd been willing to let her be in control in their last encounter, but this time he was in charge. He lay her on the bed, pinned those delicate wrists to the mattress, her black hair damp against the flush of her cheek, struggling but naturally, utterly at his mercy, and he pulled the front of her pyjama top open, popping the buttons, to reveal her extraordinary maps, drawn on her by some man's hand, a man who had literally gotten under her skin and left her marked forever. Her high, proud breasts curved so vulnerably from ribs to collarbone, pelvis rocking up to him, away from him, undetermined whether she wanted him or was repulsed. But then it came: she begged him to take her, to fuck her.

They had sex, but did not make love. Justine wanted a lion; lions maul and tear and devour. That night Wyn did things with the girl who'd haunted him for years that he'd never done with anyone in his life, and would never do again. He invaded her in every possible way, in the dark, then with the lights on because he had to see her at his mercy, needed to see it in her eyes. He wanted her fear. But she never succumbed. She would never be afraid again. She did what he wanted because she wanted it too, and would have done more. And whatever he inflicted, she inflicted on him in kind. Murder was so close on the spectrum of what they were doing. And they both knew what murder looked like.

How long it lasted, he had no idea. Sometimes he saw Anna's face, sneering at him from under the rutting body of a faceless man. Sometimes he saw Justine on the witness stand weeping, though she had never expressed any emotion. For a moment she was the child on that terrible day, but that was too much, too much. It had to be the woman, not the child. That child was always the victim, and he would not permit her to be his victim. Then he would exist in the same dimension as Kevin Wolfe.

***

He woke alone, the winter light cold and blue yet bright. He looked up at the ceiling, not knowing where he was, or how he'd gotten there. The network of ducts and pipes above looked like the innards of a great mechanical behemoth, and the mound of duvet next to him concealed something faceless and menacing. He scrambled out of bed before a rational thought could seize him and stood, naked, in the middle of the unfamiliar room, sparsely furnished with only a platform bed, an old-fashioned dresser and a stunning full-length bevelled mirror. The walls were artificial, this was the partitioned upper half of the flat. He noticed the hole in the floor from which a small spiral staircase descended. His eye fell on the heap of clothes on the floor and he dashed to retrieve them, to cover himself.

But of course, he'd been here before, only a day ago. Justine Wolfe's loft. Yesterday he had woken with a sense of contentment, even joy, and her lovely head had been near his shoulder, her arm with its dazzling network of whisper-fine veins, real and depicted, draped over his chest. Yesterday he had felt protective, tender, but with no thought of what to do next, or what he wanted. Today, however, he felt like he'd awakened on the moon. On his back and buttocks he felt hot traces of pain from what he'd endured the night before. His face hurt, but he didn't look in the mirror to see if there was any visible damage.

He put on the uniform of Wyn Rhys, Director of SPOA. Black pants, white shirt. Cufflinks – the same ones from yesterday and the day before, the blinking eyes – were scattered somewhere and irretrievable. He turned and looked at the bed finally and knew that she wasn't there, hadn't been since he woke. Perhaps she had fled, called the police, turned herself in. Because there had been a rape, it just wasn't clear who had raped whom.

Snow-soaked light filled every pane of the tremendous windows, blinding him and tilting his world on a forty-five-degree angle. He had to gather himself together, be the man he was familiar with. He had to descend the spiral staircase, take himself away from this madness, away from Justine Wolfe, never see her again or think about her again for as long as he lived. To others, his actions would look like those of a man who had lost his senses, though he knew that in fact he had found them and they had rampaged all over him.

She was in the kitchen, in front of a laptop on the counter. She was dressed in jeans and a black turtleneck, snug to the contours of her slim body. Her hair was damp – she'd bathed. He should have bathed too; his body no doubt reeked of their exertions from the night before. But he knew by the angle of the sunlight in the room that it was coming up on mid-morning. He had to get to work.

She looked up at him as he came into her peripheral vision, and her dark eyes were impassive, a threshold he couldn't cross, probably ever again. "Do you want coffee?" she asked. She had a coffee next to her, alongside his phone.

He took it and put it in its holster on his belt. "All right," he said. He couldn't look at her. He couldn't even contemplate what they had done. That hadn't been him. It hadn't been her.

Gazing at the screen of her computer Justine said, "These flash mobs are extraordinary. David Drobac has really captured the public's imagination."

Wyn glanced at the screen as he passed her on his way to the coffeemaker. In freeze frame he saw a cluster of teenaged kids all mugging for a camera, probably from a news network. "What's a flash mob?" he asked.

One side of the girl's mouth hitched up, bemused. "They're like demonstrations. Sometimes they're like mass dance performances, but other times they're political. In this case, they're building these crazy walls to protest David Drobac's death. It started with artists, and now there are kids involved. They're all over the news."

David Drobac had been seeking attention his entire career, Wyn thought, and now people were commemorating his humiliating, pointless death.

"But I feel badly for his family," her eyes flicked in his direction, "if he has any."

Wyn poured a cup and sent it, scalding black, down his throat. "Not really," he said.

His phone buzzed and he took it out. It was Nick calling from SPOA. "Are you near a computer?" he asked as soon as Wyn picked up. He sounded breathless and excited.

Wyn walked over to where Justine sat on her stool. "Why?" he asked.

"Because I need you to look at one of the videos from yesterday – the ones we collected at the incident. I found something. The girl. She was at the mall with her dad."

Heart thumping, Wyn went to Justine, requested that she allow him to use her computer, logged onto his email and opened the file. He hadn't yet watched any of the videos submitted by bystanders. He had been too distracted, pulled in too many directions at once.

"It's near the end of the clip. She's on the far left side. Pink hair, right? You can't miss her."

There was no way to watch the clip in slow motion, nor could he zoom in on any frame, but he could pause it and rewind. He didn't have to. There was no question that the figure emerging from around the edge of the large construction was Claire Drobac. She wore the same black cape, the hood pulled over her head but the pink hair showing. Even having not seen her hair he'd have recognized her by the strange finery she wore. "That's the child," he confirmed. "Are you sure she's not in any of the others?"

"Yeah, I'm sure. None of the rest of them go on as long as this one."

Wyn rewound the segment, watched it from the beginning. The person recording was originally at the back of the store and made his or her way forward, through the crowd, holding the cellphone camera overhead. The noises behind the wall were indistinguishable from the noise of the other onlookers, but Wyn thought he may have heard a shout that could be David Drobac. Then the girl, right on the edge of the frame, stealthy, head down. "If she was behind the wall, as it appears she was, then she might very well have seen her father Tasered," he told Nick.

"That's what I think," said Nick, getting more excited. "She could be your star witness. Do you want me to go and talk to her?"

"No. I'll do it. We have a rapport of sorts. I'll go there right now. Tell me, have we gotten an update on when the subject officers are supposed to come in?"

A long pause, during which Wyn looked away from the laptop long enough to notice Justine watching him, hands on her hips, frowning. Barefoot and curly hair damply plastered to her forehead, she looked distressingly young. Instantly, Wyn wanted her again, badly. His knees weakened and a flush up the back of his neck made him sweat and prickle. Places where she'd inflicted pain the night before stiffened, throbbed. He had to get out of her apartment, immediately. He turned away from her.

Nick said, "They just left. They were here first thing this morning with Tony Lucci. Frank and Stuart interviewed them. I thought you knew about it."

He hadn't checked his messages or his voicemail since last night, but Wyn suspected that there was no message from Frank. "I see," he said levelly, but felt sick, the coffee he had just drunk churning in his gut, percolating up to his esophagus. Frank and probably the rest of the team were in full mutiny mode. "Is Lucci still there?"

"Uh, yeah. I think so."

"I'm coming to the office. Don't say anything to Frank or to anyone else – not even Chantal – about the girl. We must keep her under wraps, do you understand?" No one but he and Nick had met Claire Drobac, so he wasn't concerned about anyone else in his office recognizing her. Nick agreed and rang off.

Wyn called Sasha Ginsberg. She answered but said she wasn't home, she was at her gallery, preparing for a show that was opening in the new year. Claire was at her house.

"Is there anyone there with her?" asked Wyn. Sasha said no, she was alone. "Did you know that she was at the mall with her father?"

Sasha was silent for a few moments. "Yes, I know," she said.

"Ms. Ginsberg, you should have called me right away and told me. She's a witness in this case. She should be at my office being interviewed."

"Are you out of your mind?" said Sasha. "She's traumatized. I told you yesterday, she is in trouble. This Maria person did drop by but Claire refused to even look at her. We got her some Ativan for her anxiety, and she's sleeping a lot. I think that makes a lot more sense than having her in your office, reliving the trauma."

"If she's so traumatized, she really shouldn't be alone. That's incredibly irresponsible of you." He should have had the girl taken into protective custody. Justine approached, stood right in front of him, gestured that he give her the phone. He frowned at her, turned away.

"I have taken care of Claire off and on for years, Mr. Rhys, on a very fragile income. I won't be able to take care of her at all if I can't do my job. And if you don't mind me saying, you didn't really give a shit about her well-being yesterday." She hung up on him.

"Fuck!" Wyn said, slamming the phone on the counter. Justine picked it up, swiped the lock on the screen, like she was going to call Sasha back. Wyn snatched it from her. "What the fuck do you think you're doing?" he demanded.

"You didn't tell me there was a child involved," she said, trying to snatch the phone back. Wyn put it in his holster and made his way to the sofa where he had left his jacket and coat the night before. "Not you nor any other member of the public," he replied.

She came up to him. "I'm not 'the public.' I'm–" She stopped, consternated. Closer up Wyn saw a creeping bruise near her ear, along her jaw. Had he grabbed her throat the night before? Wyn's work experience had taught him to be alert to potentially volatile situations and view them from a safe distance, through a figurative periscope. This was not going to be like that.

She recommenced. "Don't go to the office. Go to her. If she was there – if she saw everything – she's in danger. After what happened with my dad I was in a catatonic state for days afterwards. Maybe weeks, I don't know."

"Your experience and hers have nothing in common. I have to go." He struggled into his large wool coat.

This woman – who only a few hours before had been spread-eagled, naked on her bed, at his utter command but strangely so remote, every inch of her flesh at his disposal – was now suddenly pleading, for real. "She saw her father die. That's enough in common. Tell me where she lives."

"There is absolutely no way that I would give you that information." Wyn went to the door, but Justine swept in front of him, stood against it. Her eyes were damp. "Please tell me. I'm a doctor," she said.

"As much as I appreciate your concern, this is none of your business. You're being melodramatic. There is a counsellor from social services who is in charge of her case. I wouldn't walk into an ER and tell you how to close a bullet wound. Don't tell me how to do my job," said Wyn curtly. There were too many competing thoughts crowding his mind: had Tony Lucci been present when the officers had been interviewed? Were his investigators going to turn on him? Should he fire Frank? The girl was crucial, yes. He would deal with her as soon as he regained control over his office, reasserted his authority.

Into the mass of his thoughts Justine waded, persistent, belligerent. "I'm sure you'll be on her doorstep the moment you need her testimony. In the meantime, she can fuck off, just like me. You're a fucking sociopath, Wyn Rhys."

This was too ridiculous. Aggravated, Wyn pushed her aside, but she held firm, the doorknob clutched in both hands. "Let me out, now," he growled.

"Or you'll do what? This?" Justine turned and lifted the back of her sweater. The tattoos of the anatomy of her back were spotted with welts, where the buckle of his belt had landed. How to shut out the memory of what they had done, and how to prevent it from happening again? "I'm sorry," he said, and he meant it.

Justine turned back, her eyes brimming with tears. "You can do anything you want to me. Anything. I will take it. I've taken it before. But you can't let anything happen to that girl. Promise me."

But he kept his wits about him. "How I deal with this case is none of your business, Justine. I'll have you know – though I have no reason to share this with you – that I was with this girl at the morgue the other day. She wanted to see her father and I took her."

"Was it she who bit you?" asked Justine. "Don't bother answering. You are out of your depth. You have no fucking idea what you're doing." She stepped closer to Wyn, her small face upturned, and her eyes scanned his. "If you were the one who told her that her dad was dead, you owe it to her to be there for her now."

With the powerful winter sunlight casting everything in harsh contrast, into hyper reality, he saw his situation with Justine Wolfe for what it really was: a callow cleaving to lost youth and a refuge for his hurt pride, nothing more.

Moving past her to the door he said, "I'll handle this the way I see fit. Something you should know, Justine, is that I don't like people telling me what to do."

"I'm not telling you what to do. I'm telling you what's right."

"Your idealism is touching, really," he said, not hiding the fact that he was being sarcastic. "You can't understand the kind of responsibilities a person in my position has to deal with."

Justine's face expressed withering pity. "Someone in your position. If something happens to that girl – if she's found dead or in hospital – are you going to hold yourself responsible?" she asked.

"I'll deal with that problem when it arises. Right now I have a few other crises to contend with." With an insolence and slowness that made him want to slap her, Justine slid to one side and said, "I certainly wouldn't want to waste any more of your time." She straightened and walked away as Wyn exited. He didn't hear the catch in her voice. If he had he may have been reminded of Boxing Day morning, and Anna.

Chapter Thirteen

Too busy driving, Wyn didn't have time to check his messages. He hadn't been checking them regularly for a couple of days now, and he imagined them, trapped in his phone, gasping for breath, begging to be heard. Lately it had become more and more difficult, keeping up with the constant waves of information that lapped at his feet, inexorable as the ocean.

He called Maria Rosetti first, and she picked up on the first ring. After a curt greeting Wyn said, "Do you want a job with SPOA?"

Maria cleared her throat. "Is this Wyn Rhys? Are you asking me to come work for you?"

"Separate agencies for dealing with a crisis like this isn't cutting it anymore. I need a dedicated crisis counsellor, full-time, on call. I'll pay whatever you want, starting now. I need you to go to the house of the person looking after Claire Drobac, stay with her until I get there. She is a key witness in this case, and we need her in the care of a professional."

Maria said, "I went by and the girl was not ready to see me. She needs rest. You can't pressure her into talking to you. It's dangerous. She and her caregiver have a strong relationship. The woman is responsible. The child trusts her. It's not that I don't think you shouldn't have someone on staff for situations like this, but right now, I'm doing what is reasonable under the circumstances. She is not a risk to herself or anyone else as far as I can tell. I can't drop everything just because your agency is all over the news."

"I'm asking you a favour, Maria. Please, just go to the house and check on her."

Maria sighed. "I'll try. And no, I don't think I'm interested in working for SPOA. But thanks for the offer." She hung up.

After ending the call, Wyn hit "home" on the speed dial (have to change that, he thought) and a phone rang for a few minutes. Finally his daughter answered, sounding bored and sleepy.

"Bex?" he said, using, for the first time in years, his old pet name for her.

She seemed to wake up. "Dad? Oh my god, Mom's been, like, totally worried about you. Are you okay?"

Never in Wyn's recollection had Rebecca asked him how he was. "I'm … I'm fine," he said.

"Are you at work?" Probably because she already knew the answer, Rebecca went on, "Did you see all those videos about the guy who got Tasered? It's totally viral. My friends think it's, like, so cool that you're the investigator. It'll probably make you totally famous." She sounded so proud of him. This was likely the first inkling she'd had about what her father did for a living.

"Where's Mom? I need to talk to her."

Rebecca didn't seem to hear him. "Some friends of mine are building a Tower of Babel at Yorkdale Mall."

"A what?"

"You know, like the tower David Drobac built? That's what everyone's calling them. I don't know what it means, but there's this cool app you upload on your phone that gives you directions and instructions. It's, like, totally top secret. Mom won't let me go. She's afraid we'll get hurt or something, though the cops aren't stupid. They're not going to get filmed Tasering a bunch of kids, right?"

"I agree with your mother. Stay out of it."

"Why? What's the big deal? Everyone in Toronto is doing it, Dad."

"If I find out you were there, you will be grounded 'til graduation. This is not a lark. Believe me, I've seen what happens when such things get out of hand."

Her voice went back to the one he knew all too well. "Oh my *god*. This is different, Dad. This is *art*. You're always saying how I'm not engaged enough." She was exaggerating, of course. Wyn didn't give a shit about her being engaged, unless it was in earning her own pocket money.

As he waited for Rebecca to fetch her mother, stuck in King Street traffic, Wyn looked up and saw how the clouds were so low they obscured the tops of the buildings, resembling a pencil sketch that had been partially erased. Toronto: his home of twenty years. In ten, he would have lived longer outside the UK than in it. Would he go back, if he and Anna divorced?

The phone rustled, and Anna came on. "Where are you? Or rather where have you been? You were drinking last night. I was worried about you driving."

Feeling spiteful, Wyn said, "I don't really see why you should care where I've been."

A short silence, during which he could practically hear Anna's heart turn to stone. He tried to recall her fingers on his hair only the night before. "You're right. I don't really care. But you are a father, and if something happened to you, it would have an effect on your child. You left the house under the influence. That's not like you."

What did she know about him? What sort of man did she think he was? Wyn fought an urge to tell her everything: how he had fucked a strange girl, and how it made him feel more alive than he'd felt in years – decades. All the devastating details of his dominance, her submission. Anna could fuck a thousand faceless men if she wanted, they had nothing on his conquest.

"Well, you can see now that I'm fine," he said. "What did you want?"

"What do you mean, what did I want? You called me, remember?"

Why had he called, precisely? He couldn't recall. It had been a reflex, nothing more. His face burned at being caught out wanting – needing – something from his wife. "Sorry, I thought we had something to talk about, but I was mistaken," he said, sensing that this last delicate chance he had taken, fragile as a butterfly wing, had disintegrated. What was the saying Frank always used? "Don't go wishin' yer cake dough." Like a blade of light in a mineshaft, the meaning finally revealed itself to Wyn. Don't go wishing your cake, dough. Once the batter is mixed, one can't change the ingredients to make it into something else.

"Fine. I've started packing your things. You should start looking for a condo somewhere close to work when this madness blows over." She hung up. The second woman in ten minutes to hang up on him.

***

There were camera crews from all the media outlets on the street outside SPOA's offices, waiting. Had they stopped Lucci on his way in, gotten some kind of statement from him? Wyn debated avoiding them by parking in the Eaton Centre garage and using the underground passages to gain access to his building, but then thought: fuck it. He would let them ask their questions. He could organize a press conference, but something off the cuff seemed preferable somehow.

So when a reporter hurried towards him, cameraman in tow, Wyn stopped. She looked at him a bit queerly for a moment, and he wondered if she had thought he was someone else, but he was eminently recognizable. But then she recovered. "Director Rhys, Chief Lucci came to your office this morning with the officers involved in the death of David Drobac. This is highly unusual. Can you tell us what's happening? Will you be releasing a joint statement?"

God no, he thought. "Yes, the Chief is here. We are not going to be releasing a joint statement. I am deeply disappointed in the Chief's defense of his officers, who were clearly disobeying their training. Lucci is protecting them, when he should be considering the impact their negligence has had on others connected to the deceased, including David Drobac's teenaged daughter, who has now lost both her parents."

The journalist's eyes opened very wide. "She's an orphan?"

"Indeed. Naturally everyone is very worried about the officers, how they're feeling, after the shock and trauma of having killed a distraught man who was under the influence. But men like this show up in ER all the time and are peacefully dealt with. Our police force consistently uses the plea of self-defense when it shoots someone through the heart or head from twenty feet away. The most vulnerable people in our population – the addicts, the mentally ill, the poor – are being pointlessly and ruthlessly killed by men trained to protect them. People all over the city are showing their solidarity for David Drobac, who we know was an artist of some repute. You can be assured that my office will do everything in its power to ensure that justice is served and those officers pay the price."

"Will this be like the Wolfe case? Will you be charging them with manslaughter?"

Wyn did something he had never done in his entire professional career: he speculated. "I intend to charge them with second degree murder."

He took the elevator up to the ninth floor. Three of its walls were mirrored, one afforded a view outside onto the square below with the labyrinth at its centre, pale pink and skiffed with snow. It alone remained immutable as the surrounding poplars re-invented green every spring, as the summer lazed through on shimmering eddies, as fall dusted the air with regrets and as winter, like today, stilled the world in grey isolation. He saw it every single time he rode the elevator and yet had never walked it himself.

The mirrored walls taunted him; he had no choice but to look at his own face reflected, saw the long red welt down one cheek, from just below his eye to his chin. He recalled exactly the moment when Justine had inflicted it on him, not with his belt but with her long-nailed middle finger, as she straddled and fucked him. A brand on him, for all the world to see. He had gone on camera with this outrageous mark. What would the public make of it? Why hadn't he looked in the mirror in Justine's room? He could have borrowed some makeup from her to cover it up.

Barb was in the lobby, talking to the receptionist. When she saw him she looked very anxious. He motioned to her to follow him as he moved from the lobby into the office proper, shrugging off his coat as he walked. She scurried to keep up with his long strides. "Chief Lucci has been here since first thing this morning," she gasped. "Chantal has been asking me when you were coming in, and I told her I'd been calling and calling you but you hadn't picked up. We were very worried. Even Frank–"

Turning so suddenly that Barb actually walked into him, Wyn said, "Where is Lucci?"

"In the Safehouse."

"With Frank and the others? Is Chantal with them? What about the officers who killed Drobac?"

"The officers left. I think Lucci is about to leave."

Wyn looked at his phone. 11am. By far the latest he had ever come into work in his life. He had had walking pneumonia last year and still showed up at 7am. He wanted to clean up, but there was no time. "All right. Get me a coffee please."

They were waiting for him in the Safehouse: Lucci and a young man he didn't recognize, Chantal and Frank. And

Sylvia. Bloody Sylvia, he thought sinkingly. Wyn could have let the other investigators remain, but he didn't trust Lucci not to try to humiliate him, and he was already on very unstable ground with his team. If it wasn't for the enormous media impact, he wouldn't let Chantal participate, but he needed her presence, to explain to him what the deal was with all these stupid kids and their Towers of Babel and how to placate them, if they could be placated. Somehow appeal to their sense of humanity? But perhaps it was their humanity that had spurred them to action in the first place? He couldn't help but think such behaviour was disrespectful and narcissistic.

Lucci sat at the table, in uniform naturally, and as always it looked a couple of sizes too small for him. Had the force told him he was only permitted one uniform per five-year term? For all its snugness, however, he didn't appear uncomfortable in it. It was like the casing on a sausage. When the Chief saw Wyn he stood, which was discomfiting; Lucci wasn't the type to make overtures. The man next to him stood as well. Frank, glowering, remained seated. Lucci put out a hand for Wyn to shake, to show that they were in this together, partners, not adversaries. Wyn took the hand, glancing at the aide, wondering if he was a consultant or a media expert, the equivalent of Chantal.

The insincerity of the gesture was given away by Lucci's words, "Well, if it isn't the noble Director of SPOA. Is it just me, or do you get taller every time I see you?" The Chief's smile halted at the shores of his small eyes.

"Perhaps you're shrinking," said Wyn.

Lucci put his hands on his great belly and said, self-deprecatingly, "Not here, I'm not." He introduced his associate. "This is my communications manager, Brad. And you know Sylvia, of course."

Sylvia Hughes also didn't rise to shake his hand. She reminded Wyn of a brood hen, guarding her eggs. "Always a pleasure, Ms. Hughes."

Brad, who looked very much like a Brad, said, "A situation like this doesn't happen every day."

"Indeed," said Wyn, pulling out one of the chairs and seating himself next to Chantal, who shifted a little to give his height more space. He felt her eyes on the welt.

"Yes," said Brad. "The world is becoming like Jeremy Bentham's 'panopticon' – the public is the warden of the prison at the centre, and the law enforcers the imprisoned, on the periphery, unable to escape their gaze. An interesting inversion, I'd say." Because no one knew what he was talking about, no one said anything.

Sylvia shifted finally in her seat, her small, babyish hands interlaced in front of her. "Well, this is quite the situation you've put us in, Director."

It would be so easy to hobble her at the knees with the baton of his fury, but Wyn knew when he was being baited. "I think it's safe to say that bystanders at the mall put all of us in this situation, and we're in damage control," he said.

Lucci pulled his chair forward and grunted. He changed the subject. "You've been a hard man to reach." He made a small gesture to indicate Wyn's injury. "Wife tired of your carousing?"

Wyn automatically put his hand on the welt, raised like an accusation on his face: adulterer, psychopath, predator. "It's nothing," he said. He'd neglected to bring any paper or a laptop with him and felt suddenly ridiculously unprepared. "Towers of Babel," he began, looking at Chantal, then at Brad. "Did you see this coming?"

The two younger people stared at each other. Chantal spoke first, but seemed to be only telling Brad what her thoughts on the matter were. "No one can predict what will take hold of the public imagination," she said a bit hesitantly. "But in a way it's not surprising. David Drobac has some respect in the art world. His supporters are media savvy. What he built was compelling. He died pointlessly–" She suddenly looked over at Lucci as she said this, a bit fearful, but turned back to Wyn. "It is the right combination of elements to get people – especially young people on holidays with nothing better to do – galvanized to respond. I told you on the day that it could be big. It's already gone national. It could go bigger."

Lucci said, "If all the evidence had been collected at the scene none of this would be happening."

Wyn said, "Chief, there is no bloody point in arguing about the scene any longer, and who did or didn't secure it. The barn door was left open. The horses have long fled. We can't take down the videos, we can't stop people from expressing themselves. We have to wait it out." He turned to Chantal. "Roughly how long do such things last?"

Frank made some impatient movements, pushing his chair away from the table like he was about to stand and leave. "I don't really got time for this," he said. "I couldn't give a flyin' fock about these kids. I got an investigation to work on."

Raising his hand to stop him, Wyn said, "I understand the officers were just here?"

Frank's bleary eyes were cold. "Yep."

This was not the place or the time to upbraid his top investigator, not in front of Lucci. "I want you to stay, please." He had to remain calm. Frank reluctantly pulled his chair forward again. Wyn turned to Lucci. "The officers had more than forty-eight hours, with Ms. Hughes I'm presuming, to decide what they were going to say, which, as you know, goes against the mandate."

Lucci said, "It doesn't matter how much time they had. The truth doesn't go stale. As Frank here will tell you, the toxicology came back showing that David Drobac's blood alcohol level was .27. Dangerous impairment. He was making threats. And he had a weapon."

Leaning back in his large chair, Wyn said, "Right. A box cutter. From the store presumably. Was the packaging found?"

Frank said, "I'm waiting to hear from forensics. There was a lot of merchandise moved around, what with the wall and such."

"Do we have photographic evidence that it was on or near him when he was Tasered? Or is this coming from only the officers' recollections?" Wyn searched his mind for some recollection of his own of the scene, but could not bring to mind any image of where the man had fallen or what may have been nearby.

"We got photos," said Frank. "And fingerprints. The usual."

"And the officers' accounts. So, it all adds up. Very tidy. Tell me, Sylvia, do you make them memorize their stories in advance of meeting with our investigative team?"

Sylvia sneered. "I don't have to tell you anything about how I do my job. Those men are entitled to counsel. And you were on your way to the scene. There was no way I was going to subject them to a Wyn Rhys interrogation."

"How in bloody hell did you know I was going to the scene?" As Wyn said this, he noticed Sylvia, Frank and Lucci exchange glances. It didn't take years of studying body language to recognize collusion. "You told him," he said to Frank. "What the fuck..." Face throbbing, Wyn rose from his seat, turned his back on the table and bit the inside of his mouth as hard as he could. He tasted blood. He turned back. "If you wanted to go back to policing, Frank, you should have informed me. Oh, but wait, if you were back in uniform you wouldn't be able to give confidential SPOA information to the Chief's office." Wyn looked from the face of one man to the other, one smug, the other resigned. "Why in god's name did you even become a police investigator?"

Frank leaned back in his chair and stretched his long arms in front of him. The pen he held between his hands was like a tightrope on which he was balancing his words. "I've told you time and again that you were playing too fast and dirty with the cops," he said, not answering Wyn's question. "The Wolfe case, well, you were an investigator then. But the mandate – Jaysus, forcing the involved officers to remain at scenes? Not letting them talk to their lawyers?

You can say all you want about them being the same as other witnesses, but cops got extraordinary powers, Wyn. They gotta make a decision in .75 *seconds* whether to take down a suspect or go down themselves."

"The continuum of force clearly indicates how to deal with an agitated suspect."

"The continuum of force is a *guide*. Sometimes you gotta disable a potentially dangerous offender. David Drobac was under the influence, uttering threats, armed and unpredictable."

Still standing, Wyn grabbed the back of the chair he had lately vacated. "Two Taser hits? Simultaneously? Baton to the neck, preventing him from breathing? All to ensure that this 'dangerous offender' doesn't give someone a mild concussion from a toppling box of file folders? What was he going to do with that box cutter? Take on two strapping officers in fucking body armour?"

"Frank told me that the PM shows a pre-existing heart condition," said Lucci, who had hitherto looked, for all the world, like a kid with popcorn, enjoying a movie, but now he was very serious. "Even one Taser hit woulda done him in. We can't have any more Wolfe scenarios, Rhys. You are not charging my boys with manslaughter. You're gonna investigate this and say that the man died of myocarditis."

"I will draw my conclusions based on *evidence*, Tony. Don't you fucking dare tell me how to do my job."

"Shoe's on the other foot, I'd say," said the Chief. "You seem pretty happy telling me how to do mine. I filed an appeal with the Attorney General's office a coupla months ago, requesting that the mandate be left as is. After this incident, I bet I'm gonna get my way."

"What makes you so sure? If anything, the death of David Drobac is proof that the police are acting with impunity, Tasering innocent people in bloody shopping malls."

"Hardly innocent. That man has been arrested in the past," said Sylvia. "We've had calls from people he's had altercations with where he threatened them, attacked them. He *bit* a fellow artist at an opening last year. He was also banned from the United States for ten years for vandalizing a million dollar painting at an art show. Urinated on it, as I understand. He was volatile and aggressive."

Wyn said, "Tell me, Sylvia, do you have children?"

The lawyer shook her head, but it was a shake of frustration, not in response to Wyn's question. "I am not getting into a conversation about the Wolfe case. Don't bring up that awful trial."

"There's a child involved in this. The man's daughter. She has no mother. What do you think the public will think when they see the tears of an orphan?"

Alarmed, Sylvia said, "You can't bring a child into this. That's unconscionable."

"What those officers did was unconscionable. I will use everything at my disposal to turn the public against the Police Association. I will get you and Lucci fired over this."

Frank stood up, and for a moment Wyn thought he was going to leave in a huff, let the bureaucrats fight it out. "For fock's sake, you're comin' at this all wrong, Wyn! We got people protesting that the police can't do their jobs, and the pot's boiling over. It's gonna turn violent. We can't have Toronto seeing you and the police butting heads, fighting like two cats in a bath."

"We're in oversight, Frank, our job is to ensure that the police–"

Still standing, Frank waved, or rather flapped, one of his dangly hands. "We're fockin' bee-watchers," he said.

"I beg your pardon?"

"Dr. Seuss story. You never read books to your kids when they was small?"

Wyn had never read a children's book in his life. Frank said, "I don't remember which one it was, but the gist of it is, we live in a world where there's always someone watching us to make sure we don't fock things up. Cops watch the civilians, we watch the cops, the Attorney General and the Ombudsman watches us, the Premier or whoever the fock watches them. But now the civilians are bee-watchers themselves with their cellphone cameras and whatnot. Everyone's watchin' everyone else, and no one's fockin' *gettin' things done*. You recommend a charge of manslaughter in this case and yer lookin' at a mutiny in the police force. Mass resignations, strikes. Then we'll have an unpoliced province, and then you'll be wishin' there was a few Tasers around, to deal with the fockin' nightmare you'll have on your hands. Toronto's had riots before – 'member the G20?"

"That was people protesting *against* the police!" shouted Wyn. "For infringing on their rights!"

"Yeah, but you know how many officers was injured? 75. How many civilians? Three. Detentions, plenty of them–"

"Only the biggest mass arrest in Canadian *history*–"

"But fact was, the police kept the peace, even when it was them that was being protested against. No cops and you got total fockin' *anarchy*."

It was the most Frank had ever said in his life, and the most emotional Wyn had ever seen him. At the end of it, he coughed violently. Wyn and Lucci watched him in thoughtful silence. Brad looked impressed. Dr. Seuss made a hell of a lot more sense to the average person than panopticons.

"Couldn't't've said it better myself," said Lucci.

But Wyn wasn't convinced. "I suppose we don't need oversight anymore. We should just allow the police to go back to investigating misconduct themselves. That's worked brilliantly in the past." It was the perception that the police were targeting black youth in the province in the 1980s that had provoked the discussion of forming an oversight agency.

"I didn't say we don't need oversight. But now you're saying that we can't have ex-cops as investigators, then you hire fockwits like Nick Chirila–"

"You're not even giving Nick a chance. He just started, for god's sake." And found Claire on one of the videos. He had to call Maria, see if she was with the girl. There was no phone reception in the Safehouse, so he couldn't check.

"You're projecting the perception that even ex-cops can't be trusted. I know you weren't a cop for long in the UK, but it's like the fockin' army, Wyn. It's a *brotherhood*."

"I'm sure Constable Elizabeth appreciates the appellation," said Wyn, looking at Tony Lucci, but the Chief did not return his gaze.

"When you became Director we thought you was a good choice, 'cause you were an investigator. But you're no different than the lawyers what came before you. You're worse 'cause you think you know what's best for us, 'cause it's what's best for you. You're a shining star. A real liberal, out to protect the innocent civilian from the marauding hordes of cops with guns ablazing. You're great with the theory, but not so good with the facts. Cops won't put their lives on the line for your theories or what-have-you about society. And if you're in a spot of trouble yourself, do you really want the cops on the scene to have a quick conference about whether or not to shoot the guy who's got a knife at your neck 'cause they're worried about being charged with manslaughter?"

"You know as well as I do, Frank, that statistically speaking, any cop who pulls a gun on his own *mother* is unlikely to be charged, let alone stand trial."

Lucci leaned forward, and his uniform strained and winced as he put his pudgy arms on the table and interlaced his baby-like fingers. Wyn thought it incongruous that those hands had facility with guns. His voice was somber, all oiliness scrubbed from it. "You are not gonna bring a kid into this like you did with the poor Wolfe girl. That was a fucking travesty and you know it. You got lucky once. I'm no Bill Watson. I'm not gonna let your office malign the good character and standing of my force, undermine their morale, put the city at risk with strikes. You know that Jameson has never recovered from that manslaughter conviction? You ruined a man's life and for what? To leverage yourself into the Director role. You will have a fight like you've never seen in your life if you try that again."

Wyn stood and grabbed the lapels of his jacket, a show of his authority and to signal the end of the discussion. "I'm pursuing this as a criminal investigation. You should be shaking in your boots. I don't envy you your position. And Frank," he said, looking at his trusted colleague of almost twenty years. "I'm not wishing my cake, dough. I'm making a cake. You're fired. Clean out your desk. I'll send security to escort you off the premises." And he left.

Chapter Fourteen

Frank complied with Wyn's orders, silently packing his office while a security guard stood next to his door. Wyn couldn't go near that end of the building; the very thought of Frank's disloyalty sickened him, it was akin to finding out about Anna having a lover. Were the other investigators in line with his way of thinking? Would Wyn have to contend with a mutiny if he pursued charges against the police in this incident? It would appear as though he'd lost control of his own agency.

He found Nick at his cubicle, scrolling through news feeds. Chantal was with him. She turned to Wyn, furious. "Why did you do this?" she said, waving one hand at the screen. Wyn saw a headline: DAVID DROBAC LEAVES ORPHAN DAUGHTER. "You spoke to Cathy at the *Star* on your way in?"

Wyn stood up straighter and lifted his chin. "I did. It's true."

"And Nick tells me that the daughter was at the mall?"

Consternated, he said, "We have her on video, but I'm not going public with that information."

"Oh, good," said Chantal sarcastically. He had never seen her so disrespectful. "You can't do things like that without talking to me first."

"I will speak to whomever I want, when I please. Before we hired you we managed perfectly well without a communications manager." Chantal seemed much younger now than she had heretofore, but she was probably at least five years older than Justine. His skin felt hot. Embarrassment? Shame?

"Then I guess you're okay with the press being all over it. They're staking out the Drobac house."

"Well, she's not there. She's with a family friend. And I have social services involved as well. I don't want any insubordination from you, Chantal."

The young woman looked about to speak, but Nick interrupted, getting up from his chair. "We don't have time for this. Listen, Wyn, I remembered something the girl said when we came to break the news. She said that she wanted to be a filmmaker. Do you remember that?"

Wyn didn't remember. Too much had happened in the past three days. But Nick's words immediately touched a button in his mind, and a dazzling light came on. "Good Christ. Do you think–?"

Nick nodded slowly, his eyebrows raised. "I think that Claire Drobac may have filmed David being taken down by the cops."

"Oh my god," said Chantal.

Wyn took out his phone and checked for messages. There was a text from Maria sent only a few minutes before. It said, *Went to Sasha Ginsberg's house. Child not there. Would she be at the Drobac residence?* Wyn texted back: *Likely. Meet me there in 15.* He put his phone away. "I'm going to her right now."

Nick moved to get his coat from the rack next to his cubicle. "I'm coming with you."

"No, you're not. Stay here. Do not tell anyone about this. D'you hear me?"

Chantal said, "What do you want me to do? I'm getting all these crazy calls."

"Say nothing. Tell them we'll be giving a press conference later this afternoon."

***

Pellets of snow made tiny explosions on the windshield of his SUV and the wipers swished them away. The temperature was rising, the snow everywhere would slowly transform from fluff into frost, become heavier and heavier.

He tried to call Sasha Ginsberg but got no answer. Still pissed with him for not being more helpful? There really hadn't been more he could have done, under the circumstances. It occurred to him that Claire may have seen him on the news earlier this afternoon. Would that have sent her to the house, to feel closer to her father? Surely he hadn't endangered her, sharing her existence with the press? As he drove, all he could think, over and over, was *please*. He didn't know to whom he was addressing the plea. It just blinked, italicized and stark in his brain.

As Wyn advanced past Broadview, the news trucks appeared, parked all the way along Queen Street, filling a local public school parking lot (school was not in session, so they could act with impunity) and blocking several driveways. Canadian ones, a couple from the US. He could practically hear the buzz as cameramen hustled equipment out of the backs of the vans, puffing out steamy breath into the cold air with their exertions. His phone beeped and he took it out, saw another message from Maria: *Went to Drobac house. No answer. Am dealing with another emergency but call me when you get the chance.*

He parked on Queen and approached the house and saw another cluster of journalists in the park at the end of the dead-end street. The perfect place to assemble; there were lots of trees and it was a public place. No one could kick them out. Wyn chose to ignore them and made his way up the front walk. One journalist recognized him and ran towards him, cameraman at his heels. The others reflexively hurried in his wake, like they were all part of the same large and clumsy organism with a small brain. "Mr. Rhys! Director Rhys!" gasped the man as he drew closer, microphone hand outstretched. "What can you tell us about the teenager involved? Was she with her father when he died? Is it true–"

Wyn cut him off. "I want you away from this house. Don't make me bring in the police."

"We're not trespassing. We just want to–"

Wyn grabbed the microphone and yanked it, hard, disconnecting it from the camera. "Listen to me. Do you want me to have you arrested for endangering the welfare of a child? Do you? 'Cause I'm not averse to seeing you lot behind bars for a few days."

The journalist looked at him, mouth agape. The other journalists, whose microphones were functional, pressed forward, asking for a statement. Wyn said, "I am not here to discuss this case. I'm here on SPOA business and won't be interfered with. Get off this property – now." As he walked to the pale purple door, he heard the clatter and squeak of equipment being gathered up and moved off the property, back to the place from which it came. If he found her, could he get Claire to leave the building with him? How did she get in without being noticed? Would she be too afraid of the cameras and the glare?

He rapped on the door and opened the mail slot, the slot from which he'd gotten his first glimpse of her small, turquoise-painted fingertips. "Claire?" he called. "Claire, it's me, Wyn Rhys. We need to talk. Claire?" he called again into the hollows of the house. He thought he could hear his voice reverberate back to him. He turned his head to a very awkward angle to peer through the slot and made out shadows in the long hallway, but there was no evidence of movement. He then straightened and put his ear to the door, squinting as he tried to pick up a sound, any sound.

Touching the peeling paint on the cheap door, he willed it to open. Then it occurred to him to simply turn the doorknob. He did. The door sprang away from him with ease. Why hadn't Maria tried the same? Because going uninvited into anyone's home, unless it was on fire or there was evidence that a person within was in mortal danger, was strictly against protocol. But Wyn was beyond protocol. He stumbled a bit on the slippery tile of the entranceway because of the snow stuck to the bottoms of his galoshes. Silence still, but he knew there was someone in the house. And there was a smell. Tang of iron and copper, high octane scarlet. He made his way to the back of the flat, to the bathroom, dread rising in his throat.

Claire Drobac was curled up in the empty bathtub, like she was sleeping, in the same clothes he had first seen her in: the white shirt that was probably her father's, the jangly skirt. Her wrists were crudely slashed and there was a quantity of blood.

Kneeling, Wyn gathered up the girl, just as he had done with Justine Wolfe fourteen years before. She was older than Justine had been, but not much bigger. But he was older. He sat down, hard, on the bathroom floor with the child in his arms, put his hand to her neck, to the carotid artery. She was alive, still warm. Her suicide attempt was recent.

He grabbed some towels that were hanging on the nearby rack, lay the girl on the floor with her head on his lap and crossed her wrists, from which minute geysers of blood pumped where the ulnar and radial arteries had been damaged, and bound them together with the towel. She was reposeful, her pretty mouth turned up in almost a smile. Death was waxing in, life waning out. Reaching into his holster, he pulled out his phone and dialed 911 and gave them the address of the house, told them who he was. Cringing, because the press would see the ambulances – this was not good optics for SPOA, nor for him as its Director. He had been concerned about her weeping for the cameras? Now he had to worry about her dying in front of them.

Suddenly Claire stirred, her eyelids fluttering. She shivered. Wyn awkwardly struggled out of his coat and put it over her, tucking it all around her. "Please," he whispered. "Please, please." The girl's lips had lost all blood, becoming that white-lavender hue he'd seen in the morgue so many times. He had to keep her warm. "Claire, sweetheart," he said, stroking her bright hair from where it clung to her jaw and neck. "It's going to be okay. An ambulance is on its way. Hang in there. Hang on." He then bent close to her face, its moon-white transparency. "Can you hear me? It's Wyn Rhys. I know you were at the mall with your dad. I know you saw everything. Just nod to show me you can hear me." He'd done this kind of thing before, many times, leaning over gurneys, over hospital beds. He'd been the last person victims had seen before taking their last breath; him, a stranger.

The girl didn't move. "Come on, Claire. Just nod. You can nod for me, right? You were there. Did you film it? Did you?" Feeling suddenly a wave of hopelessness crash through the bastion of his determination, he banged his closed fist against the bathroom wall. He wanted to weep. This bathroom was in the furthest reaches of hell. Every decision he'd ever made in his life had led to this moment. "Claire. Please. I need your phone if you filmed it. It's evidence. Fuck."

"Oh my god." Justine.

Wyn turned. In a long grey velvet coat and red hat, Justine stood at the door of the bathroom. How had she gotten in? What was she doing here? "Have you called an ambulance?"

"Get the fuck out of here. *Now*," Wyn ordered.

Justine dropped to her knees and edged over to the girl. "She cut her wrists? Keep her head above her heart."

"You think I don't know what I'm doing? What the fuck are you doing here? How did you find out where she lives?"

"I volunteer at the street mission on the corner. I recognized the purple door on the news. Why did you tell the press about her? What were you *thinking*?"

"Don't tell me—"

"How to do your job?" Justine moved around Wyn to examine the girl. "Ever think that sometimes you do your job really, really badly?" Calm and clinical, the way he remembered her being the first night, with his own injury, she put her hand to the girl's neck to check her pulse, then carefully but swiftly lifted Wyn's coat, removed the towel and looked at the girl's wrists. "She'll live," she said matter-of-factly. Her solemn dark eyes were level with his own. "You are nothing like the man I thought you were," she said.

Sirens could be heard on the block and in just a few moments, the paramedics breached the doorway and were clomping towards the back of the house. "In here!" Wyn strangled out, his voice riven by urgency. A man and a woman in uniform came to the door. Wyn eased away from the girl, banging his hip, hard, against the bowl of the toilet. "Slit wrists," he told them as they carefully manoeuvered around the prone child and, on a count, lifted her, coat and all.

The room was so tiny they had to take her out of it to put her on the stretcher in the hallway. Justine told them she was an ER resident at St. Mike's, offered to travel in the ambulance with her, but Wyn ordered her to stay. Wyn explained he was an investigator come to check up on her. He gave them her name and saw them exchange glances. They had no doubt seen the press milling around, watched the news. "Drobac" was the most famous name in Canada at the moment.

Justine went with them to the door, but he remained on the bathroom floor. He felt exhausted, finished, never to rise again. He set his head against the wall and felt his eyes burn, his throat constrict. He was not going to let his emotions overpower his reason. Opening his eyes, he noticed the blood on the bathroom tiles around the tub, where red handprints formed a bizarre dance formation, one two, one two, in a circle. He had to get out of this horror. Grasping the cold curve of the pedestal sink and bracing against the far wall, he hoisted himself to his feet and limped out of the room, into the dark hallway, made even dimmer in contrast to the glare of the bathroom. It was empty now, but traces of the late scuffle were still evident in the slush and mud and wintery chill. A devastated girl had been whisked away, and outside the press still lingered, waiting for him to emerge, covered in an orphaned girl's blood, with the famous Justine Wolfe of almost fifteen years ago unaccountably present.

Disoriented and half-blind, Wyn shuffled along the wall, one blood-sticky hand grasping the edges of the bookshelves, back to the front room. There he found Justine on the sofa, leaning forward and putting her own bloodied hands together as though in prayer. "What the fuck were you thinking, coming here?" he hissed. "How dare you interfere in all this! It's just–" He was so angry he didn't even know how to express himself. "Just – so fucking stupid!"

Justine looked up at him without raising her head, seemingly unmoved by his outburst. "I was trying to help," she said. She opened her hands, looked down at them. The lines in her palms were darker red, tiny rivers filled with blood. "I have to wash my hands," she said, and suddenly stood and went to the kitchen.

He followed her, watched as she scrubbed mercilessly, disgusted by the blood, or herself. "I need you to get out of this house, now," he said.

Justine said nothing, her frown and jaw set.

"Did you hear what I said? You have to leave, and you can't tell anyone what happened here. Go out the back door. God, if the press saw you – did you speak to them? Tell them who you are?" Wyn turned off the water and handed Justine a towel.

She glowered at him as she dried her hands. "Of course not," she said. "I'm going with you to the hospital." She tried to move past Wyn, but he grabbed her shoulder. "Perhaps I'm not making myself clear," he said. "I want you out of this house, and out of my life."

Justine stared at him, mouth slightly open. "You can't be serious," she said.

"This is not a situation in which I would make witty conversation." He had to conduct a search of the apartment for the phone. He had to get the evidence, before the police came and seized it, and turned it over to Lucci. He looked around the room. The kitchen table looked the same as when he'd last been in it, the empty glass from which she'd drunk water still where she had set it. With mounting urgency, Wyn opened and closed cupboards, checked the top of the refrigerator. He then went back to the lounge and turned in a circle in the middle of the room, still feeling discombobulated. His face throbbed. He went into the entranceway and riffled through the pockets of Claire's velvet cape, pulling out her cigarettes, some Jolly Ranchers. No phone. "Fuck," he said.

Turning, he almost stepped on Justine. "I heard you trying to get information out of her. Wanting her phone? You think she filmed it? Is that what you were doing while she was fucking bleeding to death? Trying to get evidence?"

Ignoring her Wyn returned to the lounge, feeling aimless and bewildered. The space was too unfamiliar. So sparsely furnished, yet inscrutable. The phone could be anywhere and nowhere. Tantalizing him with its almost-thereness. "Fuck," he said again, pulling out sofa cushions, looking behind items on the mantel: photos of tiny Claire, a birthday card, an old rotary phone, the picture of the young David Drobac. Justine appeared again and Wyn pointed to the door. "I thought I told you to get out."

Crossing her arms, she said, "I said I was trying to help. You weren't going to do anything. I guess you had some time freed up in your busy schedule to attend to an orphan in danger? How thoughtful of you. You fucking asshole. All you care about is your stupid career, your stupid reputation."

Wyn came towards Justine, his fury building with each step. "This is all your fault," he said. "I wish I'd never agreed to meet you. I definitely wish I'd never gone to your house, or–" He stopped, breathless.

"Or what, Mr. Rhys? Fucked me?" Her teeth on her bottom lip when she said the "f" were like fangs. "Everyone's watching you, the man in charge of the Drobac case. I bet they'd love to know what you do with your personal time. Screwing a girl half your age who was part of the *last* greatest investigation of your career. Yeah, I bet they'd be all over it."

He grabbed Justine Wolfe by the shoulders and pushed her against the mantel, his hands on her neck, right on the tattooed maps of her carotid arteries, where two days ago his lips had sought her pulse, where indeed he had only last night placed his hands. He could feel her carotid pulse now as he squeezed, felt it accelerate in panic. A fluttering butterfly trapped just under the skin, pinned by his thumbs. He pressed harder, imagining it slowing and stilling, becoming a feathered jewel.

Justine gasped, sucking in air like a swimmer before a dive. Her great dark eyes stared at him unbelieving, that the man she fancied saved her life fifteen years ago was about to kill her. She had that look, the look Wyn knew so well, of seeing something remarkable just before death. The remarkable thing was him.

With a gasp, as though it were he who had been locked in the vise of Justine's fingers, Wyn let go and Justine crumpled to the floor, coughing and wheezing. She started to sob, her head against the brick arch of the unused fireplace, her arms wrapped around herself in a tight embrace. She coughed some more and made a sound that was the keening of disbelief.

Wyn crouched beside her, touched her shoulder. A woman with whom he was now more intimate than he'd ever been with Anna, because he had seen her not only in ecstasy but in fear for her life, and in both instances directly at his hand. "I'm sorry," he whispered. "I'm sorry." He wasn't thinking about what Justine had said, or about how she could ruin his life with one phone call to a local paper. All he could think was: I almost killed her. I didn't kill her. I almost killed her. The two phrases rotated around each other, the word "almost" preventing them from being contradictory.

Justine recovered and collected herself, not meeting Wyn's gaze as she got up from the floor. Her velvet coat, he noticed now, was crimson-blotched and stained like an animal that had been bludgeoned to death. Wyn knew his thumbs would leave bruises on her neck, just as they had the night before, imagined them bearing his fingerprints, exposing him as surely as a crime scene. He went to the blood-smeared toilet and vomited up the coffee he'd been drinking all day. Its acid scent was a black snake that, before he flushed, rose from the bowl and tried to insinuate itself back into his body.

When he emerged from the bathroom, trembling and frangible, she was gone. He heard the back door slam – if he had any luck left to him, if there was a God, she would not be seen by the press, or at least not recognized. Would she expose him? Could things possibly get any worse? What could he do to stop her? There was no way he could ever be the man she thought him to be again, and in a peculiar way, he was relieved.

Still feeling nauseous and light-headed, but jacked on adrenalin, Wyn made another tour of the apartment. He'd never been in Claire's bedroom and now felt somewhat intrusive, because he wasn't there in a truly professional capacity. The phone wasn't just evidence. It was a misplaced piece of his soul, calling to him to retrieve it. If he had it he would be Director Wyn Rhys again, not an adulterer, not a soon-to-be divorcee, not a predator of fragile young women.

Claire's room was very small, only large enough to accommodate a narrow twin bed mattress and a tiny desk. It had the loud disarray of adolescence: clothes piled in a corner, leftover bits of childhood whimsy, books, many books, and random objects that defied categorization. There was no way of anyone knowing that it had been further disturbed, so Wyn kicked around the clothes, checked under the mattress, the pillow. Nothing.

In the hall he heard footsteps, and a man called to announce that he was with the police, asked if there was anyone home. Straightening and taking a deep breath, Wyn calmly left the child's room, as official-looking as he could hope to be with his battered face and bloodstained white shirt. The officers seemed perplexed to see the Director of SPOA at David Drobac's house but were not in a position to demand answers. Wyn informed them that he had been called by a friend of the next of kin regarding the suicide attempt and that the girl was on her way to the hospital.

"I don't want this scene disturbed," he told them. "This is part of the larger SPOA investigation into the death of David Drobac. If Chief Lucci has any questions, he can address them to me." Still trembling and fearful that they might challenge him, call Lucci, demand more information, Wyn ushered them to the door and instructed them to seal both entrances with police tape. He knew that word would get back to the Chief about what he had done, and there would be angry inquiries, just as there had been after he had shown up at the scene at Gerrard Square Mall.

He couldn't leave the house by the front door and be seen by the press, who no doubt had witnessed the entire drama of the girl being borne away in an ambulance. He went to the back door and into a neglected-looking patio, closely fenced in on all sides. He called Sasha Ginsberg and told her to meet him at the hospital, asked if Claire's phone was at her house, but she wasn't at home to check. She sounded so eerily calm, it disturbed him somewhat. What had she been through with the girl's father? It seemed like there was nothing she could be told that would elicit panic.

He walked around down the street to get to his car on Queen, but was fairly certain he was spotted. He could just see the headline, which would come out in approximately eleven minutes: SPOA DIRECTOR AT DROBAC HOUSE EMERGENCY INCIDENT. Chantal would be having kittens.

***

In the reception area at the hospital, Wyn had to produce identification and explain that the girl was connected to an SPOA investigation. He was told that Claire was stable, though she had lost a fair amount of blood. He made a promise to himself to follow through on hiring a crisis counsellor to work at SPOA. If there was to be a real legacy in the Drobac case, it would be better resources for the bereaved and traumatized.

As he waited in the ER reception for Sasha Ginsberg, his phone bleated and rumbled in his pocket and he ignored it, merely sat in one of the plastic chairs wondering how the world – his world, Claire's world, Justine's – could change so much in just three tiny days. Even if Claire had not taped the event, she would still be the most valuable witness. But even the most stalwart witnesses falter and think twice about what they saw, especially when recounting traumatic events. Justine's recollection of June 28, 2000, was all over starred with her terror, her need for safety and yes, her love for the man who killed her mother and brothers. Claire's love for David Drobac would also be threaded throughout her testimony, and only the most experienced investigator, such as himself, would be able to sift out the facts of what happened on Boxing Day. No one but him would be permitted to even speak to her, once she'd recovered. But he had to wait. Waiting taught him the value of patience, something he had always lacked.

He reached into his coat pocket and felt something smooth. He drew forth the pink iPod, Rebecca's, the one with all the music he'd loved. Wonderingly, he turned it on, looked at the cascade of album covers he knew so well: The Police, David Bowie, Talking Heads, Iggy Pop, Roxy Music, Patti Smith, and of course, Joy Division. Indeed, the last song played on the device had been "Love Will Tear Us Apart."

Among the dejected and the bleeding, the not-so-emergent emergencies and those waiting for news of loved ones, Wyn put the earbuds in. The man he'd been when he first heard that song, what was he like? It seemed like all his life he'd been cynical, suspicious of other people, aloof, uncaring. Yet a woman had fallen in love with him, affixed her life to his, bore his child. He'd loved her too, entrusted her with a part of himself that wasn't afraid to be vulnerable, though it was very small, and except for those final moments, when his wife had placed her hand on his head, he hadn't felt it in years.

David Drobac probably had a dozen friends, and yet hundreds of people in Toronto and perhaps all over Canada felt love for him. And though it expressed itself so bizarrely, Wyn understood the swell of compassion; it was an innate human need, a hunger to connect in an unconnected world. He hadn't watched any of the videos of the young people who'd felt compelled to immortalize the man's death, because he'd been too consumed with the immediacy of the original event. When the Wolfe case had exploded in the media, he had experienced the same queer intimacy, removed from the public's perception of it.

The Drobac case belonged to him far more than it belonged to them, and his responsibility towards it was in keeping with his own ideas about Truth, about Justice. When he sat in that boardroom with Lucci and Frank, he knew himself for the real maverick he was; he didn't care about what the world thought of what he was doing. He'd scavenged for Truth in Claire Drobac's bedroom, but it didn't make a difference. All he had were the calculable things: blood spatter patterns, entry wounds, Taser burns, toxicology reports and the testimonies of witnesses. He had changed the mandate so that SPOA could capture and isolate the immediate experiences of the men (and they were all men, so far) who discharged their weapons, as close to the moment that they'd made that decision as possible. If only he could stop merciless Time. If only he was at the Wolfe house even ten minutes earlier, or at the Drobac's. But there was no way of preventing tragedy from charting its course, no more than one can determine the flow of water, or gravity, or the phases of the moon.

All the years he had striven for justice for the unfortunates who had been injured or perished at the hands of police had been out of love, sort of. He had more love – whatever love he had to give – for them than he had for his wife, child, parents. He didn't know if they deserved it. Truth was the thing that mattered, he thought; but Truth was, ultimately, as inscrutable to him as the love of his family. And for all that he had crusaded for relatives of victims, even though deep down he didn't know that the victims deserved their love, he'd never thought much about the love that the dead leave behind.

As the song wound its way to the final bars, he saw Justine Wolfe's eyes the night he found her in her home, when he'd stood over her and they had blinked open, announced to him that she was alive. If he'd succeeded in killing her today, it would be called a "crime of passion" and he'd be charged with second degree murder. But he hadn't succeeded. It was a good failure, one he could be proud of. Nonetheless, he sheltered an evil conceit that masked as righteous ferocity; he wasn't a lion guarding his pride. He was a lion that stalked and mauled his own kind in the dark, to remind them who was in charge, and the price that would be exacted for any infringement on his supremacy. Whatever happened next, Wyn could at least take some comfort in the fact that while he'd been harbouring a killer in his soul, he hadn't let it get away with murder.

There was a chance that Justine might try to charge him with assault. Part of him longed for it. He considered turning himself in, but what would that accomplish? All he could think was that Justine had, by her departure, determined to forgive him his transgression, and he, in turn, had to find a way to forgive himself, even if it contradicted what he had heretofore considered to be an ineluctable truth: victims want revenge.

When Sasha arrived, in her own long cape, blonde hair a halo of fat waves, her girlish face somber, Wyn stirred to rise, to meet her, to insist that she look for Claire's phone and submit it as evidence. But then he didn't. She kept her eyes straight ahead, bent on only one mission, to be with a child in crisis. She didn't see him, and he didn't alert her to his presence. Surrounded by people in various states of unhappiness and fear he decided: no. Not today.

He left via the Victoria Street entrance, passing the statue of St. Michael, his left hand aloft, his right casually holding a sword to the head of a hissing serpent. An avenging angel, but a very composed one. On one of the late nights, not unlike this one, when he'd been tethered to the hospital's waiting room hoping to speak to an injured victim, a nurse had told him that this statue had been found in a second-hand shop on Queen Street in the late nineteenth century. The marble was from the same quarry as Michelangelo's *Pieta*. People, families of patients presumably, had set flowers at the angel's feet, garlanded his head. His gaze was downcast, his upraised hand more the gesture of someone hailing a cab than summoning God's wrath.

Outside the hospital, Wyn stood for a long time at Queen and Victoria. His office was only two blocks away, behind the gargoyles and hideous red bricks of Old City Hall. Men – his men – were toiling in its cool glass expanses, waiting for the call that would send them hurtling through the night to another scene, where another confrontation had ended in a death or serious injury. The police would never stop using their weapons with dangerous and not-so-dangerous offenders, and offenders (high, psychotic, or cunning) would carry on offending. And SPOA would carry on investigating them all, and the rate of conviction would remain steady at virtually nil. Lucci would drag every Police Association lawyer into the fray to drag out the process as long as possible, until people forgot about David Drobac and his beautiful tragedy. By then, some other meme will have enthralled the country. Perhaps next time it would be a woman, or heaven forbid, a kid. As Frank said, lightning wouldn't strike twice in Wyn's career. The Drobac case could be a watershed, or it could end up like so many other high-profile cases that languish in bureaucrats' dreams.

Chapter Fifteen

June 28, 2015

The hedges on the periphery of the Road to Paradise had new leaves, as did the adolescent trees that stood trembling sentry around the square. A group of elderly people milled around outside the Holy Trinity church, a popular tourist attraction. It was one of the few nice days in June when Wyn actually enjoyed Canadian weather. Today he stood in the large lobby in his building that overlooked the square, fiddling with his pack of cigarettes, apprehensive, anxious. He didn't want to run into her. He wanted her to wait for him.

He had moved out and rented a condo only a few blocks from work. Anna had offered him some pieces of furniture from their house but Wyn declined them all, choosing to live in almost monastic austerity: a kitchen table with two chairs, a sofa and a desk in the living room, a bed and dresser. No pictures on the walls, no bookcases, no TV. Glass doors afforded a rather spectacular view of the Toronto skyline and the sunsets behind it, which Wyn had started to look forward to and enjoy as the soul-chokingly cold winter receded and spring tenderly advanced, warmed, deepened. He would sit for hours, smoking and thinking about nothing on the balcony, something he had never done in his life. Rebecca had not yet been over to visit, but they had gone out for coffee a couple of times, once for dinner. She had gotten into U of T and would continue to live with Anna, who had decided to keep the house. There was a man of some kind – Richard, Rebecca told him – who spent some time there, but there was no concrete talk of him moving in. He'd asked Rebecca about the iPod, which he'd kept, and she said that yeah, she listened to his records a few years back, constantly for a while, then got bored with them. A flickering moment, when she was thirteen, when they could have bonded over music, and Wyn had missed it.

He looked at his watch. It was 2:15pm. She had asked to meet him at 2:30.

After months of collating witness accounts, collecting and analyzing video evidence, and conducting and examining forensic tests and the testimonies of the involved officers in the Drobac case, Wyn did not have enough information to recommend a charge of manslaughter, let alone second degree murder. The videos of the onlookers were useless; they all depicted the same thing, a barrier with some noise behind it. Wyn had watched them countless times, straining to hear something that would indicate that the man behind the wall had not provoked the officers into using their weapons, had not been uttering threats, but gleaned nothing. Claire coming out from behind the wall, over and over and over again, in the one video that had captured her, taunted him every time he saw it. He knew she'd filmed it. But the phone had not been forthcoming, even after extensive searches of the family abode. Claire herself was unavailable to him because she had been taken into psychiatric care after her suicide attempt, and Sasha Ginsberg would not return any of his calls. His request for funds to hire an on-site crisis worker had not yet been approved. If the case were to go to court, he could have her subpoenaed and evaluated for competency to give testimony, but the Crown would likely advise against it if it were determined that it was not in the public interest to have her mental health jeopardized for the sake of convicting cops when there was evidence that they had been threatened by an armed man. Indeed, the chance that the case would even make it to court was meagre.

2:20pm. His heart started to beat a bit faster.

Frank came back. The afternoon that Claire ended up in the hospital Wyn called his best investigator and apologized, acknowledged that what Frank said about baiting the Chief was true, to some extent. He had perhaps gone too far, showing up at the scene in Gerrard Square Mall. Taciturn Frank accepted the apology and said he'd think about returning to SPOA, but showed up the next day and called a meeting with the men he'd selected to work on the investigation, including Nick, and they never spoke of it again. Wyn understood that, in the course of those three days, he'd done more than just failed at making his cake into dough, he'd slipped on the tightrope of his life, and there was no correcting that kind of mistake. The best one could hope for was to land safely, and Frank was his net. Frank had Tony Lucci's trust, and if he hadn't returned to SPOA, Lucci would have raised a furor over the fact that Wyn had threatened publicly to charge the officers with second degree murder, regardless of the fact that public opinion had sided so completely with the victim, and especially his daughter. Still, Wyn had to rescind his words, state that SPOA and the Police Association were cooperating. This had been very difficult for him, he who had never capitulated to compromise before. But in the end it had made the most sense, even though it meant Wyn would be unlikely to enforce the change to the mandate, as long as he had ex-cops working for him. He kept Nick, who was turning out to be competent enough, but had not sought out other civilian candidates. As loneliness set in, Wyn came to look forward to the few minutes several times a day that he and Frank would go for a cigarette in the square. It had not been only because the laconic Newfoundlander was his best investigator that Wyn had requested he return to work. Frank was, he realized, the closest thing he had to a friend in Canada.

2:30pm and Justine emerged from the Eaton Centre, directly across from Wyn's building. Her message had been very precise about the place and time, though her reason for wanting to see him was not so straightforward. She said she had something important to discuss with him, and though almost every moment they had spent in each other's presence in the short two days they were acquainted (it was the only word Wyn could think of to describe it) had been so pregnant with importance, he had to think that it had something to do with the way they had parted on that terrible dark winter afternoon. Out of a residual spite for the way they had ended things, he had not responded to Justine's invitation, perversely curious to see if she'd show up anyway. And she did.

She wore a silk dress that seemed to have every colour in it, which billowed and obscured her like a mirage. Her arms were bare and he could see the crazy pattern of the tattoos. As he knew she would, she went to the Road to Paradise and commenced walking it, just as she had that long ago day, the day of the trial. Her hair had grown out a bit, into a curly bob with very short bangs, and it bounced a little as she walked with that same determined stride. Justine was, if nothing else, a purposeful person, and fearless – so fearless – because she'd lain down next to death. Whether he showed up or not, she would walk the labyrinth. How many times had she walked it before, he wondered?

When she got to the centre (and did the same thing she'd done that other June day: looked up at the sky for answers) Wyn left the lobby, went into the square. He went to the aperture of the Road to Paradise, the embarkation point. He had intended to disregard the rules of the labyrinth and simply treat it like ordinary ground, but somehow, he couldn't ignore its demand to be obeyed. Hadn't he gotten into enough trouble, by ignoring the rules? So he followed it along the straight path to the point where it diverged sharply to the left and took him to the middle of the first quadrant, then around to the other side. He kept his head down but knew Justine was watching him now. Dizzying twists that made him feel like he was retracing his steps, maddeningly unexpected ventures inward then back outward, and taking much longer than he expected, even though he had just witnessed Justine take the identical journey. It was so compact, but it contained multitudes. After several turns and rebounds, however, he found the rhythm of it, the music even. It had meaning. It had order. He had to follow the rules of the labyrinth, just like everyone else.

Because he couldn't wrap his mind around what parts of the labyrinth he'd traversed and what parts remained to be walked, the end came as a surprise to Wyn, which no doubt was the object of the design. If life was full of convolutions and surprises, its end was always unexpected, even for the infirm and elderly. Even for the suicides. The moment decides itself when it wants to end.

Justine had watched him, he was certain, and faced him now, her black eyes finally revealing themselves in the bright sunlight to be a very deep brown with the odd golden glint. Her hand was in her loose hair. Wyn felt a sudden probing ache for her, a different sensation than he had felt upon knowing things were finished with Anna. That had been a sadness for what he knew so well. What he felt now was a sadness for what he would never know.

"I didn't think you'd show up."

Wyn took out his cigarettes and his lighter, lit up. He felt ridiculous, standing in the centre of the labyrinth, like he and Justine were on a stage together in a bizarre modernist play with no audience. People all around them were going about their business, getting things done.

He shrugged. "You made an offer I couldn't refuse." He meant it as a joke.

"So you knew?" Justine held out something to him, a black oblong. A phone. "The smoking gun."

It looked so ordinary. Just another gadget in a universe of chittering gadgets. Wyn couldn't believe it. This was not what he expected, not at all. "How...?" He didn't take it from her.

"I found it in the living room. I sat on it by accident on the sofa. It had fallen between the cushions. I thought about leaving it for the police to find, or you. But after what I'd heard you say to that poor girl I decided to take it. I was going to give it to you, but then what happened in the hallway–" She stopped and looked at the pink brick beneath their feet. "I thought about turning it in to the police, but then they would think I was a witness, and I didn't want to be involved. Anyway–" she held it out to him. "I can't watch it again. I'm giving it to you now because you're entitled to make a choice. It's not my place to prevent you from doing that."

Justine glanced down at her upturned hand, the phone lying on it like a mysterious artifact from another age, encrypted with strange secrets. "I've followed the investigation. I know you don't have enough evidence to charge those officers. I thought that by submitting it I would expose that poor kid to unbelievable pain, seeing what she'd filmed, knowing, as I know she knows, that she could have done something. She could have stopped it." Justine's eyes brimmed, and a bright, sunlit tear dropped on her cheek. "But at a certain point I had to choose between compassion and justice. This video has the truth."

Wyn couldn't quite bring himself to ask, but then had to. "Was he armed?"

She smirked. "No. I don't know what happened after the girl stopped filming, but during the confrontation his hands were open. He had no weapon. That should make you happy, shouldn't it? Nothing else seems to." She looked past him, at some children who were walking the labyrinth. It was impossible to tell if they were getting closer, or when they would reach the centre. Wyn realized something he hadn't noticed in the short time he'd spent in her company. She had a strange peace about her, an imperturbable sanctity. Not holiness, not even goodness. If anyone could figure out what truth's obligations were, it was this unusual woman. "You're the unhappiest man I have ever met, Wyn Rhys. I thought, wrongly, that I could bring some happiness to your life. I even thought I could save you, like you had saved me, all those years ago."

"I didn't—" Wyn began, but Justine raised her other hand, the empty one, to silence him. "Not in the usual way. That's not what I mean. You've had a remarkable effect on my life. I honestly don't think I would have survived the Long Night without you." Her voice changed in these last words, became smaller, tighter, more childlike. But she recovered quickly. "I hope Claire realizes what you're doing for her. It will make things a lot easier to handle, accepting that you only ever wanted to help her."

"That's not true," said Wyn. "I forgot about her. I didn't notice that she was the key witness when I should have, the very first time I met her. A good investigator would have put the pieces together. But I had other things on my mind. I let her down. When you begged me to go to her I was so furious with you because you showed me how horribly neglectful I'd been. That's why—"

The children had come to the floret at the centre of the labyrinth, where they stood. They were two girls, sisters by the look of it, perhaps twins. They turned their small chins upward and managed, in the way of children, to stare down on the adults from their lofty childhood eyrie. Then they resolutely marched back to the path, to follow it out again. The end didn't interest them. The journey was all that mattered.

Wyn had lost his train of thought, but Justine hadn't. "That's why you tried to hurt me," she said, and he noticed that she was careful not to use the word "kill." "I knew you wouldn't. Well, that's not true. I was angry and terrified for a long time. But eventually I knew that you would never do me any harm. You must have thought that I would go to the police and charge you with assault. I thought you might resort to threats, but you never did."

It had never occurred to Wyn to threaten Justine. Now that he thought about it, it was rather foolish that he hadn't, or that it hadn't even crossed his mind. But after the incident he merely did what he had always done, bludgeoned all feelings with intense work. He had a marriage to dismantle. But these distractions didn't eradicate it completely. He'd dreamt about that encounter in the hallway on several occasions, and he remembered the dreams, he, who almost never thought about sleep upon waking. In the dream he succeeded in killing her, but it wasn't always by strangling. He'd dreamt of dissecting her, burning her, drowning her, setting her alight. He always woke wide-eyed to the dark, breathless and alone. He would feel guilt, remorse, terror, love. He would reach for the phone to call her but never did. He could only imagine what her dreams looked like.

Wyn had been holding his spent cigarette. He now threw it over the hedge, off the labyrinth. It seemed inappropriate, marring the symmetry of the design with a cigarette butt. "I think we should not be in contact anymore. I hope you've gotten on with your life." He wanted to put his hand on her shoulder, not to soothe or reassure, but to assert his strength, his capacity to silence her if driven to do so. He put his hands in his pockets instead.

She held the phone out to him again. "Take it. I don't want it anymore. I started to think of myself as Claire, became her at certain moments. We are too similar."

Silent, feeling almost reverential, having this gift bestowed on him, he who was so unworthy, Wyn took the phone from Justine's hand and saw that she closed her eyes at the moment of release. Terrifying to contemplate, but this piece of evidence could give him the ballast he needed to recommend charges. Planting evidence was an outrageous obstruction of justice. And it meant that the officers colluded; they wanted no scrutiny of their actions. They knew they had needlessly and heedlessly killed an unarmed man. Even if it was accidental, they were still culpable. Negligence causing death. He could feel the familiar whoosh in his bloodstream.

From her purse the girl pulled something out, a small object, white and soft. It was a stuffed toy, a rabbit, amorphous, with only round stubs for limbs, melting ears, no tail, its coat worn down to a burnish. Well-loved, by the looks of it, and for a long time. "You gave this to me," she said.

"I know. I remember."

"You held me on your lap. And you did something." Rising to her tiptoes, Justine put her arms on Wyn's shoulders and drew his head down so she could whisper in his ear. She told him something that he had entirely forgotten about, something he had done after he'd found her in the rec room with her deceased father. He couldn't believe the memory of something so extraordinary could have escaped him, but then, he may have been ashamed of what he'd done and repressed it. He understood now why he had been so intrigued by the adult Justine, and why he'd been so afraid of her.

When she finished telling him the secret, she stood back and they looked into one another's eyes for several moments. "You don't remember that, do you," she said.

Slowly, Wyn shook his head.

"Funny, I thought you did. I thought that was why you followed me for so many years."

Thinking about it, trying to remember it but failing, Wyn had to concede that for whatever reason, his mind had decided to lock this moment somewhere inaccessible forever, but it gave him the impetus to seek her out and possess her nonetheless. "Perhaps it was," he said.

"It made everything fall into place for me. I understood why I needed you in my life – to finish off what had begun that day, when I was a child. I think I loved you from that moment. I tried to be worthy of your love, your loyalty, when I went to that girl's house."

"That was a terrible mistake."

"If I hadn't gone, would we have had a chance?"

Wyn took out his cigarettes. "No."

"You never loved me." A break in her voice, or a hitch, like silk caught on a nail and about to rip.

He lit a cigarette, squinted at the lonesome girl through the blue of the smoke. "You don't love me either, Justine. You love an idea. I loved the idea of you too. I don't know what sort of man you think I am, after what has happened between us. But when it comes down to it, I have always done what needed to be done. You were expecting some kind of hero. I'm not."

Solemn, Justine said, "You're not a good man, Wyn Rhys. But you do a good job. And that's all that matters at the end of the day, right?"

What she said hurt, deeply, but he wouldn't let her or anyone ever see him vulnerable again. So Wyn just shrugged. "Probably."

"Is that what you'll think about when you die? Will it give you satisfaction, having done a good job?" She leaned her body forward, canting on her hips and whispered, "I really hope you have someone at your bedside to tell it back to you."

And with that, Justine Wolfe stepped around Wyn and walked off the labyrinth, across the volutes, determined. She had places to be, places to which the path was more direct and on which she wouldn't encounter Wyn again. He didn't turn to watch her leave.

Epilogue

Instead of taking the third child upstairs into the pandemonium of paramedics, police officers and the homicide team, Wyn shuffled to a nearby sofa and settled on the edge of it, cradling his prize. She clung more tightly to him, and he stroked the lovely line from ankle to knee to thigh with one finger, an arabesque that made him ache. Then he touched her shoulder and drew his finger down to her elbow, her wrist, her long delicate fingers with childishly untended nails. The room was lit from above by pot lights but it wasn't harsh, even if what it illuminated was horrific. To keep her from turning her head to look at her father, Wyn drew her even closer, then kissed her cool forehead. *Alive*, he thought.

She nuzzled the space under his jaw with a sleepy unconcern, not noticing or caring that he was an utter stranger. He rocked her a little. He was never home in the evenings when his own small daughter was being prepared for bed, never held her in the rocking chair in the nursery. This girl was half grown – she seemed tall for her age – and wouldn't countenance rocking under normal circumstances. But she was compliant, and Wyn in turn was soothed by her warmth, the sound of her breath, her perfect intactness. In this bath of sensations, it didn't seem strange to him then that he needed to kiss her on the shoulder, then on the cheek, then, when she tilted her head up and looked at him from half-lidded eyes, on the lips.

In the days and weeks that followed, Wyn would not think about this moment again. Indeed, he forgot it almost the instant the kiss was broken by the sound of footsteps (the homicide team, armed with cameras, latex gloves, efficiency) on the stairs. The child was gently prised away from him and neither of them protested. Wyn had gone about his business of finding the subject officers and interviewing them, the child whisked off to a family dwelling unknown.

The memory was further submerged over the course of days and months, in hundreds of hours of collecting and analyzing evidence, in the long meetings with colleagues, interviews with neighbours, witnesses, negotiations with counsel. "Justine Wolfe" became only a name in a report, the next of kin, the survivor. The essence of her, the hereness, the nowness of her dropped into the lacuna formed by procedures and litigations. Wyn had dreams about her that he forgot upon waking. If asked, he would not be able to describe her. But when he saw her on the Road to Paradise that day of the trial, feelings he'd long stashed away clawed their way to the surface. The way she'd gazed at him on the stand: she knew, she remembered, like she'd remembered every other moment of that outrageous night. She wanted him to remember.

As was standard after attending a traumatic scene, Wyn was offered counselling, but he declined it. He was aware of the liability issues surrounding post-traumatic stress: missed days of work, a dip in productivity, even resignation, but he did not miss work and his productivity, if anything, increased. He put in more hours at the office, and to inquiries about how he was handling it, he said virtually nothing. He heard that one of the paramedics who had found the toddlers had opted for stress leave for an unspecified amount of time. He couldn't afford to take time off to recover. Holding up a recommendation that Constable Mike Jameson be charged with manslaughter became the case of his career. It paved the path to his promotion to Director. In the moment of the kiss, he had felt no desire for the girl; he had in no way intruded upon nor sullied her innocence. The kiss eradicated everything but the moment of its own existence, took on an otherworldliness that, had Wyn permitted himself to muse over it, he may have described as religious in colour and timbre. Perhaps it had been guilt or fear that caused him to forget it so completely, or perhaps he forgot it because there was no place for it in the powerfully rational part of his mind that ruled all his actions, his motivations and desires. The kiss had not been motivated by self-interest or to provide solace. SPOA Investigator Wyn Rhys had kissed the child, Justine Wolfe, because he wanted a taste of the miraculous.

Acknowledgements

My deep thanks to all the friends and family who read (or listened to me read) drafts of the book and provided feedback and support: Chris Briggs, Kate Tchakovsky, Kristin Ostenson, Peter Drobac, Polina SanFilippo, Tom Broen, my brother Jay Venner and my mother Penny Adams. Special thanks to Gareth Jones, whose book *Conducting Administrative, Oversight and Ombudsman Investigations* (Canada Law, 2008) and professional consultations were instrumental in lending the story authenticity. I would also like to thank the communications team at the Special Investigations Unit for answering my questions.

Thank you to Greg Ioannou at Iguana enough for publishing the first edition of this book, and for lending the expertise of his fabulous team. Thank you to my editors, Kathryn Willms and Meghan Behse, and to Ellen Yu for designing the cover with me. Special thanks to Jen Frankel for her support and inspiration as we release a new edition of the book under Xeno Productions.